AIRSHIPS & AUTOMATONS

AIR SHIPS & AUTOMATONS

Edited by Charles P. Zaglanis

White Cat Publications

Airships & Automatons is published by White Cat Publications, LLC.
Copyright © 2015

Cover art by Zagladko Sergei Ptetrovich
Cover & Interior design by Vasha Lewkowicz
Edited by Charles P. Zaglanis

"All the King's Monsters" *Clarkesworld* #40, January 2010.

"Iron and Brass, Blood and Bone" *In an Iron Cage*, July 2011

"A Courtly Diversion" *Aoife's Kiss*, Dec 2011

"The Unicyclist's Fate" *The Homeless Moon 3*, 2010.

"Flight of the Pegasus" *Chronology*, Jan. 2015

FIRST EDITION
Published in March 2015

White Cat Publications, LLC.
33080 Industrial Road, Suite 101
Livonia, MI 48150
www.whitecatpublications.com

To Mom and Dad, for your unwavering love and support.
I would be nothing without you.

and

Shirley A. Moore, who died the day after Christmas 2014.

~Charles P. Zaglanis

Contents

A Courtly Diversion

by Gary Cuba

THE KING'S NATURAL PHILOSOPHER, Phaidros, stomped in a wide circle around the inner perimeter of his workshop. His agitated hands assaulted the empty air around him in cadence with his plaintive groans, and unruly strands of his gray hair flew in random directions as he tossed his head back and forth.

Little Hippolyte had dared to poke her head halfway past the edge of the screen that cordoned off her tiny sleeping nook to look at him. He acted more like a man condemned to the palace dungeon than one who had been granted another royal commission.

He'd just returned to the shop after an audience with the king's chamberlain. From the philosopher's noisy ranting, she pieced together that King Aristomos had ordered up a new *makhana* to show off at an important reception he was planning — and the artifice that Phaidros was to produce had to be more ingenious, more fascinating, more complex than any of his previous works. Something beyond his wondrous singing nightingale, which fluttered its metal wings, turned its head and flapped its beak open and closed as it twittered.

Moreover, he had only three lunar cycles to complete it.

"What am I to do, Hippolyte?" he finally said. "The king will never be satisfied. Ever a new diversion, and never anything less amazing than the last. I'm at my wit's end!"

She knew Phaidros always acted distraught under these circumstances. And she had to admit: If he ever failed to please their sovereign with the result of his art, the dungeon would more than likely become his home. Despots like Aristomos had little tolerance for their minions' failures.

And where would that leave her? Hippolyte could never imagine having a better master, and she counted herself blessed by the gods in that regard. In many ways, the erudite, irascible philosopher had treated her more like a daughter than the third-generation slave that she was. She'd been given to Phaidros as a tiny helper when she was only eight years old, and she had spent the last ten years in his service.

Hippolyte poked the rest of her head out from behind the screen and ventured a soft reply.

"But you always come through, Master. Everyone in Colchis knows you have the favor of King Aristomos. The roof over our heads attests to that. He gives you everything you need to carry out your art. And you must admit, the living stipend he grants you is enough to keep us both fed ... usually."

"Only because of my *toys*! Which I spend way too much of my valuable time developing."

Hippolyte crept out of her nook and settled Phaidros into his chair. She positioned her diminutive form behind him and massaged his shoulders, trying to ease his tension. "Poor Master Phaidros. Poor, long-suffering Phaidros."

"Hrrumph."

"You know, Master, I would do anything to ease your burdens," she said. "I've helped you fabricate many of your creations, and learned much in the process. Perhaps *I* can design the next gala's automaton. To save you the time and effort, so that you can pursue your finer dreams. What would you say to that?"

"It's an utterly ludicrous notion."

"Why? Do you not credit me with the wit to accomplish the task? Or am I always to remain a dumb servant to you, doing only your bidding, hobbing gears to your specification, planing planks and beating out copper sheets at your command?"

Phaidros turned in his chair to face Hippolyte. He stared into her dark eyes for a long moment. "By Zeus, you're serious, aren't you?"

"By Hera, I am," she said, for once dropping the deference expected of a slave and directly meeting his gaze.

⚜

Hippolyte unrolled a scroll taken from Phaidros's library shelves and studied it. She could not read much of any language, nor write it. Phaidros had told her that he'd someday teach her the fuller meaning of letters—but only when she was old enoug7h and wise enough to separate the truth from the falsehoods that lurked within them.

Instead, he had taught her the understanding, measure, and manipulation of numbers—they never lied, he was fond of saying. She was also facile in seeing the sense of diagrams, and could make credible ink projections of real and imaginary things onto flat papyrus herself.

The scroll was a copy of a treatise by an Alexandrian, Heron, written a few decades prior. While its text was completely inscrutable to her, there were several diagrams showing the details of a steam-driven rotary ball he had invented.

Fascinating, she thought. All automatons needed an energizing principle. Her master Phaidros had most often used weights, suspended from hidden cords that activated the gears of his creations through pegged pinion shafts—or sometimes he employed bent slats of wood or tempered metal that released their active spirit when they slowly straightened themselves back to their original form. Could the heat of fire, transformed into steam, provide an even better source of motive power?

"Phaidros, what do you think about using this method to bring spirit to an automaton?"

The man looked up from his own work and studied the scroll briefly. "Heron's *aeliopile*? Too much smoke. Would you suffocate our king? Not a suitable approach, in my opinion. Best to copy my own proven methods — they're much more pleasing to the gods of Nature."

"But the king uses fire to warm his chambers, as do we all. And some fuels produce less smoke than others."

"Hrrumph."

So it would be naphtha, Hippolyte thought. That would burn hot and without so much smoke.

She imagined steam blowing out from the side of a kettle's lid, rattling it. In her mind's eye, she saw the billowing steam somehow confined and directed through a tube, as in Heron's machine. And as she sank into her reverie, she saw the steam impinging on a wheel. Not any kind of wheel, but one fashioned like a plucked flower, its petals twisted, spinning in the breeze — very like a maple's seedpods. And beyond it, more flowers spinning, a whole column of them. *But spinning to what end?*

For the rest of the day, she had to hob gears for Phaidros. He had obviously not trusted her to come up with a credible piece of art in time, so he'd been designing one himself. She felt a flush of anger ripple through her. This was all about giving him a chance to pursue his finer dreams, after all. Why didn't he have any faith in her?

Yet, considering the price of failure, she couldn't really blame him. And in truth — despite her brash claims to the contrary — she'd begun to have second thoughts as to whether she could create her own device from scratch. It turned out to be harder than it looked.

⊂ଓ଼⊃

Hippolyte came to understood how Sisyphus must've felt, condemned by the gods to forever roll a huge boulder up the steep slope of a mountain—only to have it come rolling back down again to its base, there to taunt him that his task must begin anew.

She pushed herself harder. She used her mathematical skills to optimize her steam outlet nozzle's contour, and finally got her metal steam flowers to spin grandly and forcefully.

Phaidros, meanwhile, was putting the finishing touches on his new falcon automaton. The clockwork bird flew along a fine cord stretched from one perch to another, back and forth, flapping its wings realistically and screeching while it traversed its defined course. It was sure to please the king and his guests.

Hippolyte saw her master cast a glance from time to time into the corner of the workshop where her own invention grew. And always, it was followed by his hallmark "hrrumph."

"Too big, Hippolyte," he finally said. "Too clunky. A waste of good material."

Hippolyte pulled her head out of the innards of her creation. She wiped her forehead with her skinny arm, and was appalled to see the grime that came off on it. She brushed a greasy strand of dark hair out of her eyes.

Phaidros walked over to her alcove and scrutinized her efforts closely for the first time. She extracted herself fully from the huge device and stood beside him while he inspected her craftsmanship.

Hippolyte smiled, seeing her magnificent creation rising in front of her: a beautiful mechanical horse whose withers were as tall as man's head. An imposing replica of a noble steed, one that any hero might be proud to ride.

Phaidros grunted. "This has got to be the most horrendous rendition of a horse I've ever seen." He pointed to the beast's belly. "This, I assume, is where your fatuous steam contrivance resides?"

She nodded. "The perforations in the side covers allow breath in, to sustain the fire that heats the water in the confined vessel above it. The fuel for the fire enters from another vessel, hidden deep in the chest, where a horse's heart would be. The means to regulate its introduction into the firebox were a real challenge. You can see the opening here, where I pour the fuel in." She removed a cap from a port on the shoulder of the horse.

Phaidros hrrumphed again, but he kept probing the machine. "Remove this section of armor, so that I may see the inner workings better."

She did so, revealing the finely crafted set of turbine blades.

"Interesting." He turned to her, his bushy gray eyebrows raised, his eyes wide in a surprised expression she'd rarely seen before. "This is not my art you're copying. This is ... something different. Where did you see it depicted? Have I missed something in my library, something that would lead a philosopher to see these things?"

Hippolyte looked down at the floor and toyed at the dirt with the tip of one sandal. "Master Phaidros, can you never admit that I may have a mind of my own? You've inspired me by your wisdom. Much of you is in this creation. But ... there is a little of me here, too."

Her master scratched his scraggly beard and slowly nodded his head. "If I didn't see with my own eyes, I'd not have believed it possible."

Hippolyte's heart swelled, and the heat of pride spread through her. "Thank you, Master. But to be honest, I've run up on a problem I can't solve: My horse won't be able to walk without falling over."

Phaidros snorted. "Hrrumph. A mere trifle. We need only break it down and assess it as a simpler series of problems. Let's look at it more closely ..."

⸎

"It's no good, Hippolyte," Phaidros said. He threw his stylus down onto the table in aggravation. "I can't make the numbers work. The gears simply won't cooperate. It's impossible!"

Hippolyte sat atop the workbench, legs crossed, arching over the wax tablet that held her master's latest series of calculations.

Her vision fogged, and in her mind's eye she imagined a tall stack of tablets, each calculating one variation of the gearing solution for a given aspect of the horse's movement. They suddenly collapsed back into a single one, their differing solutions merging.

"Master, what if we approached it with a different sort of *mathematike*? One that deals solely with the *change* in the horse's balance point as it moves. And with gears that could engage and disengage and slip freely, according to what was needed at any given moment. Like this ..."

She reached out and snatched the tablet away, scraped its surface smooth and began scratching strange new numeric expressions and diagrams upon it in a frenetic blur of motion.

"No!" Phaidros exclaimed. "That can't work. It's unnatural. It ... it goes against everything I know to be true."

Hippolyte lifted the stylus and looked over at her master. His face had become flushed. "Phaidros, you told me that you wanted to pursue finer, higher thoughts. Did I not hear you correctly?"

"I was distraught. I misspoke."

"The great philosopher Phaidros, admitting to having made a *mistake*? By Hera, *that's* a new one! I don't believe it for a moment."

Phaidros slammed his fists down hard against the workbench, jerked himself up off his chair and glowered at Hippolyte. Then he strode off and stood at a window overlooking the courtyard, his back turned to the slave girl.

"This is not about the horse, is it?" she said. "This is about something else. You're afraid, Phaidros. Afraid of what? Of trying something new? Of seeing farther?"

She saw Phaidros's shoulders rise and fall back again as a huge sigh escaped his frame.

"You're right, Hippolyte. I *am* afraid. I'm afraid of taking risks. As we all should be, living in this time and place. There is no room for failure in this land. Everyone but you seems to understand that."

Phaidros turned back around to face her, tears leaking from his eyes. She'd pushed him too far. She ran to him and threw her arms around him. They wept together in the fading afternoon light, he from frustration, she from guilt.

And then they went back to the workbench, lit a lamp, and worked on into the night, exploring the ramifications of Hippolyte's "new mathematics."

⋐⋑

"By Zeus, the blasted thing *actually works!*" Phaidros said, watching her trot the monstrosity around the enclosed back courtyard of the workshop. He had to yell to make his voice heard over the clanking and whirring of the machine's internal mechanisms.

Hippolyte, sitting astride the beast's broad back, pulled back on the throttle lever and disengaged the transmission gears to bring the monster to a halt. She beamed. "Of course it does, Master. Did you ever have any doubts that it would?"

Phaidros rubbed his beard, moving his head slowly from side to side as he gazed at their contrivance. Then he leaned back and roared in laughter, and Hippolyte joined in with her own high-pitched giggles. After a few moments, Phaidros became serious again.

"Nevertheless, Hippolyte, it'd be best to use my mechanical falcon for the king's gala tomorrow. Your horse is a marvelous prototype, to be sure. But even you have to admit that it's the *ugliest* thing ever birthed by the mind of man—or woman. I'd be too afraid that the king's consort and all the noblewomen of the court might expire on the spot from the sheer horror of the beast's visage!"

Hippolyte felt her grin drop into a frown. But he did have a point. Truth to tell, it *was* an ugly, noisy, smelly baby.

Phaidros smiled gently. "But perhaps we can discuss its military applications with the chamberlain and arrange a demonstration for him after the gala. In truth, I'd be surprised if he didn't already know of the horse's existence. His spies are everywhere."

Cⳝ℘

Finely dressed nobles and their wives filed into the royal palace's main hall. Hippolyte helped Phaidros finish setting up his falcon display, stretching the mechanism's guideline tightly across the hall in front of the throne where King Aristomos would sit to give his invocation and kickoff the celebration.

It was indeed an important occasion, intended to impress an ambassador recently arrived from a powerful kingdom to the south, which Hippolyte learned was called Persia. In a case like this, Phaidros explained, demonstration of a suitable level of cultural attainment would greatly influence their future economic and military ties.

They made their way past the empty royal throne to an antechamber behind the reception hall, avoiding the scrutiny of the gathering guests. Hippolyte saw that Phaidros was sweating profusely, and she suspected it was not from physical exertion. He was more nervous than she'd ever seen him before.

Phaidros wore his finest toga—a Roman dress style that had recently become popular within their otherwise Hellenistic culture. As elegant as it was, the garment still hung sloppily on his bony frame. Hippolyte clucked at him. Here was the realm's greatest natural philosopher, and he looked little better than an old, starving beggar. She reached up and tried to straighten the raiment on his shoulders.

"You'll knock them off their feet again, Master Phaidros," she said. "You always do."

"Hrrumph. Leave me now. Your fussings and flutterings distract me. Go tend to your horse, and let me lay my fate on the line once more, alone and naked before the world."

She hugged him and he grunted, then she left him. But she didn't return to the workshop. Instead, Hippolyte climbed a servant's stairwell and settled into one of several spying niches that ringed the hall below.

She peeped out through the slotted opening there and watched as King Aristomos, accompanied by the short, corpulent Persian ambassador, entered the hall from the royal quarters, followed by the king's consort and family members, his tall chamberlain, and a number of other high-ranking dignitaries.

The assembled guests rose and dutifully acknowledged their king's entrance. To Hippolyte, their reaction sounded somewhat more tepid than she would've expected. Almost as if they didn't really want to be there.

Then there began an interminable round of boring speeches and testimonials that made Hippolyte's eyelids feel like they'd gained the weight of metal. At long length, after having talked himself hoarse, the king gestured roughly toward Phaidros, who stood peeping around a curtain behind the throne.

It was his big moment.

The natural philosopher shuffled out of the alcove, stumbling momentarily over the end of his toga—which had somehow slipped askew again. He walked around the throne and stood in front of the king. Phaidros fidgeted with his garment for a few moments, then started speaking.

"My gracious king, esteemed ambassador, noble court members, and honored guests. I ... I have a small diversion to present to you tonight, a new work that I hope will amuse and amaze you all. It will demonstrate certain complex facets of the mechanical arts, whose expression and craftsmanship in this case are not exceeded in the known world. I give you ... my metal falcon!"

Phaidros stood on his tiptoes, reached high over his head and, with a shaky hand, removed the silken veil that had concealed the bird. He waited while the crowd's buzzing settled down.

At that moment, Hippolyte felt the guests' palpable emotions to her very bowels; the specter of fascinating dread swirled and permeated the hall in a cloying miasma. Its wordless message proclaimed: Pity poor Phaidros; his fate is being weighed yet again. *There but for the grace of Zeus go I!*

Failure was not an option. Not for Phaidros, not for anyone else there.

Phaidros raised his face toward the ceiling for a moment, eyes closed, mouthing a silent prayer to the gods. Then he sighed deeply and pulled a pin loose from the falcon's mooring.

The bird lifted its bronze head, uttered a screech from somewhere deep within its body, extended its wings and began to traverse the thin cord toward a turnaround post on the far side of the room.

It managed to travel no more than the length of a man's arm before the cord broke, sending the bird plummeting directly to the marble floor with a loud crash. There it turned round and round on its back in tight circles, its wings flapping discordantly. Then it began to self-destruct, its screeches turning into caws, into raspy mews, finally into a series of clicks as small gears began spilling out of its body, rolling in all directions. After a short time, it gave up the last of its active spirit and lay still.

Phaidros stood dumbfounded, staring down at his ruined device.

Hippolyte heard a communal groan escape from the crowd. She clamped her hand over her mouth, suppressing a wail that threatened to erupt from her; she knew what this meant for Phaidros. And seeing him standing there — alone in front of his king, his face ashen, his hands fluttering at his side — she knew that he did, too.

There was little sense in explaining to the king how flawlessly the bird had performed in their workshop. Perhaps they had frayed and weakened the cord from too many trials there. Or, she thought in horror, perhaps I distracted him too much, making him help me with my own stupid piece of junk instead of taking the time to identify every potential weakness in his own design. A wave of nausea rolled through her. Yes, it was so. In the final analysis, she and her foolish dreams had brought this awful result down on him.

In the now death-quiet room, she heard the Persian ambassador chuckle, and watched him turn toward the king — whose face, she noted, was a vivid shade of red.

"Very amusing, Aristomos," the Persian said. "Of course, it'd be quite impossible for my nation to engage in mutually beneficial congress with ... *backward* societies. But maybe in your case I can convince my king to grant you the gift of a *real* philosopher, so that you may at least enjoy courtly diversions that *work*, eh?" He pursed his lips for a moment, then added: "That is, until such time as we decide to send our armies here to bring you pretenders a *proper* form of civilization." His chuckle became a boisterous laugh, his huge belly undulating up and down in perfect rhythm to his loud guffaws.

Aristomos' face turned from red to a darker magenta shade. Hippolyte could see the veins bulging in his forehead even from her distant vantage point.

"And I'll show you what we'll do to them, should you ever try that," Aristomos sputtered. "The same thing that we do to *anyone* who displeases me!" He stood and pointed at Phaidros, who trembled under his fiery gaze. "Guards, take this man out and execute him at once. And let this be a lesson to anyone else who fails to do honor to their king."

⋘⋙

Hippolyte could bear to watch no more. She raced down the back stairs and out the servant's entrance of the palace, her head spinning. She had to do something to help Phaidros. *Think!*

She sprinted to their workshop and burst into it, panting. The metal horse stood in the corner, lazy tendrils of steam still drifting out of the exhaust pipes in its nostrils. She expelled a sigh of relief. Thank Hera I only banked the firebox earlier, she thought, and didn't close it off completely.

She hurriedly checked the water and fuel vessels' level indicators and grunted. Plenty of water left, but the fuel was low. Hippolyte hefted a heavy amphora holding their supply of naphtha and poured the ropy, viscous liquid into the fuel port frantically, spilling much of it down the horse's left leg. She tossed the vessel aside in her haste; it smashed apart, the remaining fluid in it running across the floor of the shop.

Hippolyte scrambled up the foothold depressions along the horse's flank to mount the beast, and jerked the fuel feed valve fully open. The firebox roared and, without warning, the spilled naphtha ignited on the horse's leg. Droplets of the flaming liquid leapt to the puddle on the floor, and she suddenly found herself engulfed in a blaze that raged through the workshop.

She sat atop the steed, helplessly waiting for the steam pressure to rebuild, crying out as the flames licked at her. After a seeming eternity, when she could no longer stand the searing heat, Hippolyte jammed the horse's transmission into reverse gear and drove the lumbering beast backwards toward the only exit available to her, the big doors to the shop's rear courtyard. It smashed through them, showering her with wooden shards and splinters.

She had to keep moving, else the flames that had now spread across the horse's side would burn her badly. But how to exit the courtyard? Its solid stone walls were at least as tall as she was, and its tiny gate was much too narrow for the horse to plow through. She moved the horse in a wide circle around the courtyard, trying to think, then straightened it out and shoved the drive throttle forward. The horse gained speed, its legs rising and falling in perfectly synchronized arcs, its body tilting from side to side to maintain its balance.

Hippolyte headed the charging automaton directly toward the far wall of the yard. At the last instant, she pulled a lever to short-step the trailing leg, let both rear legs bend low, raised the front legs, gunned the throttle—and leapt over the barrier.

Hippolyte felt a shudder roll through the horse; one of the rear legs must have grazed the capstone of the wall, she thought. She struggled with the control levers to get the front legs down and forward into a landing position. If the machine fell over, she knew that she wouldn't be able to right it again by herself—if she survived the tumble. They'd had to use a portable crane back in the shop to lift the horse up after their less successful testing trials. And that was certainly in flames by now, along with everything else inside the shop.

But her bigger problem at the moment was staying atop the steed. She'd never tried to make her horse jump before—had never ridden a real horse, for that matter—and didn't know what to expect. Her body rose from the leather pad affixed to the horse's back, seeking its own arc through space, one that was different from the path that Nature had proscribed for the horse. Hippolyte clutched at one of the curved metal bars that spanned the beast's withers as her rear end and legs lifted skyward. "Hera preserve me!" she cried.

Her rump hit the leather pad with a force that knocked the breath out of her. The horse tipped forward precipitously, and she scrambled to regain her senses, pulling back on the throttle and manipulating the control levers in a panic. A nerve-grating gnash of metal against metal came from somewhere beneath her. She fought the controls and slowly brought the machine back to stability.

"No more jumping tonight—I promise!" she said. A few lingering flames still crawled along the horse's side, so she re-engaged the transmission and got the horse moving apace again.

Hippolyte drove the beast at as close to a gallop as she could manage, heading for the main avenue to the palace. She exited an alleyway, and there in front of her was Phaidros, flanked by two armed palace guards, being marched to his final destination—which was, she surmised, the barracks at the edge of the city.

The guards turned and stared at the fiery metal monster that sped toward them, frozen in their tracks, their mouths agape. One had the presence of mind to draw his sword a moment before Hippolyte rammed into him, knocking him hard onto the road. He lay there, senseless, his weapon ending up in the dust a dozen feet away. The other guard took off into the night, screaming to Zeus to protect him. She turned the steed around and brought it to a clanking stop next to her master.

"I thought you'd never get here, Hippolyte," Phaidros said, wiping his brow with his hand.

"You knew I was watching the demonstration?"

"Of course. Why should anyone in the land miss seeing my ultimate shameful moment, had they but half a chance to view it?"

"Quit flagellating yourself and get on, Phaidros," Hippolyte said, patting the saddle behind her.

He clambered aboard the steed, sat behind her and wrapped his arms around her slender waist.

Hippolyte turned her head to talk over her shoulder. "I'm afraid I managed to burn down your workshop, Master," she said. "Please forgive me."

"Clumsy girl. But no matter. My career here is ended, my life forfeit. Best we head down toward the docks. Maybe we can steal a boat there and delay our demise for a few pitiful hours before they finally catch up with us."

Hippolyte swiveled the automaton around and pointed it toward the palace. "I had a different sort of notion. I think we need to put a finer point on this whole venture. One that will either cause the king to recognize your true genius — or take us both out in a blaze of glory." She paused for a moment, then chuckled. "If nothing else, perhaps one of the palace musicians may compose a fetching ballad about our exploits."

She pushed the throttle forward and set the beast off on a trot, bringing it to rest at the foot of the tall marble stairs in front of the palace. She felt a huge sigh escape from Phaidros, blowing against the back of her neck.

"You always were a clever girl, Hippolyte. I'm sorry I didn't spend more time telling you that, over the years. I am proud of you, no matter how this misadventure turns out."

Hippolyte engaged the transmission and deftly manipulated the mechanical steed's legs, ascending the stairs carefully.

Once at the top, they advanced past the strangely unguarded entrance. Well, she thought, that should not really come as a surprise, considering the terror their approach must have evoked in the palace soldiers' minds. They strode unchallenged through the archway that led into the reception hall.

The king had obviously conquered his anger and had resumed the festivities as though nothing had gone awry. Hippolyte saw his goblet slip through his fingers to clang on the floor when they entered the hall; beside him, his consort swooned and the Persian ambassador jumped to his feet, his eyes bulging. The fat man moved behind his chair and hugged its back, as if believing it could afford him some kind of protection from the monstrous metal apparition that advanced toward him.

The crowd shrieked as the loud, clanking contrivance made its way into the center of the grand hall. Steam billowed from the horse's nostrils. The naphtha fire on the outside armor had mostly died away, but a few flames still licked up from the beast's front hooves. In a flash of inspiration, Hippolyte manipulated the controls in a new way and the horse reared, rising up and waving its front legs in the air. She cracked a pressure relief valve at that instant and released a blast of steam; it made a deep, deafening whistle that echoed throughout the hall.

A few of the guests fled the room, screaming in terror; most seemed too paralyzed with either fear, or wonderment, to move. Hippolyte walked the horse forward and brought it to a halt directly in front of the king, its front feet resting on the top step of the platform that supported the throne, its nose barely a foot's length away from Aristomos's face. The automaton's turbine continued to whir, sounding like the buzzing of a hive of agitated bees. Exhaust steam from the horse's nostrils blew past either side of the king's head as he sat there, frozen, his eyes wide with terror.

"My Lord," she said. "With your permission, I'd like to petition against the judgement you have lately rendered upon my master, Phaidros. Upon calmer reflection, a wise king might come to see that it was rather unfair and extreme, don't you agree?"

Aristomos could only grip the arms of his throne chair. He opened his mouth as if to speak, but no sound came from it. From her perch high above him, Hippolyte leaned forward and saw that their grand sovereign had peed in his toga.

"Yes, I see that you do. All honor to you, King Aristomos." She bowed her head once toward the king and then looked over at the ambassador, who stood trembling behind his chair—but she continued to address Aristomos as she glared at the porcine foreigner. "And perhaps you may wish to remind our esteemed Persian guest that we really don't waste too much of our chief philosopher's time on courtly diversions and toys, when his true calling is designing more practical contrivances—like unstoppable war engines, for instance. Of which this is but a trifling example, compared to the many other, more fearful, ones we have in development."

Hippolyte studied the ambassador; he seemed to be trying to swallow something bigger than his fleshy throat could handle.

She manipulated the transmission levers and backed the horse a step away from the king. Then she turned it around and pranced it proudly out the entranceway of the hall.

ෆ෫ඊ

They had no better place to go, so she marched their steed around to the stable yard behind one of the city's lesser-frequented inns. There it died, releasing the balance of its steam pressure in a plaintive whistle that descended steadily in tone as the monster lowered itself, inch by slow inch, to the ground. When its belly finally touched the earth, the beast fell over sideways with a final vaporous sigh, spilling Hippolyte and Phaidros onto the ground next to it.

It was plain to see that their creation would never rise again. But as to its better, more robust progeny, those that might benefit from the prototype's lessons in materials science, in mathematics, in power transmission, in adaptive control systems? Neither Hippolyte nor Phaidros would venture to speculate on that now—since they didn't even know if they'd live to see the morrow.

Phaidros had a few coins in his purse, and with them they secured a room for the night. They collapsed on the sleeping mat inside it, both of them utterly spent, neither of them much caring what the next day would bring.

CS80

The chamberlain found them in the early afternoon, while they were breaking their fast alone in the inn's public room. Hippolyte saw him enter, tugged at Phaidros's arm, then stood quickly, knocking her bench over. She backed away, bowing low. Phaidros hardly reacted to the man.

"Ah, there you are at last!" the chamberlain said. "We've been looking for you all morning." He took a seat next to the philosopher and motioned for Hippolyte to rejoin them at the table.

Phaidros turned toward the man and bent his head down. "I'm prepared to meet my fate now. I've long been prepared to do so. It was only a matter of time before I finally failed my king. But I beseech you, my Lord, please let Hippolyte go free. It was all my doing. She is an innocent party in this."

The chamberlain chuckled. "No, no. It's nothing like that, Phaidros. In point of fact, the king has been deposed. We're now engaged in setting up a Republic. I'm acting as regent until we can establish freely elected Senatorial functions."

Phaidros and Hippolyte both gasped as the chamberlain continued. "It seems that Hippolyte's eloquent words last night brought inspiration to our leading citizens — along with some measure of shame, I might add. They finally came to realize it was time to address the, ah, *distinct disadvantages* of living under a despot's rule. Aristomos is on the road with his family at this minute, headed for exile."

"But what of the Persian ambassador, my Lord?" Hippolyte said. "His disdain for our culture? His military threats?"

"It seems that our esteemed Persian emissary has reassessed his position in both regards. He signed a trade agreement and a non-aggression pact with me early this morning. He too was swayed by your ... impressive demonstration last night. And truth be told, he too didn't like Aristomos very much. So he's a fairly happy man today — if only because he managed to survive our grand reception for him last night!"

The new regent leaned back and laughed. "We have a great future ahead of us, in no small measure because of you two. Phaidros, we'll rebuild your workshop and library, and double their original size. Plus we'll give you free rein and resources to research anything you want to, free from bureaucratic pressures. No more time wasted on toys and courtly diversions. We all realize now how that can serve our new society best in the long run. And there's more!"

He turned toward Hippolyte. "A few of my ... *informants* had already told me that the fearsome mechanical machine we all saw last night was your own conception, Hippolyte. To be honest, I've long believed that everyone in the land has something important to contribute to our culture, regardless of their standing — if we could but simply nourish it and let it flow forth freely. In time, the majority of our citizens will come to understand that, and I'm betting they'll soon vote to abolish slavery forever within our borders. But I can at least take one step along that path now. On behalf of us all, I gratefully thank you, *Citizen Hippolyte*, for showing us the way forward."

Hippolyte felt the blood draining from her head, her mind unable to absorb the sudden swirl of events. She opened her mouth, then closed it again, unsure of what to say. One image alone re-centered her thoughts.

"But what of the horse?"

The regent smiled. "Yes, what of it? I see that it now lies in a heap behind the inn, and children are already playing on its carcass. Surely, it would please us if you could share its detailed construction plans, so that we may build a whole cavalry of them. But it hardly matters. What's important is that our potential enemies come to know that we *might* construct them—and never be sure what other advanced defensive engines we may pull out of our sleeve. In any case, Hippolyte, we would be pleased to have you help direct our future military strategy as Ministress of Weapons Research. What would you say to that?"

Hippolyte gave a glance toward Phaidros, and saw that his normally dour expression had disappeared, replaced by one of complete, childlike amusement.

"My Lord," she said, still looking into Phaidros's wide eyes, "I'm honored by your offer, more than I can say. But I could never imagine myself working apart from my master—rather, my *father*, the great philosopher Phaidros. Never."

The regent rose. "So be it. In any case, I'm sure we'll benefit from whatever arts you chose to pursue in the future." He strode to the exit of the inn, paused, then turned back to them. "In the meantime, until we can get a proper residence and workshop constructed, there are unused rooms at the palace for you to live in: the king's old quarters. I trust that will be satisfactory to both of you?" He left the inn, laughing loudly.

Hippolyte and Phaidros clasped hands across the table.

"Phaidros—has this all really happened, or am I still asleep and only dreaming it?"

"Hrrumph," the philosopher said. "Better to ask your ugly horse the answer to that. In truth, it would know more of such things—considering that it was your dreams that gave birth to the beast in the first place."

Phaidros reached over and brushed a wayward strand of Hippolyte's hair away from her face. "But more importantly: What shall we work on next, daughter? That is, after I finish teaching you the meaning of written letters?"

Hippolyte's vision clouded from the tears that suddenly welled in her eyes. "How high can our thoughts fly, father? How high?"

The Dog-Faced Cannibal

by Christine Purcell

THE CONCEALED EXIT from the Chief's hale was close by, hidden in a stone wall under glossy maile vines. Papa-ena grunted under the weight of the broken automaton. His muscles strained as he navigated the treacherous path forward. Even with Mohihi carrying the other end of the machine, he fought the urge to stop and rest. Not here. Not now. He needed to be steady. Ena was always steady. He concentrated on how grateful he was Chief Kahanai hadn't found the machine and discovered that a wooden doppelganger had taken the place of a Menehune worker.

Ena's foot caught on a hapu'u fiddlehead and he lurched forward, throwing Mohihi off balance. She stumbled to one side, but her thick legs kept her from falling. Somehow, they both maintained their hold on the automaton.

They stood motionless among the dense ferns as Ena's breath came in wheezes. Less than ten feet away, Chief Kahanai sat on a stone bench entertaining his daughter, Ailana, with stories about the gods of the mountains. There had been no pause to indicate Kahanai heard them.

Mohihi touched her heart in relief. "You galumphing fool," she hissed.

Ena put a finger to his lips. He cocked his head, studying the tall chief and his beautiful, tall daughter. The bench, which was very large, was almost crowded with the two Tahitians, who sat with their legs pressed together and made the bench appear very small. While Kahanai talked, Ena could just make out the words.

"So, you want to know about the Menehune?" Kahanai teased his daughter. "Someday you will be Chief and will need to know all of the island's mysteries, but that day is not today. Now, all you need know is you will never see a Menehune. True, they built this house. True, they continue to improve my hale. But they do their work at night and insist that no one watch them."

"Why's that?" Ailana's voice commanded like her father's, but with a gentle warmth that made the order seem a request.

"They are funny little fairies."

Mohihi's eyebrow shot up with violence. "Fairies!" She spat on the ground. "He calls us fairies. Try exiled slaves. Try survivors of a secret massacre."

Ena grunted his agreement. "Keep calm, my queen. Soon he will learn how vicious the sting of a fairy can be."

Ena carefully unwrapped the fiddlehead from his leg. At his nod, they hurried toward the wall, leaving through the low opening under thick leaves, and then continuing to the edge of the forest. They passed into the darkness of dense foliage; their shelter and their prison, eager to drop their burden.

C3§O

Ena watched Mohihi bent intently over the dog-faced automaton. Her fingers moved deftly across the wooden jaw, fitting the sharp pointed rocks that would be its teeth. Next, she moved on to the curved claws, tightening the hinges. This machine was built for lethal speed, pincers to catch and cuff, teeth made to gnash. Finished, Mohihi turned to him with a wicked smile and a slice of moonlight illuminated a smoldering eye. She looked feline and feral. Ena backed up a step. He could taste the hate pouring off of her, salty on his tongue. He was overwhelmed by her anger. Of course, they both wanted reprieve from their exile, but he wondered at her motivation. For Ena, this wasn't about revenge. It was a matter of will. Something he would need in the coming days as he dragged this cumbersome killing machine from island to island.

He looked from the twisted face of his beautiful Mohihi back to the exquisite craftsmanship of the automaton. They had worked on it for such a long time, deprived of rest and leisure. They had worked on it with a fervor that far exceeded reason. And now that it was finished, the beauty of the dream evaporated and a breathless horror filled his heart. Ena leaned against a tree, his teeth chattering.

Mohihi snatched his wrist. Her brown eyes blazed and her mouth set in a tight line. "Find strength, my leader," she said. "You alone can do this, and I demand it of you."

Ena swallowed hard and nodded. A slight smile quirked the corner of his lip. Mohihi was impossible to refuse.

CB&O

A fortnight had passed since Ena retrieved the automaton from the hale. Many days ago, the initial terror of the dog-faced automaton had been unleashed on Kauai. Now, Ena stood on the Maui shore. A thread of moonlight painted the beach with splashes of dim streaks and shadow. He watched as the dog-faced automaton chewed off the face of a Tahitian descendant. Mechanical jaws tore skin and ripped out bleeding muscles. The Tahitian moaned, and made a feeble bat at the wooden automaton from his supine position in the sand. Ena's stomach lurched and he felt the heavy mashed taro eaten earlier rise up his throat. He cursed at himself for pitying the man. These actions were necessary. Kahanai needed to be afraid when Ena made his move. No. Kahanai needed to be more than afraid; he needed to be terrified with blind panic. The strength of generations of the oppressed lifted Ena.

Afterwards, Ena retrieved the automaton and stepped boldly to his koa canoe. With a silent push of his oar, Ena paddled evenly out across the black water toward his forest.

☾☽

After years of careful crafting and three final nights of feverish work, there were two hundred and fifty automatons, exactly. And two hundred and fifty Menehune. While the automatons worked to build the stone road, as Kahanai had commanded, Ena and Mohihi lay in wait, hidden by darkness in the ferns outside the Chief's hale. The rest of the Menehune hid a distance off among a low field of lush plants, ready for a desperate war if anything went wrong.

From atop the lookout tower that loomed inside the garden wall, a glint of metal caught Ena's attention. He imagined Kahanai peering through his looking glass as he made his tally. He would find every Menehune accounted for. Ena had checked every cog and cylinder himself. There would be no breakdowns tonight. No mistakes.

Ena wondered how Kahanai's nerves were. With stories of the eepa—the dog-faced cannibal—spreading faster than lava, Ena guessed Kahanai's nerves could not be good. Ena put on his own dog-faced mask. He stroked the taut pig skin and the coarse hairs tickled his fingers. He would surely look a fright. Ena hurried through the small hole in the garden wall.

He and Mohihi, whose face was draped in a veil of black feathers, moved almost soundlessly. Ailana's room was on the second floor, near the fishpond. The guards relaxed, or dozed, or played pebble games. There was no need for heightened alert. The Menehune were working. The dog-faced cannibal was said to be terrorizing Maui. Or perhaps Kauai.

No one noticed two short figures as they climbed the stones that made up one wall of the hale. Ena and Mohihi found tiny nooks and recesses for handholds that would be useless and insignificant to the larger Tahitians. And though Ena's fingers pulsed with pain, and his knees scraped the rough-cut rock, he made slow, burning, upward progress as his shoulder blades knit and his toes strained with effort. When his hand caught Ailana's window sill, Ena allowed himself a small smile.

Inside, Ailana slept gracefully in her bed, black hair melting into the darkness. The floor creaked under Ena's step as he drew just near enough to grab her. She sat up with a start. Her mouth opened, ready to scream at the sight of the dog-faced eepa invading her bed chamber. But Mohihi was already behind her and both hands clamped fast over Ailana's mouth. Ailana struggled, thrashing like a fish.

"Your flailing is making me hungry," Ena growled in his most feral voice. "I'd advise staying still if you want to keep that pretty face."

Ailana's wide eyes trembled. Ena felt bad for scaring the lovely girl, but she stopped moving in response to his harsh words. While Mohihi bound the girl with coconut-husk rope, Ena pushed aside the stand that held her washbasin and pried back a floorboard. Then he helped Mohihi hoist the girl up and over their shoulders. The Tahitian beauty was heavy, but they were strong. They took her down the cramped secret passageway and out of the hale by another unknown exit in the walls of the kitchen. But before he left, he let a frightened cook glimpse his face. The dog-face of an eepa cannibal. The chief's daughter was theirs now. By morning, Kahanai would feel the sting.

 CR&O

That night in the forest, under the cover of the banana leaves, Ailana sat stiffly in her bonds. Another length of rope wrapped snuggly around her slim waist, securing her to a sturdy tree. Her honey-colored legs stretched out long and lean from under her kapa-bark skirt. For a moment, Ena couldn't take his eyes off her. It wasn't just that she was beautiful; there were a lot of pretty women on the island, both Menehune and Tahitian. It was that tilt to her chin as she cautiously watched the forest bustle with activity. The young women and men gathered taro and bananas, the older ones tuned up the automatons with animal oil and koa winders, and the children chased each other through the plant decay and sprawled on the ground, calling for their mothers. They were an exiled people, but they had made a good life and Ena was proud to show who he was, who his people were, to this Chief's daughter.

She watched Ipo, one of the young men, repair an automaton. He sat in the dirt surrounded by a hoard of wooden cogs and spindles. Up close, the automaton smelled of the faint sweetness of warmed kindling. The little machine was expressionless on the outside, but its inside was filled with moving parts. Ipo's hands moved expertly over the gears, intuitively finding a cracked shaft.

Ailiana's guarded gaze shifted from Ipo back to Ena. Ena's dog-mask was slippery with sweat. He pulled it off and wiped his brow. His face now revealed to be plain and not that of an evil eepa, the wariness in Ailana's eyes turned to fury.

"You little termite," she spat. "What do you mean to do with me?"

The sneer on her lips was endearing and Ena found himself grinning.

"You think this amusing?"

Ena adopted a properly serious expression. "No, I think this necessary."

"Are you Menehune?"

"Yes."

She mulled this over a bit as she chewed a bottom lip. "What are those markings on your face?"

Ena ran a finger over the grooved spiral on his cheek. "Ta moko. They tell our story in ink."

"And the machines?"

"They do our work so we can rest."

"You mean so you can kidnap me." When Ena didn't challenge her, she asked, "Why?"

"We want our freedom," he responded automatically to her commanding tone.

"Freedom from what?"

Ena related the history to her, tracing out the journey that was marked in ink on his face and chest. How they had come from Marquesas only to have the Tahitians arrive years later and slaughter them. "Your father's ancestors banished those who survived to the forest hundreds of years ago. And every night we must work so the Chief can make his count and know we are not plotting against him. But we made machines to replace our numbers. And your father is not wise to us. And now we have you."

"If you can make such machines, why not build more? Take them to war and be done with us." Her voice broke with the last word.

"We are not like your people. We do not wish for massive bloodshed. We only want our freedom. But we will do what we must."

"And how do you plan to get it?"

"We will negotiate with your father. Our freedom for your life."

Her eyes hardened. "He won't deal with you. Not that way. Let me go and I'll talk to him. Shame him into telling his people the truth."

"You understand why I cannot trust you with that task."

She nodded grimly. "I'll just have to think of a way to make you."

ೞ৪৹

When Ena arrived at the Chief's hale wearing his dog-face, he creeped through the hidden gate entrance, then through secret passageways. It would be more dramatic this way, his mysterious appearance. Like magic.

He came up through the floor outside the Chief's receiving room. Two guards stood wide-eyed in a moment of frozen shock before they crossed their spears to block his way.

"I want to see Kahanai," Ena growled.

The younger guard's eyes darted to his elder, his spear trembled slightly. Behind them, across the room, the Chief's face was cold and his white knuckles clawed the arms of an enormous teak chair.

"Let him come," Kahanai bellowed.

The guards dropped their spears and stepped aside. Ena swallowed hard and shuffled forward. He stood hunched-shouldered, pinned under Kahanai's stare.

"Menehune freedom for your daughter," he managed to croak. His voice came out eerie, much better than he had planned.

"I know eepa ways," Kahanai said. "I know what you have done on the other islands. How can I believe Ailana safe?" The Chief's mouth set into a hard line.

"Declare the Menehune free and I will deliver her unharmed."

Kahanai shook his head. "I have no guarantee that if I made such declaration, you would return her."

"Our massacre, our enslavement has been hidden for generations." Ena's voice was strong. "Right the wrong done to us and be rid of your shame."

Kahanai closed his eyes briefly and they crinkled with exhaustion. "You ask the impossible." Kahanai dismissed Ena with a wave of his hand.

There would be no negotiation, the cold bastard. Ena went back to the forest.

CREO

It was early morning as he returned, and everyone was sleeping. Everyone except Ailana.

She smiled at him brightly. "Any luck with my father?"

Ena shook his head in frustration.

"I thought not. I have something to cheer you up." She pulled a slender toe from the dirt to reveal a dark spiral on top of freshly red and swollen skin. "It hurt much more than I expected."

Rage rolled inside Ena. "How dare you moko yourself like one of us." He pulled his arm back to strike her and she turned her head to brace for the blow. Guilt washed over him that he would harm a girl who was bound and unable to defend herself. He unclenched his fist and let his arm drop to his side. "I shouldn't be angry with you." There was another who deserved his wrath. "Who put ink to your skin?"

"I did." Mohihi moved serpentine through a small cluster of banana trees. "She suspected you would fail at your talking and that we should have another plan. She was right." Mohihi stepped to him and handed him an albatross bone and pot of burnt timbers. "Maybe you should listen to her."

Ena saw the hope in Ailana's eyes along with the desperation. He turned back to argue with Mohihi, but she had slipped away.

"What is your plan then, girl?"

"Sit with me and I'll explain."

As Ailana explained her plan to tell their story using their ink and her body, Ena began to feel encouraged. "Every time my father sees me, he will feel shame. Every time our people see me, he will feel shame. How can he not grant you freedom to live where you wish?"

It seemed worth a try. Or perhaps Ena was just desperate. If this plan failed, he could always move in on Kahanai with his automatons. No. He was just fooling himself. Even an army of five hundred was no match against the thousands of Tahitians. Kahanai could already be plotting to invade the forest. But then, Ena's people would have the advantage of picking them off in small groups as they tried to funnel through the trees.

The albatross bone-chisel shook in his trembling hand. He inhaled, consciously stilling his body as he pressed the sharp end coated with burnt timbers into her cheekbone. Her skin shone in luminescent patterns where the sun filtered through the fringe of the banana leaves. As he struck the chisel with a hammer, droplets of blood welled to the surface of Ailana's skin. The sight of the welt blossoming on her face stirred passion in him, but for Ailana or for his people it was impossible to determine. He was carving their story into her flesh. Perhaps his desire was a response to the joining of such beauty.

Her skin was soft as an orchid under his thumb and his heart quickened whenever he felt the energy that crackled when he brushed her with his fingertips. As he bent over, her breath tickled his ear.

He worked steadily for hours, 'till sweat dripped from his eyes and his forearm ached. Ailana never once cried out, never flinched. She held her posture erect, and kept that proud tilt to her chin.

"We should break until tomorrow," Ena said.

Ailana nodded and then promptly passed out.

He smiled at her bravery. Perhaps with her help, the Menehune would be part of the sunshine again. Free from the darkness.

C3&O

Ena worked slowly on Ailana's ta moko for most of the next day. When every part of her vast amount of exposed skin was covered in images of his people's history, he stopped. A silent tear slid down Ailana's face and pooled in the corner of her nose. On impulse, Ena kissed it away. Coming to himself, he pulled back in astonishment.

"I'm sorry. It is just, I am so grateful for what you are sacrificing for my people."

Color came to Ailana's cheek that was more than could be accounted for by the repeated taps of the chisel. "It's been a long process for both of us. No need for apologies."

Ena turned to put the chisel down and met Mohihi's little angry eyes burning in the darkness. She turned and stalked away from him. Ena knew that when Mohihi was furious, trouble would follow. Regardless, there was work to be done. Ena put on his dog-face, untied Ailana, and escorted her back to her hale.

C3&O

Only two days passed before the news came. Ailana's ta moko had shamed Kahanai so deeply he'd wandered away in grief and jumped into the sea. Ena felt pain for Ailana. This was not what either of them had foreseen.

He went to tell Mohihi the news only to find her sleeping place empty. Along with the deserted pallets of many others. Ena looked around their forest dwelling and supposed that nearly half their numbers had disappeared in the night. Along with most of their koa canoes. Mohihi had taken those loyal to her in search of a new home. The hatefulness of Mohihi's desperate action and the lack of faith of the others hurt deeply. The journey to other land was immense and arduous. Many of his people would die on the way. But, Mohihi was impossible to refuse. It seemed Kahanai was not the only one to feel the sting of a fairy.

⋘⋙

A messenger arrived from Ailana's hale. He was tall and thick as a tree. "An invitation!" he cried. "There will be a feast tonight to celebrate Chief Ailana's decree that the Menehune be freed."

Ena smiled a smile that went around his face two times and then ran to tell his people.

⋘⋙

The forest slipped away and Ena felt a hollow throbbing in his chest. They had a good life in the forest; a dark existence that was brightened by the closeness of the Menehune family. He wondered if Mohihi and the others would rebuild that bond again somewhere else, perhaps on a small island free of outsiders.

When Ena and his people arrived, they were met with an enormous party. Lauhala mats were rolled out and centerpieces made of ti leaves, ferns, and bright flowers covered the ground both inside and outside the walls of the hale. Thousands of Tahitians sat eating from gourd bowls filled with poi or from wooden platters of meat, fish, and sweet potatoes.

As the Menehune passed inside the garden, Ena felt the smallness of their presence. The hundred or so of them barely garnered notice among the guests who kept arriving all the while. Steam rose from the underground imu oven. The smell of roast pig wafted from the river rocks. Dancers performed the hula kahiko to the musicians chants and drums; a steady background to the raucous laughter and conversation of the attendees.

Ena nodded to four of his young men who carried a large parcel wrapped in kapa bark. The men took the offering over to the oven, peeling back the covering, revealing the still form of the dog-faced automaton.

A collective gasp rose from the crowd. A susurrus of "eepa" spread out through the guests in steady waves. Then, the young men tossed the automaton onto the coals. The Tahitians cheered in their ignorance and orange flames began to melt away the Menehune's sin.

Ena spied Ailana on the other side of the fishpond, sitting in her father's teak chair that had been moved outside for the occasion. She wore a feather cloak as a sign of her new status, the vibrant reds and yellows woven into intricate diamonds. She was a beautifully regal bird of prey and Ena's heart leapt with happiness at the sight of her.

He gradually wound his way through the sways and stumbles of the contented guests, until he found himself kneeling in front of her. He looked up at her with a grin. "Thank you. Your strength in keeping your promise is a rare gift to my people."

She looked down on him, the moko around her eyes emphasizing her sadness. "I could do no less." Her voice was distant.

"I am sorry for the loss of your father," he whispered. "I can't imagine the pain this must have caused you."

Ailana shrank; her shoulders hunched, and her chin dropped. Her gaze withdrew from him until she stared at nothing. The vastness of her heartbreak smothered him until it was hard to breathe. His body was heavy as he stood. Turning away from her was difficult, like the air conspired to resist him.

He walked over to the stone wall near the secret exit concealed by the maile vines. He took one last look around the lavish garden. His eyes locked with Ipo, one of the good-looking young Menehune who was always quick with a smile or an offer to help repair the machines. Ipo grinned crookedly; a mixture of joy and mischief. He nodded to Ena, then turned away, extending his hand up to a stunning Tahitian as they started to dance. Ena chuckled softly, then slipped outside the wall.

ᎤᎦᏅ

That night the quiet of the forest haunted Ena. He was used to the murmured voices of his people, the squeals of children, the knocks of tinkering. Now he could only hear his breath and the blood rushing past his ears. The pallets were all empty, the cooking coals cold. Ena dragged his feet over to where the automatons were piled. Their shapes were the same as his people, but their features were crude, their hollow eyes lifeless. Ena sat on the ground, his back resting against the cold wood of his machines. He felt an immediate connection with their emptiness. It sucked at him with such heaviness that when he tried to stand, his knee only cracked and dust rubbed inside his joints. His body was too big. Too big to dance. Too big to gather up the empty pallets. He was tired anyway. So, so tired.

He wondered if his people would ever come back to the forest. Or if they would stay happy in their new world. Maybe he would become a legend, one told over and over again—a myth about how Ena decayed along with the machines, or maybe one about the dog-faced cannibal—until his story was carved into the ta moko of forever.

ALL THE KING'S MONSTERS

by Megan Arkenberg

THE MONSTER IN THE CELL across from me is Hunger. He is a young boy, brown and slight, with long crooked snatching fingers and thin greasy hair. All day, he plucks bits of straw from his mattress and digs them into the dirt floor or the flaking mortar between wall-stones. Sometimes he chews on them.

At night, he screams.

We are going mad, slowly, all of us. The monsters have taken everything, everything but themselves.

০৪৪৪

When Uri was dead, they brought me his things in a scarred leather bag that smelled of blood and burnt flesh and, unbearably, of him. There were his clothes, the torturer's thin bloody handprints on the sleeves and collar; and the miniature of me that he had worn in a silk bag around his neck. The final item was a stained, half-finished sketch of a monster, its long neck decked with tassels and jewels like a King's, its single horn barbed like a spear, its sharp teeth jaggedly overlapping its jaw. Worst of all were the eyes, like black holes bored in a sheet of iron, ragged-lidded and dim.

Two words were written on the back. *Pride*—though whether it meant that pride had killed Uri, or that it would kill me, or simply that pride is a monster, I do not know—and *Soon*. They need not have written that last. I knew they were coming.

C3&D

Before Hunger came, I shared a cell with Grief.

Her child was dead. She called his name at night, weeping into her ragged white hair. I could not comfort her. She flinched from my hands, from my voice, from my offers to comb her hair or share my half of the gritty gray bread the guards brought us.

I whispered to her sometimes, telling of Uri, but she did not listen—or else she did not hear. I learned long ago that Grief is a monster without ears.

C3&D

I wake at dawn. That word is almost meaningless here, but I have kept it, as I have kept the words *sunlight* and *rain* to describe the weak colors and sweet smells that sometimes reach us through the bars. Dawn is when the guards walk down the block of cells, looking to see if any of us have died during the night. That is the way they discovered Grief, frozen in her sleep.

No one is dead today. We are not that lucky.

She is with the guards today. I hear the click-click of her boot heels, like claws clipping against the hard earth. Her waistcoat and sleeves are clean now, pale blue and purest white, but by nightfall she will be covered in blood.

Of all the King's monsters, she is the only one I fear.

C3੪0

"The King came to Abaddon on our wedding day," I
told Grief.

This is how I remember it; Uri and I standing beneath
the canopy on the riverbank, the gentle rumble of his voice
as we read our vows and scatter tulip petals to the current.
Suddenly, the creak and snap of metal joints. An iron monster's shadow falling on our faces. The break in Uri's voice as
the King flies overhead.

In the middle of our wedding vows, Uri paused. He was
a man who put his hate before his love.

"It is not well to speak ill of the dead," I said, "so I will
say only that I wish he had chosen differently. I wish he had
not paused."

Grief turned her face to the wall and shivered.

C3੪0

She stops in front of my cell.

"What is your name, prisoner?" Her voice is very harsh;
it comes from breathing in smoke all day. They say she was
a blacksmith before the King came, that she is the one who
built his iron monsters. I am not sure of that, but I know she
is a monster in flesh.

"My name is Miriam," I say.

"Why are you here?"

"Uri of Jordan was my husband. The King wants me where
he can watch me." *With all his other monsters*, I think but do
not say. She wouldn't understand, which would be bad; or
she would, which would be worse.

"Uri," she repeats. "The famous rebel."

Let that be all, I pray, but she does not move. I am kneeling
on the floor, my eyes level with her waist. I see the steady

swell of her chest with each breath and feel my own heart hammering like horses' hooves.

"Tell me what he was like," she says.

"You know what he was like," I whisper. "You killed him."

She says nothing for a long time. Her body tenses, her chest heaves as if with pain. For a wild moment, I think she will kill me too.

Then she turns and walks to the next cell.

⋆

Uri told me once that the iron monsters have names. I asked the name of the King's and he said a strange, brittle word, a word that means power and authority and soundness in the language of the King's people. That is the monster Uri set out to kill.

Pride was Uri's monster, as Grief was the white-haired woman's and Hunger belongs to the boy across the block. Pride killed Uri. Pride made me a widow.

Pride is my monster, too. Its other name is Vengeance.

⋆

There is a new boy in the cell next to me. The man who was there before went out with *her* and did not come back. That man's monster was Fear. The new boy is Anger.

"We'll teach those bastards," he says. And when he comes back from questioning: "We'll kill them with their own weapons." He is questioned a lot. I wonder how long it will be before someone who loves him is given his things in a scarred leather bag.

One day, when the questioning has been especially brutal, he falls against the bars that separate our cells and mumbles through swollen lips, "We'll kill them. With the weapons they've given us, we'll kill them."

I look at him and laugh harshly. "What weapons have they given us? They've taken everything."

"Everything but themselves," he says.

She comes for him the next day. Then his cell is empty.

⊂3⊃

When they arrested me, they would not let me keep Uri's things. They went through the house, collecting his clothes for the fire, and when they could not find his portrait of me they took me into the cellar and beat me until I told them where it was. But they did not ask for the scrap of paper with its half-finished sketch of a monster.

The day after she comes for the boy, I see a scrap of paper sticking out of his mattress straw. If I stretch, I can just close my fingers around the corner. I glance down the block, making sure the guards are not coming, and take the paper into my cell.

It is a picture of another monster, this one complete. Its neck is short and powerful, its eyes narrow, its jaw tight in a hideous grimace. Rough, graceless rivets hold its thick teeth in place.

There is a faint bloodstain along the bottom; the boy had this picture while he was being tortured. I think of the marks on the sketch they brought me with Uri's things.

The boy's family will never have this picture. Thinking of them, I fold it and tuck it into the silk bag at my throat.

⊂3⊃

"What do you think of me?" she asks.

She has come alone, her clothes already red from the day's work. I look at her face to avoid seeing the stains. It does no good; her eyes are the color of dried blood.

"I think you are a monster," I say.

"Did it occur to you that monsters might be kept on a leash? That they have to eat what they are fed?" Her skin is too dark to show a blush, but the way she turns her head away makes me think she regrets the question. Her throat tightens as she swallows. "Miriam," she says, nearly whispering, "hold on to what the King gave you."

"He gave me nothing," I say. "Nothing but pain, and grief, and hunger, and fear."

"He gave you vengeance," she says.

She looks a long time at the silk bag, and before she goes, she slips a bit of paper between the bars.

It is a picture of Uri's monster.

∽

Hunger did not scream last night, and this morning he sits quietly on his mattress. He reaches for the straw sometimes, not as though he is going to play with it, but as though it is hiding something.

The guards are agitated. They chatter in their brittle language, the sound like metal on metal. *She* is nowhere to be seen.

Perhaps I am mad, but I think I heard her voice last night. It sounded like she was singing.

∽

There is something I did not tell Grief; Uri sang, the night he was captured.

Old King Folly sat on a wall, Old King Folly had a great fall, and all the King's monsters and all the King's men could not put the King back together again.

"Children's rhymes," I said, kissing his forehead. "Hush, love. They'd kill you for less than that."

He laughed, drawing me down into his lap. "They'd have to find me first."

"You're so certain you can beat them."

"They've given me my greatest weapon."

I wrapped my arms around him, pressing his face against my chest. His lips lay against the skin that rose and fell with my heartbeat. "You can't trust them, love," I said.

"Them?"

"Whoever's telling you these things — your greatest weapon, the names of the King's monsters, these foolish children's rhymes. The *King's* monsters, Uri. You have to remember whose they are."

"I'll steal the King's monsters away from him," he said.

I shook my head. "Who wants to own a monster?"

CR&O

In the end, he was wrong. We do not need to steal our monsters. Sometimes, they are handed to us in a scarred leather bag.

CR&O

The men who brought me my food take Hunger on their way out.

This is the first time she has not come for the prisoner herself. I strain my ears; sometimes when I do this, I can hear them screaming. This time, I hear nothing.

My appetite is gone; the bread tastes like ash in my mouth. I think suddenly that I am about to die. This feeling has been with me every day since my arrest, but now it is overpowering.

Every breath becomes precious to me. The moldering straw, the fetor of the dungeons seem suddenly as sweet as perfume.

I do not want to die.

The guards come to my cell next.

⋈

When he was dead, I went out into the riverside garden he had loved so well and ripped up the tulips, scattering their petals in a mockery of the wedding ceremony. I chopped down the cherry trees and burned them in a fire hot as a blacksmith's forge. I stood over the flames, choking on the ash and wishing I could die.

"Here is your monster," I said, and threw the sketch onto the fire. "I was wrong. It is yours, after all, and what's yours can die with you."

The picture burned, and even though I wished to, I did not.

⋈

This is where he died, I think as she locks the door behind the departing guards. I want to say it out loud, because I cannot make myself believe it any other way. This room is too dark, too dry, like a cell made of old bones. There is no smell of blood here, only rust and dry sweat.

"You asked me what he was like," I say. She turns to me, her eyes blunt and penetrating like awls. "It should be enough for me to say that if you hadn't killed him, this place would have."

"This place did." She rests her hand on her hip, hooking the iron keys around her thumb. "He brought himself here, Miriam, and I did what I had to do. The time was wrong. He was to lay low, wait for me to tell him—well, you'll understand soon enough."

She walks to a part of the floor that is smoother than the rest and kneels. I follow slowly. "The time was wrong—for what?"

"You'll have to take his place. Pride was his, built for him, but she will serve you just as well." Creaking, the paving stones beneath her begin to sink. She catches my wrist roughly and pulls me onto the platform. "This is it, Miriam—Uri's rebellion. For the first time in months, the King is without his monster. We must catch him while he is weak."

"We? What's happening?"

And then the floor opens away above us, and I see.

The room is full of monsters. Short and corded, tall and sleek, glittering iron claws and fangs, rippling silver scales. I could name them at a glance: long-toothed Hunger, crooked dark-eyed Grief, Anger with his graceless jaw and powerful neck. The King's monster crouches at the end of the hall, a mighty emperor among his subjects.

She takes me by the hand and leads me up to Pride.

I brush my fingers along the monster's graceful tasseled neck, and the dull iron against my skin feels as hot and vibrant as the torturer's hand—the blacksmith's hand, the hand that shaped all the King's monsters. Pride is beautiful. Her deep eyes flicker as I look into them; her breath on my cheek is cool and sweet.

The blacksmith hands me her reins. "Mount up," she says. "The others will join us soon. But I wanted you to be the first—you've lost so much you didn't choose to give."

I have no voice. Pride nudges her iron head against mine, cruel and gentle at once; this pain is hers, too. She belonged to Uri, and Uri to her, more than I ever did.

The blacksmith turns her back, and leaves Pride and I to become each other's.

෬෩

We take to the skies, all the King's monsters, with drawn swords and cruelly-tipped darts, with steel fangs and claws gleaming. Our queen and mother rides at the head, cutting through the air on the King's own monster like a ray of light.

The King has taken much from us, but he will learn to fear the things he's given, the things he's made of us.

We are all the King's monsters, and we fly.

The Thing with Feathers

by Cora Pop

ALL OF THIS HAPPENED BECAUSE OF THE BIRD.

Perhaps, also because of my father's gambling and death. Of my brother deserting *me* to join Queen Victoria's army. Of becoming penniless and alone at nineteen. Though, really, mostly because of the bird.

The door behind the clematis vine had led me straight to Lady Grey's bedroom upstairs. My target had proven identical to the previous two—a cabinet adorned with monkeys, birds, and Hindu gods—and the same panel had sprung open when I pushed one of Vishnu's hands.

Every time I had a hint of hesitation, the thought of my employer chased it away. And if the shame of being caught with a stranger's wallet in my hand wasn't enough, the memory of the man who'd caught me urged me on. A former army man, big as a door, a deep red scar marking his face from forehead to jaw. He had stared at my brother's trousers and coat, both too big for me, then at my face, at the curls escaping from my cap, had run his fingers roughly over my forearm, and then he'd grumbled, "You'll do ... Miss."

I knew now why. Even a big child, well fed, would have had trouble putting his hand through this hole. But I had slender limbs, and I was starving.

"Do the job," he'd said to me, "and I won't call the police, and you'll be paid nicely. Double-cross me and rot in jail."

Then he'd taught me how to pick a lock, open any window from outside, and a few other thieves' tricks.

So now I was about to steal the ruby for him when the bird began singing.

It was the most exquisite canary song, at once joyful and melancholic. Distracting me. Beckoning to me.

At arm length within the secret compartment, there was a tiny door with a ring. To open it, I had to pull slowly on the ring until I heard a click, then turn it two clicks to the right and four to the left.

But, this time, I miscounted the clicks. I had to start over, then one more time.

In size and cut, the ruby was the twin of the other gemstones I had acquired, the sapphire and the emerald. Perfection. Yet when tracing its contours with my finger, I noticed it was chipped.

I marveled at this only briefly before I hid the ruby in a small pocket inside my corset. Now I was done. My heart sang a little song of joy. Like a canary's.

Except the bird was a robin now. *That* was odd.

I should have left right away. Instead, I glanced outside. The many guests of Duchess Grey were frolicking on the distant lawn next to the water fountains, dressed in their *fête champêtre* costumes. Five o'clock was one hour away. That meant that no maids and valets were yet rushing everywhere in the woes of tea preparations. I had time to see the bird before seeking my escape.

Listening intently, I stepped into a plain corridor. At the other end of it, a door had been left ajar. The bird was a skylark now. I hurried quietly.

And stepped into a place of wonders. An articulated doll, its porcelain face exactly like Queen Victoria's, stood on a tea table. On a mahogany desk stood a globe with oceans of turquoise and continents of agate and quartz, surrounded by a spider web of fine gold wires. Everywhere, clocks with tiny mechanical peacocks and shepherd girls were insistent reminders of the time I was wasting.

Somewhere among all that, the bird was a canary again. Only ten past four. *Where are you?*

At last. Perched on a rose, in a magnificent flower arrangement, was a plump yellow bird with ruffled feathers and a tiny beak. It poured out a nightingale's song now.

Carefully, I lowered my head. And gasped. At the novelty. At the perfection. The bird's body was of gold filigree with a miniature skeleton inside. Its gold wings showed every barb of every feather.

The song ceased. The bird turned to me an eye of lapis-lazuli and the fine gold feathers of its crest fluttered briefly as if with disquietude.

"Oh, my beauty," I whispered.

The bird hopped onto my hand. Minuscule claws from articulated gold fingers dug into my skin.

"Are you alive?" I said, wonder pressing my chest. I looked for a spring to be wound like a clock's to convey movement but there was none.

With the bird on my hand, I sat on the floor. I forgot about my employer, about the ruby, about being in a stranger's castle. All I knew was the bird and, for some silly reason, I thought that all it knew was me.

Until a concert of chimes startled me out of my reverie. … Four … Five … Five o'clock already?

I jumped to my feet, my heart racing madly. The guests were flocking across the lawn towards the castle. I ran to the next window. They were gathering in the shade of the side terraces for the afternoon tea. But they were not supposed to be there. Not yet. Blocking my escape route. So many of them with their children, their dogs, their maids, their butlers. Perhaps I could find another way out. Perhaps I could wait.

No, I couldn't wait. Lady Grey might return to her bedroom. Somebody might come to the study. And it was six miles on foot to the village where the man with the red scar was waiting for me only until eight o'clock. "*If you're late, the deal is off.*" It wasn't fair, after four months, to be given only a few hours and I had pleaded with him, but in vain.

So I tied the bird's beak with a ribbon from my hair while it watched me, blinking with eyelashes of gold.

"I'll take good care of you," I whispered, hiding it inside my shirt.

Just then, a door clacked, close by. Hurried steps followed, heavy but cautious. I dropped to my hands and knees, praying that whoever it was wasn't coming to that room.

Whoever it was, it came in.

At least two people. Hushed voices.

Thieves, I thought, holding my breath, and almost laughed. *Other* thieves?

A man spoke harshly in a foreign language. Maybe Italian.

All at once, noises of overturned objects rose from everywhere, mingled with more angry words in Italian. Whatever they were seeking, it was eluding them. Something broke, one armchair away from me.

I crouched lower, started crawling backwards, underneath tables, behind armchairs, catching glimpses of black trousers and shoes moving around frantically. At the door to the corridor, I stood and just before I squeezed out of the room I glimpsed an oversized Humpty-Dumpty, in a suit with bold vertical stripes, white and black.

I dashed from behind the clematis vine into the mild sun of late afternoon, a few yards away from the closest tables. The fresh pastries smelled heavenly.

I stole along the old walls, keeping behind the flower beds, taking courage for when I reached the open lawn. With luck, my clothes could pass for the garb of a stable-boy or an under-gardener, and nobody would notice me in them. But when I turned the second corner, there came a boy, rolling his wooden circle. I swerved to avoid him.

"Who are you?" the boy asked loudly.

I smiled to him.

"You're not a boy," he cried. "Why are you wearing boy clothes? Nanny Jones! Nanny Jones! Come and see!"

I looked at the gate far across the open lawn and I looked at the old oak trees which were much closer. I didn't wait for Nanny Jones to see me. I took to a run straight to the forest.

Some children darted after me, and their nannies alerted the valets, and soon there was a mob chasing me.

Past the first oak trees, past the hazelnut bushes, breathless, I kept glancing back. My foot caught in a root.

I stumbled, my arms flailing, grabbing the first thing for support, and hung onto it, swaying.

For it was a soft ladder, suspended out of thin air. Surely it was hanging from a tree branch, only I couldn't see it for the leaves. My right heel was caught in the braided silk of the first rung. I stooped to reach it, clumsily.

"Let go of the ladder," came a voice from heavens.

Just as a low growl rose not one yard to my left. I froze. A gray dog, enormous, was fixing me with glassy eyes.

"Well, I can't," I said, my eyes on the dog. "My heel is stuck. I have to–"

"Take off your boot and go," said the voice from the heavens.

"I won't do such thing."

Voices resounded at the skirt of the forest. More rustlings stirred the bushes. On my right, a second dog bared its teeth, its lips quivering.

"They'll bite me!"

"Step on the first rung then and hold on tight. I'll pull you up."

"Well, I cannot—I really have to—I assure you that—"

The dog on the left moved closer. A shiver chilled my spine.

"They'll tear you apart ... "

Did I sense a drop of humor in that tone?

"Are they your dogs? Call them off!"

"There's no time for this. Do what I'm telling you. Quick! I *will* pull the ladder up regardless and you'll be hanging upside down."

Reluctantly, I put my other foot on the silk ladder. With a strange whirr the ladder started moving up.

"I can't see you," I called, holding hard onto it. "Are you in the ... tree?" but there was no answer.

In seconds, I was above the hazelnut growth, shielding my face from the oak branches. And soon I was above the treetops also and staring into something that was there and could *not* be there.

There was a square opening in the sky, like a glimpse into a room, and the devil was looking down at me from within it.

I didn't believe in the devil, but what else could it be, black, with huge round eyes, glimmering in gold, maybe from the fires in Hell, and a face like a ghost's. When I was within reach, he held his black hand out to me. I took it, mesmerized, and more than certain that I was going to die. The devil pulled me up through the opening.

Then I was on my knees, on a perfectly polished wooden floor, the color of a dying sunset. It was chilly in there, like in a room with the windows left open in winter. The devil was untangling my high heel from the braided ladder.

"Have you borrowed your sister's booties?" the devil said, a hint of laughter in his voice.

I stood up, not quite gracefully, leaning into his hand. In the mirrors of his goggles, I could see the twin boys that I resembled, frightened and disheveled. I took off my cap, shaking my curls free.

"You're not a boy … " the devil murmured, his hand still wrapping mine. He tore off his goggles, undid a chin strap and took off a black leather cap with large earflaps.

I saw unruly black hair, eyes like two pieces from the sky, a cruel mouth, but smiling, and, oh, so beautiful.

"You're not the devil … " I whispered.

He was unrecognizable in his bizarre spectacles, but I had met him in London, at my first ball. He had swept me away in a waltz, cut short by strange men running and by his precipitous departure. After that, my dance card had been a simple formality without meaning. Two years ago. In a different life. No wonder he didn't recognize me.

"Lord Grey," I said and curtsied out of habit, taking a bit longer for my bow as I was attempting to compose myself. The bird stirred underneath my shirt. *His bird …*

"Please, call me Damon," he said. "Have we met?"

He eyed me with that blue ice in his eyes, one dark eyebrow lifted as if in doubt, with a curious insistence that I would have thought rude under normal circumstances.

"I'm Amelia Thomson." *Viscountess Valentia, completely broke.* "I'm Lady Bassett's personal secretary." *When had it become so easy for me to lie?* I was almost certain I had seen the old baroness among the guests.

"Well, Miss Thomson, as much as I'm enchanted to make your acquaintance, I apologize for making of you my unwilling guest."

"Sir, I am grateful to you for rescuing me … from the dogs, but–"

"Tell me," he said abruptly, "were you *supposed* to be here?" His blue stare was almost unbearable.

"I'm *supposed* to be in the village, with lady Bassett's letter." *To meet the man with the red scar who will find me at the end of*

Earth if I fail. Eight o'clock was not two hours away.

"The post office is the other way ... "

"I was distracted ... "

"Do all Lady Bassett's assistants wear men's clothes?"

"I do, when I need to move fast."

"You could've asked a valet to deliver the letter."

"Lady Bassett trusts *me.*"

He opened his mouth to speak more, then only bowed his head.

"I'm sorry, Miss Thomson, I got carried away ... "

"Amelia, please."

He smiled to me, an enigmatic smile, at once sweet and predatory.

I took a step away from him. We were in a room, long and narrow, gleaming with rich woods and smooth metal. Oval windows with brass frames lined the long sides and every empty spot on the walls held instruments of copper and glass. There was a red leather sofa and a small desk scattered with maps. On the desk stood a globe of turquoise and onyx, wrapped in gold and silver wires. At each end of the room, wooden steps led to a door.

The door in the floor was closed now and Lord Grey was standing on it. All I could see through the windows was the blue sky with small clouds rolling on it. I dared not approach them to look down.

"What is this, sir? Your house in the tree?"

"Damon, please ... My airship."

He seemed to have said that with reluctance but also with pride. And then he smiled, for my eyes must have grown wide with bewilderment.

An airship? I had heard of them, steam-powered machines that could be steered in the air, but to actually be in one ... *Afloat? Hanging in the air?* I suddenly needed to sit down and the couch seemed far away.

"I'm sorry," Damon said, catching my elbow. "I haven't offered you a seat."

The next moment I was on the couch and he had a bottle in his hands.

"Champagne? It's perfectly chilled. I always take a bottle with me when I go up…"

He popped the cork deftly and poured the bubbly in two crystal flutes.

"To airships … " I said, already dizzy with all these new things.

"To unexpected encounters," Damon said.

The champagne was freezing cold and delicious, but I hadn't eaten since the night before.

"When you go up …" I mumbled.

"I go very high above the clouds. It is very cold there … Better than a cold room … "

He brought out a plateau of cold meats and cheeses. I was ravenous. I couldn't remember when I had last eaten properly.

"Shouldn't you entertain your guests instead?"

"They are my mother's. And I'm not much of a mundane inclination …"

"Are you hiding?" I laughed.

He lowered his head towards me with a conspiratorial smile.

"I'm hiding from a young lady that my mother wants me to marry."

"I see … You don't want to get married."

"Only to the right person …"

Damon's gaze drifted slowly over my face, almost like a caress, making me blush, then out the oval window behind me. He stood up abruptly, picking up a field-glass.

"Bonzardo!" he said after a moment.

"May I?"

The powerful lenses brought the hideous face, all layers of thick skin and fat, much too close to mine. And for one second, the tiny eyes, too vivid for such a face, stared at me directly. I gasped, almost dropping the field-glass.

He couldn't have seen me, could he? I coiled up on the sofa, below the window, my heart and thoughts racing wildly. The sinister Humpty-Dumpty in his ridiculous suit. And two gaunt men dressed in black like undertakers. Standing on the lawn, looking in our direction. But I couldn't tell Lord Grey where I had seen them.

Damon appeared just as distressed as I was. He consulted his pocket watch then started pacing, his dark eyebrows knotted over the ices of his eyes.

"Who is he?"

"My rival, Count Bonzardo."

"As your mother's guest?"

"He's Italian. He's a beloved of all gullible rich women like my mother."

"Still ... Here?"

"He must be desperate ... He's after the bird ... For his airship ... "

The bird ...

The hollow inside me grew into a black precipice.

"But the bird will not allow anybody to find her," Damon said as if from far away.

"His airship ..."

"Amelia, forget about the balloons you've heard of. Those are simple toys, feeble attempts at not being blown away by any wind. They can reach ten miles an hour, perhaps, with luck. I'm referring to *real* airships. Machines one can fly around the world. Or to the Moon ... "

The passion in his words made him so beautiful that I forgot to breathe. This wasn't the best moment to meet him again, when I was in such dire straits and he so unattainable.

"Have you been to the Moon?" I whispered.

"Not yet ... " He smiled, his eyes shining. "But I will ...

However, there is a race this Saturday, from Paris to Shanghai."

"Tomorrow ..."

"The prize is a book of ancient knowledge, one that teaches how to reach the Moon, the stars ... I know Bonzardo wants it by any means."

"Then why aren't you in Paris?"

"I'm waiting for my assistant."

He took the field-glass again.

"Bonzardo looks displeased," Damon said.

A fluttering of fear stirred inside me.

"Can they see us?"

He shook his head.

"The airship is shielded. We are invisible."

"I need to leave," I said abruptly, "lest I shall lose my employment."

Bonzardo lurking in the forest was an unsettling thought, but the man with the red scar was real.

Damon raised his eyes from the dials he was reading and smiled.

"I will excuse you with Lady Bassett, do not worry."

How about the man with the red scar?

"Please, take me to the village. I *must* be there before eight."

"You cannot appear out of thin air in the village. Besides, I cannot leave here before Geoff returns. After, if you want... Don't worry, he's been in the army. He's very punctual..."

I started pacing from one window to another, still unbelieving that I was in this ... *airship*, above the treetops. Maybe it was a nightmare. Maybe I was at home, the proper girl I used to be. But every deeper breath pressed a stolen ruby into my breast. And a strange golden bird was nestling underneath my shirt.

"Would you like to take your chances with the dogs? Of course, there could be other beasts in the forest ..."

He *was* laughing at me. I turned my back to him. On the far lawn bonfires had been lit for the evening dances.

"I thought so," Damon said. "I will not risk you stumbling upon Bonzardo. I cannot fight him here. Please, be patient. I'll take you to the village tomorrow morning."

His hand hovered over the gold and silver wires surrounding the globe.

"I have to choose my winds. Adjust my instruments. You have the room. Call me if you need something. There is a bathroom over there ..."

I wondered if the wires represented a map of steady winds.

"Am I a prisoner here?"

"No."

"Yet there is no ladder for me to climb down."

He nodded, pensively.

"No ladder. For now. Good night, Amelia."

"Good night." *Damon.*

When he was gone, I took the bird out and put it on the window sill. The ribbon I had tied around its beak had fallen, but the bird had kept silent; it started preening its golden feathers, occasionally watching me with one of its lapis-lazuli eyes.

I laid my head on the soft, cool pillow.

"What shall we do?" I whispered. "You'll not betray me, will you?"

I thought of Lord Grey in the other room, of his ice-blue eyes, of his smile. He was intangible, part of a different world. His interests where so elevated, so pure, so ... scientific, and I was now just an ordinary thief.

CREW

I woke up shivering, in the pink light of dawn, my breath drawing white clouds in the air. Heavy wool blankets were covering me to my ears.

I stood, wrapping the blankets around me. Damon wasn't

there. Worse, the bird wasn't there.

I climbed the stairs, opened the door, and stepped onto … a balcony. In the wind. In the sky.

Inadvertently, I took two more steps.

Very far below, underneath moving clouds, I spied a city, split by a large, bent river.

The clouds began spinning, or maybe it was the rising sun glinting playfully in the roofs below, or the rush of air, the smells, the cries of seagulls. My vision blurred. I leaned over the parapet, ready to fly on my own.

"Welcome to Paris," Damon said, one arm around my waist, the other in front of me on the railing. "Turn around … Look at me … "

Trembling, I looked up at him, at his blue piercing eyes, and the pitch-black hair falling over his forehead, at the bird on his shoulder, chirping merrily, at his mouth half-smiling, half-scolding, so beautiful, and I wanted to die.

"Listen to me, my airship is solid. And I will *not* let you fall."

"I've never been to Paris …" I whispered.

"Let's try again," he said softly. "Imagine you're seeing a map … There's the Louvre … And over there, Baron Haussmann is destroying the city to build it anew …"

I took his advice, fearfully. Yes, I could see tiny doll-houses, squeezed into labyrinthine streets, and large, geometrical gardens, and even ant-like people, and carriages with ant-like horses. Slowly, miraculously, everything had steadied.

Damon wasn't next to me anymore.

"Geoff has been found dead in the village. I had no reason to wait longer …"

Was he apologizing?

"But you said …"

"Put this on."

He handed me a leather jacket, too big for me but good to keep the wind out.

The bird flew onto my hand. Damon smiled, a playful, enigmatic glimmer in his ice-blue eyes.

"She likes you."

"Yes, I like you," the bird said.

I jumped, with my heart beating wildly.

Damon burst into laughter.

"Obnoxious creature! She's not uttered one word since I've made her."

"I have been waiting for *her*," the bird said in the melodious voice of a young girl.

"*You* made it?"

He led me to a chair decked out with bizarre instruments. The Pilot's chair? In front of it stood a small opaque window, brass-framed, with plenty of vertical tubes and spheres underneath. Numbers appeared and disappeared on it as if by magic.

"My analytical engine," Damon answered the question in my widened eyes. "The airship's *computer* ..."

He lifted a panel to reveal another tangle of silvery tubes and wires. A silver ring was spinning underneath. Above it, like glowworms in a spider's web, were three gems, a diamond, a sapphire, an emerald.

My heart sank. Two of them I had given to the man with the red scar.

A fourth place was empty. *Waiting for the ruby.*

I realized how hard I was shaking only when Damon steadied me again, his arm around my back.

"Have you heard of *vimanas*?"

His stare was burning my face but I couldn't get myself to look at him. Why did he have the stones?

Vimanas? The flying chariots from the Vedas, from the Ramayana.

"No ... What can a poor girl–?"

"You're *not* a poor girl." he said, his eyes on the red scratches that my hands bore from the narrow holes.

"You are beautiful," the bird said in Damon's voice. Uncanny bird, making me blush.

"The gemstones are part of an ancient flying machine," Damon said, his blue gaze piercing mine. "The diamond defies Earth's pull, gravity as Sir Isaac Newton called it, a thousand-fold the power of steam. The sapphire is for stealth—hence we are invisible at will. The emerald commands a weapon—a most powerful one at the height of its abilities. Each of them will partially work on their own but the missing one is meant to bring true life to the ensemble. The ruby ..."

He knows, I thought, my chest hollow.

"I've learned about them from a Vedanta mystic in Calcutta. He has given me the ancient engine, the spinning ring you've seen, and the diamond. He also had a chip of the ruby. That piece gives life to the bird. Such will the ruby do for my airship..."

He knows, I thought, *though he won't confront me directly. He is a gentleman. Although one who has ordered three thefts ...*

"The stones were kept in a temple in the jungle, stolen by a Company officer, gambled away, lost ... It took me years to locate them, in the most unexpected places ... months to prepare their acquisition ... Geoff was waiting for the ruby in the village. He was killed. The ruby was not on him. If Bonzardo has it–"

Something was floating inside me, tears, anger, fear, defiance.

"I *could* take it out of the bird ... It won't be as powerful, but it could work. I need the ruby for the race."

And kill the bird?

"Can you make the bird alive again after?"

"Can you put the heart back into a human being?"

"So the bird will die forever?"

He nodded, his gaze heavy on my face.

"What will you do?"

"I will ... do my best. Even on steam alone, this is an amazing airship. The race starts tonight. They're here."

He pointed to the west, to the north. Three shadows were floating over the buildings, of giant birds with outstretched wings. A gray shape materialized briefly, shimmering, and a man saluted us.

"Who is that?"

"That's Count Von Stegel, from Prussia," Damon said, waving back to him. "He's a friend." Higher up, I caught a glimpse of red and gold. "That's Xiao Hui. Sometimes, he's a friend also. And that's Gaston Tissandier. He keeps to himself."

"And Bonzardo?"

"Bonzardo must arrive at night. He hasn't achieved proper invisibility yet."

At that precise moment, a howling pierced the sky.

"Down!" Damon yelled, throwing us to the floor, he above to protect me. Splinters flew from the parapet where the projectiles bit above our heads. More followed, their hissing insufferable, like of hot stones thrown into water, one after the other, only at inhuman speeds.

"Stay down!" Damon cried, scrambling to the pilot's seat.

A rumbling rose from the floor. Pneumatic hisses stirred tubes I hadn't noticed before.

The airship maneuvered abruptly, lowering itself on the left side, pushing me into the parapet. And then again, soaring upwards, making me skid the other way, on my knees and elbows.

"Go below the deck!" Damon yelled.

"Go to the cannon," the bird said, in my voice.

I clambered onto what had to be the gunner's chair, high in a little dome. The armrests held strange metallic gauntlets, with straps and buttons and I had no idea what they could do; but the small cannon was something I could use.

"Amelia, what are you doing?" Damon cried over his shoulder. "Stay down!"

"I know how to fire a gun!"

Shells, long as my forearm, were attached to a leather strap going into the cannon. I tested the trigger. The recoil was a hard punch to my palm. While the machine-gun pulled another shell inside, I tied myself into a harness.

In the whooshing sounds, I swung around until I saw it. Behind and above us, loomed a bulky monster with humongous wings, a colossal owl darkening the heights. Snakes of white fire charged at us from its split belly, animated innards undulating across the sky, like wailing, meowing lightning. And from within them rushed swarms of fire wasps, their screech excruciating, numbing. Where they touched, hisses, splinters, ashes rose into wild dances.

"Damon!"

The urge to flee, to burrow was twisting my belly. I clenched my teeth, pulling the trigger.

"*Damon!*"

"Aim upwards!" spoke the bird.

"Are you tied?" Damon yelled.

Before I answered, I was upside-down, the harness cutting hard into my shoulders. Paris became a city in the sky, then the sky reclaimed its place, but where was Bonzardo, then Paris and the sky switched places again, and again, and again.

In the mayhem, Damon and Bonzardo circled each other, switching positions continuously, up and down, close and far. *Let us just run away*, a litany in my mind, *please, Damon, please*, as I pulled the trigger each time I glimpsed the monstrous owl.

Had Geoff been there, I imagined we would've stood a better chance. But I did my best. My aim improved with each shot. And then one shell clipped the tip of Bonzardo's wing. The owl tottered. I yelled with joy.

Fire licked my shelter.

"Down!" the bird cried and I obeyed.

The glass dome snapped around me. Something pinched my cheek.

"Stay still," the bird said and something pinched my cheek again.

I glimpsed sideways to see the bird holding a bloody shard in its beak.

"Thank you ..." I murmured.

The airship dropped on its side again. Now I could see silver and brass wings too, so beautiful. I shouldn't have been able to see them.

"I can see us!" I cried.

A force like nothing I could've imagined pushed me back in my seat then, pushed the skin off my face, pushed my eyes behind a curtain of darkness, ever thickening. Damon shouted something about gravity but he was far away, somewhere else entirely, and I must've been dying, surely I had been shot and that was death. Tiny needles pierced my neck. The bird's claws?

"Come around!" the bird said, pinching my ear next.

"Ow!"

I came around in an eerie silence. We were in the clouds, still climbing, more gently now.

The air stuck my nostrils together. Ice crystals have grown on my eyelashes.

"What's happening? Damon?"

I could barely articulate.

"The mandrake cannot function in the cold."

"What?" *You're mad. Can we?*

He unstrapped himself, stumbled towards me.

"The homunculus! Bonzardo's airship has a mandragora at its core. It's slept thousands of years under the sands of Egypt. It withers in the cold, it dies. He won't follow us here. We have a few minutes ..."

Blood was flowering in the torn black leather on his shoulder. He pulled my seat up, brushed shards of glass off my clothes.

"Amelia, it's time to give me the ruby."

He was standing right next to me, his beautiful face like stone.

I was all soft, shaking.

"Is this where you chill your champagne?"

"Give it to me now," he said sternly, only his eyes warming my heart. "I *know* you have it. You think I would kill the bird? We will both die here, Amelia, *Viscountess Valentia*."

I brushed away snow from my eyes.

"Who's piloting the airship?"

"The analytical engine. Amelia–"

Fire serpents swept the deck like lashes of a whip handled by God Himself. They lingered, whispering, searching maybe, then retired with a hiss. A Kraken of the air feeling its prey.

"You said he wouldn't come this high!" I shrieked.

The airship shook brutally and for two seconds it fell.

"Damon, what's happening?"

"He's pulling us down. He's acquired new weapons–"

"Don't *you* have better weapons?"

His gaze brushed the brass gauntlets on the gunner's seat.

"I need the ruby! They won't work without it."

A low creak stirred the depths of the airship. Again we sank.

Yes, we'll fall from the sky and die.

I pushed my hands inside the gauntlets.

"Amelia, how could you think I did not recognize you immediately?"

Why was he still talking?

Eerie colors were running on the clouds. Something was brewing around us, maybe the Kraken, gathering strength. The gauntlets were tickling, warming my fingers.

"How could you think I could forget that dance, that *mere* half-dance you gave me? I ignore how Geoff has forced you to do this and I apologize deeply for everything ... Including the scratches on your hand ... Give me the ruby *now*. Please ... "

Fire serpents irrupted over the parapet. The airship jerked to the side, all its parts shifting.

"I know nothing about a ruby," I murmured, my eyes half-closed. A white luminescence shifted over the gauntlets.

"Very well," Damon said. "My apologies ... I will endeavor to outrun him, then."

He turned towards the pilot's seat, his pace unsteady, like a drunkard's, his left arm rigid, drops of blood staining the snow on the deck.

Tears pricked my eyes, melting the ice. When I lifted my hand to wipe them, a beam of light spouted from the gauntlet, barely missing my face. The beam sliced through the parapet, sliced through the tentacles of fire. Where it happened, they fell on the deck where the snow extinguished them. *This* was the weapon. I could use it.

"Don't be stupid, Amelia," the bird said in my voice again. "Give him the ruby."

"What will he believe of me?" I murmured. *Of a thief ...* Wasn't he a thief too?

Now that it was certain that he knew who I was—who I'd been—was there anything left to me, anything to defend to Damon's eyes the noblewoman that I was born, anything except for the semblance of my honor? Was it worth dying for? Stupid Amelia.

"He won't care," the bird said. "He's smitten with you, can't you see?"

The fire snakes lashed the deck again. I sliced at them furiously, with both hands, but where one fell, two appeared with renewed impetus, and the beams from the gauntlets were

shortening, weakening, and we were falling, fleeing and falling, and falling, into the wailing, painful wind, towards Paris.

Then Damon yelled in pain. I saw smoke rising from his
leather jacket. He couldn't take shelter; he had to steer the
ship, to save us. He could be dying. I couldn't let him die. I
had to save him. I slid my hands out of the gauntlets and,
with numb fingers, I squeezed the ruby out of my corset.

In a single moment of calm, I untied my harness. Then the
airship shifted, dropped again. I fell off the seat, slid roughly
and barely managed to grab something with my free hand, a
ring on the deck, clutching the ruby in the other.

No foothold was possible now on the steep slope. How to
reach Damon? Could I throw him the ruby? What if I missed?
I looked at the bird, still perched undisturbed on my shoulder.

"Oh, I'll take it to him," she said, sounding almost bored.

She darted with the ruby in its beak, against the wind, into
the thickening fire, until I didn't see her anymore.

Still we fell. Still we spun. Still we shook.

I held as tight as I could, my eyes shut, waiting for the end.

⊗

The end was late.

I still held tight, my eyes squeezed shut, grasping the subtle
changes in the air, in the humming of the wood against my
face, in the pull of gravity, unbelieving.

Then, I realized that sun, not fire, was stroking my face,
sweet, quiet sun. A shadow passed over my eyelids, strong
arms pulled me up, had me take a few steps, stayed around
me as shelter.

"Remember what I told you about looking at a map?"
Damon said softly.

Slowly, but not fearfully this time, I opened my eyes onto
brilliant blue under the bright light.

"The Mediterranean …"

"Is this how you'll fly to the Moon?" I said, through crazy laughter, crazy tears.

"Better," Damon laughed. "But first to Shanghai."

"Yes, with you," the bird said.

MEMPHIS BBQ

by Cat Rambo

AT THIS POINT IN THE MEMPHIS SPRING, wisteria overflowed the roadside ditches in frothy purple drifts. The dogwoods were in full bloom and the landscape looked idyllic.

Nonetheless, Postman Chaz McCartney was reasonably sure corpses moldered somewhere in those green-lit woods. With the Civil War less than a decade old, scars of war still marked this terrain where fighting had occurred. And Doc Lightning's bandit gang, which operated in a pirated zeppelin, had hit only two towns over a few days back, and were surely still in the area. He sniffed the air, steamy from last night's rainstorm coupled with the morning's hot press of sunlight.

But it wasn't the scent of death that met his nostrils. He smelled something else long before his horse got within sight of the Brown's cabin, hidden away among a tangle of redbud trees, wild blackberries, and kudzu. BBQ, hot and spicy and greasy, a pepper-laden whiff that scraped the bottom of your lungs and set them tingling. He breathed in appreciatively, mouth watering, stomach sending up a grumble saying the biscuits and sawmill gravy he'd had for breakfast were long since dearly departed, and it was well past time to be sending in reinforcements.

It was almost enough to make him forget about Mandy. Almost. He'd pretended to himself that his errand didn't involve her or her mother's cooking, but it was getting along to lunchtime and he'd offend Ma by turning down the lunch that would inevitably be offered.

His horse snorted and jerked its head at the bit, full of spring-spangled impatience. He patted his mount's shoulder. "Steady on, Comet."

Forget about Mandy. But when he got closer, there she was, standing out front among what looked like a small crowd, shouting at her father. Not people, though, making up the crowd, but attempts at mechanical men, the kind her father, Timothy Brown, had been working on for three decades now, all of Mandy's life and then some. He'd raised his own lab assistant in the shape of his daughter.

Chaz couldn't catch what they were saying, now that Mandy had stopped shouting, but the way she was pointing at one of the mechanicals would seem to indicate the topic.

She and Timothy had identical expressions on their faces, puzzled and irritated and as though their fingers were itching to get at the root of the problem. The expression was more appealing on Mandy; the faint freckles on her nose and cheeks formed a perplexed constellation under her fine, gingery brows. Her father's hair had once been the same color, but gray was overtaking it, or more accurately had won that race a good decade ago.

"Still having trouble with that loobey-stuff?" Chaz asked, dismounting with a genial nod to the pair. Dr. Brown nodded back before returning to his contemplation of the mechanicals.

"Lubricant," Mandy said, not sparing him a smile. Her eyes studied the mechanical as though telepathically dissecting it. "Lessen you got something genuinely useful to say, Charles McCartney, you might as well get back up on Comet there."

Chaz scratched between his horse's ears, one of which flicked forward at mention of his name, before continuing to tether the reins to the porch rail. "Well now," he said, drawing the words out carelessly. "I reckon I would if I'd come to see either of you, but truth is, I'm here to talk to Miz Brown."

"Mother's in back, boiling," Mandy said. For the first time she looked at him, a little irritated and a little impatient and a little something else. His face, regarding her, was steady and placid. Her eyes were the first to drop. At that motion, he stirred. "Then I'll go find her. G'morning to you both."

He wanted to look back as he went around the side of the house, but he knew it'd be a tactical mistake. He'd been trying to get Mandy to warm up to him for years now, and she remained fixed on her work. His only consolation was that she dismissed her other suitors just as easily. He didn't mind that she'd taken up a profession or even to following Lady Suffrage. He didn't want a doormat of a woman. But she'd taken the words of that Susan B. Anthony to heart, swearing not to marry, to devote herself to science.

The thought soured his expression, and when he swung into sight, he was scowling.

Ma Brown was a burly woman, with farm-raised muscles, honed from chopping wood, birthing calves, and above all else, stirring the kettles, famous through the countryside, that stood to her waist. In the depths of the one she was standing beside now, murky red fluid bubbled and popped.

"Mind you don't stand in the steam!" she snapped as Chaz ambled up. He sidestepped the steam hastily, expression easing as he peered into the kettle.

"What is that? You coming up with a new kind of BBQ?"

"Hot sauce. My cousin in the Territories sent seeds last year she got off a trader there, calls 'em phantom chilies. Hottest thing you ever tasted."

"Why do they call them phantom chilies?"

"Eat one and that's what you'll be." She smirked to herself. "Anyway, why are you back here talking to an old lady and not the one you're sweet on?"

"They're too busy figuring out their dilemma to be talking to the likes of me," Chaz said with a sudden grin.

"I already told 'em how to fix it, but they won't listen to me." Ma snorted. "Tim ain't never paid attention, but Mandy used to, at least."

"I came to see you, actually. You got a special delivery letter, so I'm special delivering it." He fished in the pockets of his coat, drawing out a thick vellum envelope.

She propped the long wooden spoon across an arc of the kettle in order to take the envelope, using the edge of a fingernail to slit it open. She squinted at it despite the sunshine blazing down over her shoulder.

"Want me to read it?" Chaz said. He was used to this exchange.

She handed it to him.

"Dear Ms. Brown, We regret to inform you of the death of your cousin Vaughn ... "

She snatched the paper from him before he could read further. "Vaughn dead!" She crumpled it in her hand. "Good riddance to bad rubbish."

"Don't you want to read further? You might have some sort of inheritance coming."

"Ain't nothing I'd inherit from that man that I'd want."

Chaz had never seen her so angry. But before he could say anything, a shout from the front of the house caught his attention.

He turned around to answer that cry, but an upraised gun stopped him. Two men stood there with steam-pistols at the ready.

"What do you hellions want?" Ma exclaimed.

"Sssh, Ma," Chaz said. His eyes were fixed on the nearest steam-pistol's muzzle, a round hole deeper than oblivion. He could hear the gentle hissing of the guns, even over the crackle of first beside him. "These are Dr. Lightning's gang, if I'm not mistaken. Can I ask you fellas what business you have here?"

"Nothing a yer concern," the closest said. "But we're not the killing type unless pressed to it, as you've no doubt heard. So, if'n you'll lie down and let us undertake to tie you up, we'll do our business and be gone so you can start working yourselves free."

"That's my daughter shouting round to the front." Ma squared her fists on her hips. "I ain't lying down till you promise no harm to her."

The bandits exchanged looks. "I'm afraid you're not in a bartering position, ma'am," the second said. "If you don't lay down, I'll shoot you in the foot, and if that don't do the trick, in the head to follow."

"Hold on now," Chaz said. But Ma was already in motion.

The bandits didn't expect the attack; that was what saved her. They weren't used to resistance, let alone from a woman. Their expressions wavered before hardening to the trigger-pulling stage and in that moment Chaz followed Ma's lead.

She plowed into one first, bowling him over and grappling for the gun. Her arms, covered with the brawn necessary to farm work, wrapped around him.

Chaz hit the second as his gun swung towards Ma, hugging him ferociously. This close, a steam-pistol could do a lot of damage, and he knew from the sound that both were well-primed. In a half hour, the chemical reaction powering them would be spent and they'd be useless until reloaded, but he didn't have that sort of time. Blue sky and ground flashed by as they rolled. He heard the pop and hiss of a shot, but couldn't see whether Ma or her opponent had been hit. He wasn't much used to fighting, but grim determination made up for lack of experience.

They crashed into the other combatants, who reeled towards the kettle.

Hands locked around each other's throats, Chaz and the bandit struggled. Breathing was hard now, and an agonizing stab as he tried to gasp for air told him he had at least one broken rib.

The other bandit screamed, yanking Chaz' opponent's attention sideways and Chaz let go in order to punch, a straight hard jab that snapped the man's head backwards and closed his eyes.

Chaz pulled himself to his feet. Pain banded his throat, constricting it, and his heartbeat drummed so loud in his ears that he could hear nothing else. Now he could see why the first bandit had screamed. The man's head had been shoved into the kettle and was submerged, a sticky red mass of BBQ roiling around his motionless shoulders. He was clearly dead, or else he would have reacted to the flames licking up his legs.

Ma crouched nearby, hands on her knees, watching him.

"Are you all right?" Chaz asked.

"For now." She rose, dusting off her hands and eyed the supine bandit. "That fellow out for the count, or should we dump him in too?"

Ounce for ounce, a woman could out-savage the hardest man, Chaz thought, but all he said was, "Leave him there, I reckon. Let's go check on the doc and Mandy."

But all they saw on the front porch were the motionless mechanicals.

"Took em," Ma said.

"But why?"

Ma's eyebrows knit in query. "Something to do with Dr. Lightning." She glanced down at the paper in her hand and started to speak, then reconsidered. She went on, "There's something we don't understand."

She looked towards the back of the house. "But I bet I know who can tell us."

They trussed the bandit in a sitting position, his back against a hitching post. The man's head hung limp at first. Ma roused him with a bucket of water, which brought him sputtering back into consciousness.

Chaz knelt beside him. "I ain't going to take up too much of your time," the postman said in his most reasonable tone. He jerked his head towards the kettle. They'd pulled the dead man away from the pot and extinguished the flames licking at his pants and boots, but he still lay in an unsavory, motionless heap. "All I'm saying is you can talk to me, or I can step aside and let Ma be the one getting answers from you."

Terror filled the man's face as Ma smiled meaningfully at him. "What do you want to know?"

"Your friends took the doc and his daughter. Why?"

"Yellow fever took Lightning, couple weeks ago. He was the only one who knew how everything worked, so we figgered we'd take us a new mechanic. Townsfolk said the girl was just as good as him; thought we'd use one to persuade the other."

Chaz' jaw went tight, but all he said, his voice mild, was, "And where are y'all holed up, that they'd be taking her to."

"The Pearlie slough," the man said.

Chaz rose. "Fair enough," he said. "I'm going to go get Comet and get him saddled up. Guess you can entertain him till I'm ready, Ma."

He didn't ask what she'd done when he returned, but he could see the bandit's threat had been removed for good.

"What are we going to do?" Ma said.

Chaz tilted his hat back on his head, rubbing at his brow.

"There ain't no room in this for you, Ma, as I see it. I've got to ride to Pearlie, fast enough to catch up with em before they get their ship fixed and float away."

"You're going to face down a pack of bandits by yourself?" she asked. "Don't be ridiculous. You'll need assistance." She pointed at the mechanicals.

He tried to make his tone patient. "Those ain't working. That's what the two of them were arguing about."

"And I know that, son. As I was saying, I have some ideas on that."

CB⬥ⵚⵕ

At first he thought her insane, but she backed her theory up with hexological reasoning. The Law of Similarity. The Law of Contagion. And the fiery heat of the phantom chilis. It all boiled down to BBQ.

She used a fine sieve lined with cheesecloth to strain the steaming liquid into a clear glass jug before using a long thin funnel to drip it into the appropriate receptacle on each mechanical, talking all the way as she did. "Told you they'd regret not listening some day," she said. "They think if you don't have a string of letters after your name, your opinion's worth no more than a half-et ear of corn."

Chaz thought privately that perhaps they hadn't been too crazy if they'd rejected the notion of exposing their machines to a liquid composed primarily of vinegar and peppers.

Ma's sparker snapped, igniting the last mechanical. Like the others, it shuddered into motion, emitting oily whiffs of smoke, a red gleam shining in the bulbous glass lenses serving it as eyes, giving each a strange, bug-eyed appearance. She set each one into motion with one of the big brass toggles on each side. They trundled after her in a nosy mob as she came back to Chaz.

"That's a sight better," Ma said. "I'll get my hinny saddled up and we can be off."

"Hold on," said Chaz. "I don't remember anything about you going with me."

Ma eyed him. "You need me to operate the mechanicals."

"Whyfore?"

"They're voice controlled."

Chaz harrumphed, but nodded, shifting in his saddle. He glanced up at the relentless sun. "Let's go, then."

He kept Comet to a swift trot, but the horse, sensing his impatience, kept outpacing the mechanicals and Ma, so he'd have to wheel and wait for them.

They made an unlikely army. A rain barrel shaped one boasted four scythe like arms, the one beside it swinging three hammers of various size. A fragile-looking, attenuated one sported clippers and shears. Struggling valiantly to keep up, one dragged a box on wheels behind it, its many arms hugged to its side with the effort.

The bandits hadn't feared pursuit. They'd left a swathe of trampled bushes and cracked sapling, smelling of fresh new growth. As they left the road, Chaz slowed to a pace that allowed the mechanicals to keep up; Ma brought up the rear on her raw-boned, long-eared mount.

Chaz paused and held up a hand. The mechanicals clustered around him. Ma came up and he beckoned to her, leaning close in order to speak quietly. Comet eyed the hinny sideways; she returned the look with disinterest.

"We're coming up on the slough," he said, glancing down at the mud squelching around their mounts' hooves. "Keep back, Ma. I don't want to be worrying about you." He undid the strap on his holster, glancing down at his pistol to check it.

Ma gave him a reluctant nod. He crept forward, slapping away mosquitoes, hearing the squashy footsteps of the mechanicals, making him wonder if there was any actual point to stealth.

As it turned out, there was too much commotion in the bandit camp for anyone to notice him or the mechanicals.

The zeppelin dominated the center of the circle of lopsided, dun tents, sagging, hovering half-inflated in the air, ropes tethering it to circular metal objects on the ground.

Everything was mud – each tent was set up on a platform of wood whose neat accordion folding showed a scientific nicety.

The oddest thing about the scene was the line of purple light, its origin unapparent, that surrounded the tents. Like the zeppelin, it hovered, but where the vast balloon was some twenty feet above the glistening puddles, the line lay a scant inch from the ground and water. Above it, sporadic sparks indicated some presence in the air. As he neared, Chaz realized the sparks were insects encountering some invisible barrier.

Mandy was squared off with half a dozen bandits. Hands on her hips, she stood over a slumped form that Chaz recognized as Dr. Brown. Chaz counted over the opponents. An older Negro man with a pistol, two blonde young men near enough in looks to be twins, currently not brandishing the pistols that rode holstered at their hips, an older white, a middle-aged Chinaman, and a scowly black-bearded fellow who looked to be the leader, or making a try at it, at least.

Everyone was shouting.

"I tell you again, I won't cooperate until you bring him medical attention!" Mandy announced over a hubbub of "See here, Missy!" "You'll do as you're told if you know what's good for you!" and "Get that thing away from her!"

The last of those made Chaz note that Mandy brandished a small brass-plated device in her hand. She was as animated as Chaz had ever seen her, tendrils of strawberry-blonde hair escaping her usual tight bun to curl in the early spring sunlight.

"Stand down, boys, and let the lady have a little breathing room," Chaz said, ambling forward and speaking with much more nonchalance than he actually felt. He hoped that the mechanicals behind him would impress the bandits. Farm machinery was capable of doing damage–Chaz wouldn't have wanted to be hit by ol' Shovel-arms by any account, but still there was a certain absurdity about them that diminished the overall menace.

Everyone whirled, Mandy included.

All the faces held an identical surprise.

Mandy was the first to recover.

"I'm glad you're here," she said, holding herself poised as a parasol, "but your presence is unnecessary. These gentlemen and I are in the process of reaching an agreement."

"What sort of agreement?" Chaz glanced around. "I hear your ol' boss ain't feeling so well."

"Daid," a blonde twin said. The other elbowed him in the ribs.

"Do ya need tah tell im alla our business?"

"How'd he come to die?" Chaz queried. Most of his attention was on Mandy, but he was tracking every gun clutched in a hand, as well as the small machine Mandy held, a knobby, button-covered thing of brass and scarlet glass.

"That's aside the point," Black-beard snapped.

Chaz held up his hands in a placatory gesture. "I'm just trying to ascertain all the facts, son." He swatted at the back of his neck. "How about I come inside your circle, sit down, and we discuss how we can all part amiably?"

"Ain't going to be no amiable parting," the black man said. "You take the old fellah and we'll be taking the leddy."

"You don't need to worry she'll be subjected to no hankypanky," Black-beard added, glaring at the other. "We just need someone with the knowhow, now that we don't got the doc no more."

"Mandy," Chaz said. "Did you want to go with these gentlemen?"

The question was rhetorical. His fingers itched towards his gun. The denial would be his signal to move.

But she said, "Yes."

He blinked. His fingers froze. "Beg pardon?"

"I want to go with them." Her look was steady as a shot.

"Don't be ridiculous!" Ma snapped. She'd come up from behind as well. "You still got a passle of learning to do before you go off to become queen of the air pirates."

Mandy's chin titled upward. Stubbornness crept into her eyes. "I know plenty."

"Not where it matters. Trust your mama, I still got a few tricks up my sleeve." She jerked a thumb at the mechanicals.

Mandy blinked as though noticing them for the first time. "What are you using?"

"Never you mind!" Ma snapped, even as Chaz said, "Barbecue sauce."

"Barbecue sauce?" Incredulity pitched Mandy's voice even higher. "How ... quaint."

"Doing the trick, ennit?" Ma gestured the mechanicals closer.

Chaz was aware of a gentle hissing, a sound that tugged at his attention. It had been doing on for some time now, he thought. Movement tugged his attention upward. The zeppelin held considerably more gas than it had before, its sides rounder, the ropes tethering it straining now.

The Chinaman intercepted his gaze and snapped something. Everyone exploded into action.

Mandy pressed a brass button. With a snap, the ropes holding the zeppelin retracted, slithering back into their metallic casings. At the gesture, her father's head slumped down even further, then onto the ground fully as she released him. The mechanicals around Chaz clanked forward, but the bandits moved too swiftly. Black-beard grabbed Mandy about the waist, pulled her up the rope ladder with him, ascending even as his fellows swarmed after him.

Ma ran forward to claim her spouse. Chaz drew and aimed. But the ladder bobbed and jerked in the air, swaying as the zeppelin ascended, its engine now barking harshly.

He jumped. For a sickening second he thought he wouldn't

make it, and then in an even more sickening moment, he realized he had and that he was moving upward as rapidly as the zeppelin. He spared a glance down and his stomach clenched. He set his jaw and began climbing, the rope fibers biting harshly into his hands. Up above, the bandits had climbed into the cabin and one was goggling down at him.

He expected with a certain fatality that they'd start shooting. But they let him haul himself upward until he emerged through the hatch and into the crowded cabin where Mandy stood with hands on her hips in a way that was indisputably her mother's. The air smelled musty and the interior was in bad shape, brass dials and trim overcome by verdigris.

"You get back off now, Chaz," she said. "I'm seizing my destiny. This used to be my second cousin, Vaughn Lightning's, airship and crew and now I'm taking over."

He gawped. "You're related to Doc Lightning?" He remembered the way Ma had snatched the letter away before he could read more. It made more sense now.

She nodded.

"But I came to rescue you," he said.

"You thought you'd come rescue me and I'd fall in your arms a-fluttering my eyelashes."

"That was among my hopes, yes." He swallowed hard, looking her straight in the eye. "I've loved you ever since I first saw you, Mandy Brown. I'd build you a home and your own laboratory and all the tubes and sparkmeters and gewgidgets your heart craved. I'd lay the moon at your feet, if you wanted."

Was that regret in her gaze? His heart leaped, only to be dashed by her next words.

"Sometimes," she said, and her voice was gentler than he'd ever heard it, "sometimes that isn't enough, Chaz."

Under her direction, they set him down near the outskirts of Pearlie. By now the engine was purring like a cat that had been given its own cow for dairy purposes, the dull brass of the zeppelin's interior fittings was starting to shine, and the bandits looked like hopeful men rather than desperate ones. They lowered him down on a rope, and as he hung there, he stared up, willing Mandy to change her mind at the last minute, hoping until he saw her face vanish as the hatch slid closed.

Doc Brown was at the chirugeon's, Ma with him. She glanced up as Chaz entered, question in her eyes. When he shook his head and sat down beside her, she only said, "Timothy thinks my idea for the lubricant was mighty smart."

"Didn't say that exactly," Doc Brown murmured, although his eyes were closed. "Said it was unique."

"Much of the same," Ma said. She patted Chas's elbow. "You come round tomorrow, Chaz. Love may break your heart, but good barbecue'll build it back into operating shape."

He could only think of Mandy's eyes, filled with a pity that was worse than any other expression he could have seen. He looked at the sprig of wisteria someone had put in a little vase beside the sickbed, a touch of purple, delicate and light as air, and shook his head.

But Ma knew as she watched him. She might not have the book learning her husband and daughter did, but she knew there were things in life you could count on and things you couldn't. Love was in the latter category, but there would always be barbeque.

A Horrified Mind

by Ferrel D. Moore

IT WAS THE GREAT PAUL MORPHY, world chess champion, who invited me to Miskatonic University. I was there to referee a match between Morphy and the infamous chess-playing automaton, the Turk.

"Behind that door," said Professor Pickett with an exaggerated flourish "stands the enigma of our age. But you"—he pointed a crooked finger at me—"you, Mr. Herriot, declared it to be, in kindest terms, an illusion. You have publically intimated it is nothing more than a fraud."

I'd immediately distrusted the eccentric professor of metaphysics, and his irritating manner did nothing to change my opinion. In the dancing gaslight, he looked entirely scholarly, yet obscenely feral, like an educated snake.

"Perhaps I was excessively severe in my judgment of the … contraption," I said.

Of course, Professor Pickett was referring to my essay about the mechanical chess playing charlatan. In 1826, when the Turk was first exhibited in America at the New York Exhibition and caught on like the plague, I speculated in print that it was nothing but a hoax. In Baltimore, I'd seen too many Snake-Oil salesman pitching their false cures for consumption, while all around them people lay dying. I knew a fraud when I saw one.

"I will not," Morphy said off-handedly, "be party to a deception."

I watched as he extracted an elaborately scrolled pocket watch from his vest and flipped it open, noting the time as an irritable expression curled the corners of his mouth.

"Precisely so," I said. "If I find fault with the science of this enterprise, then we will leave here at once."

Professor Pickett seemed to be taken aback, but recovered after a moment's contemplation.

"But, Mr. Herriot," he said smoothly, "as you will soon enough see, the Turk is more mystery than science, more magic than fact."

After having vanquished Paulsen so decisively and even the mighty German Master Anderson, Monsieur Morphy had issued a world-wide challenge to all chess players of master rank. No one had risen to accept the twenty-two old prodigy's challenge since all by then knew of his prowess. Time passed and the young man was about to retire, crowned with the acclaim of all as the King of Chess, when he received a letter from Professor Pickett, who had accepted the champion's challenge. Morphy had expressed his outrage to me that the professor himself had not risen to accept Morphy's challenge. In my judgment, he lacked the temerity. No, he was accepting the challenge on behalf of the Turk.

I thought Morphy's annoyance at the prolonged conversation was compounded by what he considered Pickett's insulting behavior in demanding that he, Morphy, honor the Turk's challenge. The very idea that Pickett believed a machine could out-calculate and thereby defeat a human being in the most demanding mental contest known bordered on an affront. On the carriage ride to Pickett's home, Morphy had even expressed his distrust in the man's credentials and worried our journey might ruin his reputation.

Yet, Pickett was in fact, a man of some prominence at Miskatonic University, no doubt due to his fortune. Even though the Miskatonian Metaphysics department was combined in those days with the Theology department — a holdover, perhaps from its days as Arkham College — no professor without substantive means could afford to live in such a mansion.

"Professor Pickett," I put in, "I am quite familiar with the Turk. Although in my essay, I did in fact declare my belief that its chess play was mere theater, I was never afforded a free hand to closely examine the … machine. So it is true there is some small chance"—I emphasized the word small—"that I was in error. Therefore, tonight, although I am here at Monsieur Morphy's behest, I pledge to you both I will thoroughly examine the automaton's structure before and during its operation to ensure that this match is entirely free from artifice. By the end of the day, I'm sure we will have discerned the truth, and quite put away mystery and magic in favor of science and fact."

Professor Pickett stroked his dark goatee thoughtfully as I spoke. In the fashion of our time, it was trimmed to a sharp point, his moustache waxed and curled, and both, as there is no reason now not to speak frankly, looked entirely out of place on his square face. His features were remarkably similar to the man who sold me the Snake-Oil guaranteed to cure my wife shortly before she died.

"You understand," said Monsieur Morphy, seemingly irked at not being the center of attention, "I had never seriously considered anyone would accept my challenge, because I have already defeated everyone of repute save that coward Staunton. His refusal to play during my last trip through England angered even the Queen."

"Your reputation at the game is enough to wilt the nerve of any would-be opponent," I said soothingly.

"The Turk," said Professor Pickett dismissively, "has no nerves. He is comprised entirely of cedar wood, cables and pulleys, gears and screws and agate marbles."

"Agate marbles?" inquired Morphy.

"The eyes," replied the professor. "Come, see for yourself."

After a deep bow, our ungainly host removed a brass key from his pocket, unlocked the double doors which led off his study, and threw them wide. His arms held high as they swung open, he appeared as a priest proclaiming the word of his God to followers assembled in the room. But in the center of that magnificent chamber there was only one personage — *the Turk himself.*

ᨏᨒᨔ

"Well, Mr. Herriot? Will you share with us your observations?" asked Professor Pickett.

Although I heard his question, I did not answer. Instead, I stood transfixed.

It sat high upon a deep red velvet cushion, above and back from the wheeled cabinet upon which it was affixed. As I remembered from my earlier investigations and interviews, brass bands wrapped around its mannequin body beneath purple-starred robes. These bands were in turn screwed to the side of the structure. Its face was pale, white paint, and its eyes shown bright as polished bloodstones. Reflections of the room's shuddering candlelight shimmered uneasily in those eyes. A smile slit the mad face, formed by slightly parted scarlet lips. All this was topped by a glittering gold turban which gave the Turk more the look of a gypsy fortune teller than of a chess automaton.

"My God," said Morphy. "It seems alive."

"Ah," said Pickett. "That observation leads to the metaphysical puzzle of the age, does it not? Can a machine be alive? Can a machine think?"

"Hardly," I said. "Because such a thing would clearly violate the established *Chain of Being.*"

"Your knowledge of philosophy surprises me, Mr. Herriot," said the Professor. "And while most academicians would accept your observation, at Miskatonic University we are perhaps more skeptical."

"And what," said Morphy, "has any of this to do with my being here?"

"It has everything indeed to do with your journey and the match. Perhaps, as Alfred Russell Wallace has postulated, one species may over time be replaced by another, superior species. I find a certain macabre joy in the idea. Could machines someday be the species that replaces us? Heresy? It may be, but you are here, my dear sir, to demonstrate for now the superiority of the human mind over the mechanical thinking of a machine. That is, of course, if you are up to the challenge of maintaining Mankind's place at the top of Wallace's evolutionary ladder for the time being."

The angry flush which colored Morphy's face came as quickly as the sudden ocean squalls I witnessed while posted on the *Waltham*. He was of Spanish ancestry, and the temper of their men is well known. His agitation was in fact so great I felt I might soon enough need to step between them or the young man might issue another, more deadly challenge to the peculiarly obtuse Professor Pickett.

"Professor," I said hurriedly, "Have you forgotten it is Monsieur Morphy who has issued the challenge, and it is your machine, as it were, that must rise to Mr. Morphy's consummate level of play?"

"Forgive me. I am overwrought. Mine is a world of abstractions, you see, and I beg you, therefore, to make allowances."

There was no contrition in Pickett's cold stare, but I pressed on. I felt an overwhelming desire to put him in his place.

"If it pleases Monsieur Morphy," I said.

There was a moment's pause while Morphy shifted his stare from Pickett to the Turk. The man and the machine seemed to lock eyes with each other. Morphy's face was tan, his eyes large and dark, and his thick black hair hung to his shoulders cut in the European fashion then so popular in New Orleans. The Turk stared at him through his unblinking marble eyes with the precipitous expression of an insane puppet.

Neither blinked.

"If it pleases Monsieur Morphy," I repeated.

"It does," he said finally, absently brushing his coatsleeve, and looking irritably at Professor Pickett, "if we may get on with it."

"Of course," said Professor Pickett. "Mr. Herriot, are you ready to proceed?"

"I am."

"Then, Mr. Meridian, bring the Egg."

Before I could question the identity of Mr. Meridian or the Egg, I heard bootsteps advancing toward us from behind. A lumbering giant in servant's clothes approached the double doors through which we had entered. Morphy started and stepped back after following my stare and seeing the slope-shouldered creature approach. Arms stretched slightly forward, his thick hands supported a royal blue velvet cushion upon which lay an oblong cylinder bristling with iridescent hues.

"What on earth is he carrying?" I demanded.

"Why, it is the Turk's brain," answered Professor Pickett ingenuously. "A genie trapped within a seamless metal bottle, condemned to a life of servitude, indentured to a mocking mannequin constructed of wood and metal."

೦೩೮೦

An hour passed before I pulled myself out from inside the Turk's cabinet and announced to Morphy, "I have carefully examined every facet of the Turk's construction, and can find nothing untoward."

"And the Egg?" asked Morphy impatiently.

"Yes, there is still the Egg."

The dynamics of the great room had changed since the introduction of the Egg. Four of Pickett's unusually large assistants were now present. Two stood without the door and two stood within. The professor had explained they were introduced as a means to both protect the contest from disruption by unexpected visitors, and to provide us with witnesses willing to guarantee what was to transpire during the match game was accurately reported. When I questioned whether his employees could fairly be said to be unbiased, he merely smiled and said they were provided to us by Miskatonic University. Yet they had the sloped forehead, the beady eyes and the bulky bodies one associates with workmen. One look at their thickly knuckled hands even suggested experience in fisticuffs. I had seen many such men in my Army days, though none exuded such a sense of menace as them.

"There is hardly much one can hope to divine when examining the Egg," observed Pickett. "There appears to be no fissure, no hinge, indeed no opening or crevice of any kind anywhere on it."

I brushed off my knees and went to examine it.

The assistant who had carried it in had laid it and its cushion on a square wooden table not four feet from the Turk. There were no wires of any sort connecting it to the automaton, and its color-variegated surface was too diffuse to act as a reflecting mirror. My initial thoughts were it was to be used as some kind of a distraction. However, when I waved a hand between it and the Turk, my fingers experienced a numbing sensation and my mind was besieged by an image of oily, roiling, dark waters and glutinous monsters appeared in my mind as though placed there. I jumped back and, after catching my breath, became aware Professor Pickett was staring at me with the intensity of a mesmerist.

"My dear Herriot," said Morphy. "Whatever is the matter? Your face is pale. Are you ill?"

Still the professor kept his gaze on me. He knew I had experienced something incognizable. Yet he said not a word. A slight hint of humor even tugged at the corner of his mouth.

"A momentary chill," I answered shakily.

"A gentleman should not pass the entire day without brandy," said Professor Pickett. "I shall not proffer the same to you, Monsieur Morphy, as you shall presently be summoning all your mental faculties. Mr. Herriot, however, needs only be alert enough to detect foul play, and since there shall be none this evening, a fine stock such as I have can only help drive away his chill."

Liquor had not passed my lips for more than two weeks. Was it possible this metaphysician knew my reputation? The approbation of humility is something for which I lack the facility, yet it had never occurred to me that Professor Pickett may have made inquiries concerning my habits. More people than I would like to consider were well enough aware of my struggles with drink in the past, especially so since the death of my wife. And yet, there seemed to be no reason for Professor Pickett to investigate my habits save the consideration Monsieur Morphy had selected me to determine if the Turk was a fraud. Could it be the professor was digging for ways to prejudice my judgment or a basis to dispute it when the match was concluded?

Another possibility vexed me, and that was the disquieting permutation that the professor had divined my weakness merely by studying me. The direct knowledge of a man's soul is wonderment in a saint, and stark terror when gifted to a madman. Was it possible he knew how dreadful my cravings for a mere snifter of brandy were? For a man whose boyhood teething pains were soothed with bread dipped in gin, three days can be a long time without drink. My hands trembled so I had no other choice but to conceal them behind my back.

"Mr. Herriot?" he asked politely. "May I presume your answer to be a yes?"

My fingers intertwined behind my back like a brood of snakes. I could feel Morphy's questioning eyes on me. The journey to Miskatonic had been arduous but the true reason I suffered so to refuse the professor's offer was the uninterrupted haunting of my days by the melancholy memories of my lost wife. Each day without her was more distressing than the one before. I endured her absence with nothing to distract or enlighten my mind. The journey with Monsieur Morphy was my first interruption, but still I judged her loss by the lassitude and apathy by which I bore my life. Without Abilene, the time between birth and death was no more than a man waiting in an abandoned station for a train which would never come. And there before me, offering me something to ease my nerves was a man who bore such a startling likeness to the swindler who had sold me Snake Oil claiming it would save my Abilene's life.

"No," I said with an effort. "I will require my full faculties in my role as advisor to Monsieur Morphy. His confidence in me shall not be forfeit."

"Bravo," said Morphy. "What have you to say then? Is the Egg a trick? Have we come all this way for nothing?"

There was something not right about the Egg. I could hear or perhaps feel a slight, faint buzz in the air, as though a distant swarm of bees were approaching. The vision of dark, oily waters and glutinous creatures filled my mind again. I thought of Abilene's sweet voice and pushed aside the hideous menace of lurking monstrosities. I filled my internal eye with an image of her singing.

"You may proceed," I told Morphy, straightening my back and looking him squarely in the face. "I recant my earlier suspicions of this device and I have every confidence in you. The reputation of the human mind is brilliantly represented by your genius."

At no time until that moment had I seen any indication of trepidation on the part of Monsieur Morphy. He was a supremely confident young man who had beaten the best the world had to offer. It was at that moment, however, when he looked from the Egg to the Turk, that I first saw the recognition birth in his eyes that this whole affair of the professor's was not a trick. When he looked back again at the Egg, it was clear he finally understood the Turk really was a puppet. The intelligence he would now confront over the chessboard rested not in the turbaned marionette, but in whatever thing dwelled within the Egg.

"Well then," smiled Professor Pickett, rubbing his hands together with poorly hidden delight, "shall we begin?"

As Morphy and the professor turned to approach the Turk, I saw, from the corner of my eye, one of the hulking assistants surreptitiously avert their eyes, and then the image of Abilene coughing up blood onto her alabaster dress rose in my mind like a leviathan breaking the surface of a malevolent sea.

CঙଞO

Sweat trickled down Monsieur Morphy's broad brow as the game entered its second hour. He sat hunched forward on a stool, an elbow propped on one knee, his fist wedged firmly beneath his chin. Though the temperature in the great room was cool and the great chess master hailed from a warm clime, he had yet removed his coat as though his over-heated mind was afflicting the rest of his body. After he made a move, Morphy wrote it down and did the same with the Turk's responses, using the notation of the

Syrian-born Philip Stamma, a system he much preferred
to the cumbersome method of the legendary French player,
Auguste Philidor.

The Turk was exact as ever; the automaton's only movement was the graceful, almost noiseless machinations of its
incredibly crafted hand reaching out with unerring precision
to move a piece to counter Monsieur Morphy's own. The
eerie countenance of the puppet-like contrivance grew more
formidable with each passing move. It showed no emotion
at all; indeed it possessed none to show.

In deference to the silent struggle, neither Professor Pickett, I, nor the assistants inside the doors made any noise at
all. It was as though we stood guard in a sepulcher observing
a man contesting for his very soul, the effort as cold and still
as white marble.

From my chair perched off to the side of the Egg, I saw
nothing whatsoever to suggest trickery or deceit. The only
movement, as I have related, came from the two contestants
making their moves.

Whenever I looked over to the professor, I saw his face had
been transformed. The man's interest was more than keen.
He watched the match as though his own life hung in the
balance. His eyes burned with a predatory stare, and his lips
were formed into a cruel grimace.

Even without glancing at the Egg, I could feel an unpleasant, almost unholy energy pulsating within it. My mind
fermented with horrid memories and disquieting, even repul-
sive images; I was convinced I had accompanied my young
friend to a place beyond madness.

ᘓᘔᘓ

"I will have him," said Morphy. He held his fists before
me and shook them vigorously. His eyes were bright and

he appeared fevered. "But I tell you the Turk is no machine, Herriot. It is an *abomination*. There is no man controlling its moves. It plays like a demon. I assure you—I know the play of mere men. I make my own case fairly when I say there is no man alive can beat me when I set my mind to be victorious. That machine is not, however, controlled by a man. I tell you again, it is a demon."

Monsieur Morphy paced energetically back and forth across the small room to which we had retired after the end of the second hour of play for a short respite. His forehead was wrinkled with concentration.

"Have you looked into its eyes, Herriot? Have you truly done that?"

"Marbles," I said. "They are only marbles."

"Are they? Hah! And yet I will defeat the creature. Cassiopeia, the very goddess of Chess herself, watches over me. She saw me from afar when I was a boy and claimed me as her own. I will not disgrace her." He raved and gesticulated and I grew more worried with each of his passing declarations that the Egg was affecting his mind. By the time the professor returned to inquire whether Monsieur Morphy was ready to resume the match, I had begun to fear that before the night was through, the exemplar of American chess would be utterly vanquished by a turbaned machine with no more soul than a locomotive.

CƷ੪Ʋ

I was about to follow Monsieur Morphy into the match room when Professor Pickett said to me, "A word, perhaps, Mr. Herriot? I will not detain you long."

"I have a responsibility."

"You will not only indulge me if you take a moment to converse, but I assure you it will neither impugn your honor

nor discredit you in any way. What I have to tell you is something you already most surely desire to know."

Monsieur Morphy was already on his stool, all his faculties directed to the game. It was abundantly clear he would have no knowledge of whether I, or anyone else for that matter, was present in the room with him. For his brilliant mind, there was only the struggle of man against machine.

"It will be for only a brief moment?'

"Of course," said the professor. "Let us return to the room from where you and the young master departed so we may speak freely without disturbing the match. We will miss little as they move so infrequently, and I fear the game is far from over. It is therefore appropriate I use this moment now to unfold for you the true magic and mystery of the Turk."

"Is there trickery involved?" I demanded. But I knew a man like him would never confess.

"No. There is no trickery, although I have no doubt that when you know what I know, you may wish there was."

At a word from the professor, the two assistants which had before guarded the doors to the match from outside intruders followed behind us and stationed themselves to guard our secret conversation. As Professor Pickett closed the door behind him, I saw one of the men standing without room transfer a small bludgeon from one pocket to another.

CS80

"When I learned Mr. Morphy solicited your assistance, I was at first incensed," said Professor Pickett. "Complications never bode well for an enterprise."

It was clear from the professor's agitated demeanor that *the enterprise* might be in difficulty. My own opinion was the same. Morphy and I were secreted in a remote estate and at the mercy of a university faculty member who seemed unstable.

"Did you publicize this match to other members of the Miskatonic faculty?" I inquired casually.

He looked at me keenly.

"You are a perceptive man, Mr. Herriot. To answer you as directly as you have put the question — no, I did not. Certain of the faculty are more open minded than others. Did you know that when the infamous Salem witch trials occurred many of the accused fled secretly to Arkham? My own grandmother, I am grieved to say, was crushed beneath heavy stones while her neighbors looked on in approval. She had been found to possess a copy of the *Vigiliae Mortuorum secundum Chorum Ecclesiae Maguntine*, and her neighbors, you see, mistook her obeisance to the Old One to be servitude to the devil of Christianity. There is no devil, Mr. Herriot, as I'm sure you know, but there are indeed devils within us all. The devil is myth, but the Old One my grandmother worshipped is very real. Although she did not escape, there were others from those dark days who did. Their descended families have close ties to the university."

"What all this to do with my question?" I demanded.

"A great deal," said the professor. He smiled indulgently. "A very great deal indeed, but I will elucidate that issue soon enough. All will become clear when you learn the true history of the Turk and the Egg."

"Can you get to the point, Professor Pickett? My charge is in the other room locked in competition with your machine, and I would very much like to return to my duties."

As a former soldier, I sensed not only was I in difficulty, but I also realized I needed to lay hand on a weapon without being caught in the act. To that end, as he continued to speak, I looked furtively around the room as he walked about, sometimes looking at me and sometimes staring out the window. I sat at a writing desk, my back to it and facing him.

"Are you familiar with the Yemeni poet Abdul Alhazred? No, you say you are not, but it is my intuition you are well familiar with many things both Arabic and Arabesque. I see recognition in your eyes. No matter, for the moment.

"Abdul Alhazred was more than a mad poet—oh yes; he went quite mad and was the apparent author of the Necronomicon, although certain of us dispute which caused which. Ah, I again see the light of recognition in your eyes."

"What has this to do with the Turk? If you do not tell me, professor," I said sharply, standing bolt upright as I did so, "I will return immediately to stand by Monsieur Morphy."

"Sit down."

"I will not."

"You will sit down at once or I will have my two assistants force you to remain seated. Yes, you see that now, too, don't you? I am in command here. If you wish to live out the night, you will do as I bid."

"Live out the night?" I asked, but I did so as I was returning to my seat.

The professor waited a moment longer, and then continued his divulgence.

"Abdul Alhazred was more than a brilliant poet; he was a savant equal to the English occultist and academician Dr. John Dee. You are familiar with Dr. Dee's Monad? Of course. Like you, both Abdul Alhazred and Dr. Dee were masters of intricate puzzles that were essentially cryptograms brought forth into the world of pictographic conundrums. Your reputation as a cryptographer, Mr. Herriot, might just save your life this very night. It surprises you I know this? Fah. Every army has its need for men like you. In fact, were it not for wars and political intrigues, ciphers would scarcely be necessary in this life. And do not worry that your assignments within the military are known to my associates and myself; we have connections even within the Army."

When he turned his head to pause and look out the window for a moment, I looked behind me at the writing table and saw to my relief a sharp-edged letter opener. I immediately grabbed it and secreted it beneath my jacket. The professor was too lost in his thoughts to notice.

"Dr. Dee," he continued, "was a remarkable man. There is, perhaps, only one like him born each generation and mayhap each century. Poet, explorer, cryptographer, and mechanical genius. It was he in a moment of monstrous betrayal that actually created the Turk. Von Kempelen acquired it when he purchased a lost cache of the doctor's estate. He then presented it to the Empress Josephine as his own invention. Many scholars mistakenly believed Dr. Dee's translation of the Necronomicon and his other papers telling the true story of the astounding automaton's creation were never put to paper. They were wrong. I now have those papers. Just as importantly, I, as you have seen, have the Turk itself."

By holding my arm at my side, I was able to conceal the letter opener. While the professor continued his exposition, I worked desperately to conceive a plan. The indisputable fact I was outnumbered five to one was not bad enough; worse still, I had never killed a man in my entire life. Never during my military career had I fired a shot at anyone, much less plunged a knife into a mad academician. But his resemblance to the man who had sold me the bogus tonic for my wife was so great that I felt the urge to kill him just for that.

He stopped directly in front of me and propped his fists against his hips. Looking up at his towering figure, I realized that if I failed in an attempt to kill him, he would promptly snap my neck like that of an unwanted kitten.

"And what exactly is the Turk?" I asked, and then altered my question. "No, what I meant to ask, sir, is what exactly is inside the Egg?"

An unpleasant smile played across the professor's face, and he actually reached down and demonstrated his approval by slapping me on the shoulder. This unwanted contact stoked my hatred.

"Excellent. I tell you again how much I admire your mind. The Egg is truly the question. What is it residing with the prison of the Egg? I spoke the truth earlier, Mr. Herriot. Within the Egg is a djinn, what we might today call an evil spirit, or a genie, albeit with a slight degree of inaccuracy. In point of fact, this genie will grant any command given to it. The Old One left it for us that we might use it to raise the lost city of R'lyeh from the depths. Ph'nglui mglw'nafh Cthulhu R'lyeh wgah'nagl fhtagn. Which is to say, *In his house at R'lyeh, dead Cthulhu waits dreaming*. When R'lyeh rises, the great Old One will return to its former glory and I will be the new High Priest. I will have unlimited power."

He was mad, of course. But could I, in good conscience, take the life of a madman?

"And why," I asked, "have you not claimed that power? Why have you not yet commanded the thing within the Egg to do your bidding?"

Professor Pickett gave a strangled epitaph and moved toward me with a terrible glare in his eyes. I leaned back in the chair and for a moment all seemed lost. Then, by degrees, the red flush that colored his face gradually disappeared and he shook himself as though to throw off his rage. Finally, he spoke again.

"No man can command the djinn until it is freed from the accursed Egg. Dr. Dee be damned. He used his genius both to create the Egg and to imprison the djinn. The Turk was created to lock or unlock the door to its cell." He leaned forward and peered at me. "You see the diabolical genius of it don't you?"

"No," I said carefully. "Pray reveal the difficulty to me."

"Obvious," he said, straightening to his full height. "Is it not obvious? After creating the Turk, that hideous affair of cables, gears and wood, he sealed the djinn inside the Egg with one last instruction— it was to remain sealed within under the command it could never be freed unless the Turk was beaten in a simple game of chess at which the djinn could never be beaten. You see it now, don't you? He condemned the greatest power in our entire world to play chess and not to be beaten. It was a plan both insidious and insane. Only if the Turk is beaten will the djinn be released from the Egg to be commanded by anyone else. He created this infernal puzzle in the belief that if the djinn were ever needed to serve humanity in an hour of dire need, someone of great intellect would arise and solve the riddle. If Dr. John Dee were alive today I would rip his head from his body."

Had I not so resolutely feared for my life, the imp of the perverse would have caused me to laugh outright.

"And you hoped Monsieur Morphy, who is without a doubt the greatest chess player who has ever lived, would be able to defeat the Turk and thereby free this *djinn*?"

"Precisely."

"But what in God's name do you think I might do to help you?"

In truth, I was arguing with a madman.

"You are an ingenious cryptographer, Mr. Herriot, and have a certain flair for analytical constructions—as your former Army Captain tells us. However, in your examinations of the Turk, your preconceptions caused you to miss the salient element of the Turk's construction."

"And that was?" I asked.

"You did not ask yourself how it was the Egg communicated with the Turk. Had you considered that perspective, it might have become clear to you it was the chess board itself by which the djinn was communicating his moves to the machine."

The knife-like letter opener I held by my side was beginning to feel excessively heavy, and I had to shift my weight and press my arm still harder against my side to hold it in place.

"I fail to understand the point."

"The point is that a winning sequence of moves is the coded algorithmythic which will open the Egg. Should Morphy fail in his effort to defeat the Turk, I will next rely on your genius to examine the cryptographic code which these moves represent. You will not attempt to defeat the Turk in chess, Mr. Herriot; you will instead attempt to decode the winning sequence."

"And if I should refuse? Surely you understand you cannot propel a man's mind to its highest performance by force?"

The professor laughed; it was a surprisingly musical sound.

"It is my thought to tempt you, not force you. I have something to offer I believe will cause you to exert every effort to decode the sequence."

His confidence was unnerving. I could not imagine what this madman might offer me.

"What might that be?" I said. "Pray, tell me."

He leaned back against the wall and said, "The return of your wife from the dead."

I swear for a moment, my heart stopped beating. My face drained of blood. I could actually feel its departure. This man who looked so like the fraud I blamed more than any other for the death of my wife, was actually offering to bring her back. I saw a blood vessel throb in his throat and it was all I could to keep myself from lashing out at him.

"The djinn can grant any wish, my melancholy friend. Yes, I know all about your recent loss. When I learned you were coming, I probed every aspect of your life. I made discreet inquiries of your friends. Creatures such as Porter and Wilson I ignored. I have no interest in your personal life at all unless

I can profit from it by better understanding you. No, indeed. And our investigations revealed your deepest need. Yes, it was your weakness I sought to understand. Finally, I understood. You truly grieve your wife. I tell you, Herriott, the djinn can return her to you from the grave itself."

Was it possible? Could this thing called the djinn return my beloved Abilene to me? Did such power exist in the universe? Could this vile man provide me a chance to be with her again?

"Ah, I have your attention now, do I not? Think on this — when the winning sequence of moves is executed by the movement of the chess pieces, the Egg will begin to open. But I warn you, in that instant, you must not look at its radiance. To gaze upon the djinn will bring the curse of insanity down on your head. Abdul Alhazred learned this. Dr. Dee avoided repeating the same mistake by heeding the mad poet's warnings. Do not mistake this for myth. To look at the djinn brings madness as surely as each day ends in darkness."

"Abilene? This creature can return my wife to me?"

"As ever she was," intoned the professor.

"What devilry is this?" I cried.

"No devilry," he said, his voice rising. "My grandmother died because the masses believed in devilry. The Old One possesses science and powers beyond our wildest dreams. Science, not devilry. He shall confer upon me the power to revenge my family and wreak havoc upon humanity. My body will be freed from the tyranny of disease and death. What god could deny his high priest?"

Tears began to trickle down my cheeks. How many nights had I begged God and his angels to return my wife to me? How many days had I passed in drinking myself into a stupor to forget my loss? Now Professor Reynolds Pickett was declaring that the djinn could resurrect her from her death shroud and clothe her in the finery of life. Was it his fault that he looked like the Snake Oil salesman who caused her death?

"Now you see, Mr. Herriot, why I and my family before me have worshipped the Old One and labored for his return?"

Wrong. It was all wrong. What he was telling me was evil itself. Such power should never be placed in mortal hands. But to bring back Abilene, my own sweet love — could such a thing be wrong? Could it be wrong to re-unite a man with his wife?

"What say you? Will you join me? If Mr. Morphy fails, will you lend me every assistance in opening the Egg?"

I could think of nothing to say. My every heartbeat was a surge of grief. Finally, I blurted out, "How do I know this is possible? You ask my help, but you offer me no proof."

"M assistants are your proof," smiled the professor.

"I beg your pardon?"

"They are not human. Surely you felt there was something *wrong* about them. They are homunculi."

"What are you saying?"

"They are creatures made from dust and the science of the old ones. They are soulless laborers I formed using the spells set down by Abdul Alhazred and translated by Dr. Dee himself. All that can move them is the sound of my voice. They are slaves to my commands. The science of the Old One gives them form and movement."

He reached into a pocket and withdrew a piece of oddly colored metal which caught the light in such a way I felt immediately nauseous.

"With this amulet, I am linked to them in a similar fashion to that of the Egg and the Turk."

"This is beyond belief," I said.

But in fact I did believe him. The assistants standing guard outside the doors were more creatures than men. Like those of the Turk himself, their motions were mechanical. I began to despair for both my own life and that of Monsieur Morphy. This man was infinitely more evil than I had imagined.

"Make your decision, Mr. Herriot. I have told you the true history of the Turk and its Egg. You asked me for proof of the powers of the Old One and I have given it to you freely. Now, I ask, what say you?"

My hatred of the man crystallized at that moment. By offering me the hellish possibility of resurrecting my Abilene from her true death he had violated that which I held sacrosanct— he had debauched my memory of her life. I loathed his very existence. His cold eyes had measured my grief and thought it for sale as had the Snake Oil salesman before him. Yet, for a moment, I controlled my rage.

"I am yours," I said.

"I have your word on it?"

"You have my hand."

I turned away slightly as I rose, then took hold of the knife and pulled it from beneath my coat. His eyes widened when he saw it, but before he could cry out for his creatures, I plunged it beneath his ribcage, then thrust it up into his heart.

"But," he said in a strangled voice, "I was to be immortal."

When I twisted the knife higher, he gasped and with both hands reached for its hilt. A manic fury gave me strength and I moved into him, driving him back against the wall. I sobbed as I performed this heinous deed but yet I thrilled to plunge the blade deeper. Blood washed my hands like guilt; the warm, thin liquid of his life dripped from my fingers.

It was too much to hold him upright forever by the knife and the force of my grief. He tottered for a moment when I stepped back, and then dropped to the floor with the noise of a steamer trunk hitting the ground.

Professor Reynolds Pickett was dead.

CʒꝏD

With a soft push, I opened the door to the room and peered at the homunculi the Professor created. They, too, had fallen to the floor and lay there unmoving. I wondered if they were dead, but realized that, having never had true life, they could not actually die. The professor had not had sufficient time to summon them in his defense before I murdered him.

Warily I opened the doors to the great room. The two remaining homunculi lay still on the floor also, having fallen one to either side of the door frame. Morphy was actually standing when I entered, running one hand through his hair, and with the other he grasped a piece and snapped it down on the chessboard. I moved across the floor like an Indian scout through grass, making as little sound as I could, although to this day I do not know why. It was imperative I gain his attention and dissuade him from finishing the game. It must be stopped, no matter the injury to his pride. The risk was too great. I had come to believe that no man could defeat the Turk.

When I got close enough, I said softly, "Monsieur Morphy? If you please, it is time to stop the game."

He turned and looked at me as though I were mad.

"Stop the game? Have you been drinking?"

Past his shoulder, I looked into the agate marble eyes of the Turk. The automaton's hand slid forward, grasped a piece and made its move.

Morphy whirled around and clapped his hands.

"Hah!" he cried. "You are undone."

"Monsieur Morphy," I said, grasping his shoulder, "you must stop the game. It is time for us to leave. We have little time."

With one hand and surprising force, the young chess master pulled free of my grip and picked up another piece.

"Checkmate," he howled and slammed the piece down onto the board.

I stepped back in horror.

"My God," I said. "Whatever have you done? All is lost."

"All is won," laughed Morphy. "Nothing is lost and everything is won. I have defeated the Turk. I have not only defeated every man on the planet worth playing, I have now defeated the devil himself. Truly now I am the King."

The room filled with an unearthly keening and a faint yellow-green light. Immediately I pulled Morphy away from the Turk with the force of a man twice my size.

"Cover your eyes," I said. "Don't look at the Egg; whatever you do, don't look at the Egg."

But the imp of the perverse held court that night, and Monsieur Paul Morphy looked. I quickly placed my hand over his eyes so he, in fact, saw very little of the emerging light. With my face close to his ear, I said firmly, "You must trust me at all costs. You have won. You are victorious. Now if you do not wish to lose everything, you must leave this house and never look back."

CZ8O

It was with great difficulty and a brutal effort that I both restrained and convinced the chess master to leave. He railed and cursed me every step of the way and swore he would never pay me even a single penny for attending him. We parted mortal enemies, though I bore him no malice. He had only done what he was born to do; exercising the talents Cassiopeia herself had gifted him to defeat the greatest challenge of his life. I bought his silence with the threat that if he spoke of the match to anyone. I would declare to my dying day the Turk was a mere contrivance, which declaration alone would diminish his reputation. Of the death of the professor, he knew nothing. As I watched him huff away, I wondered what would become of his mind after enduring even such a brief exposure to the djinn.

ᘓᘔ

I returned to the great room, which was by then filled with the disquieting radiance of the creature. My movements were slow and tentative, since each step of the way I had my head turned away from the djinn and my eyes covered with one hand. In the other I carried an andiron I had discovered in the house.

When I finally stood before the Turk, I enacted the plan I had devised. In the struggle, Monsieur Morphy had left behind his written record of the game's moves. With a trembling hand, I played each of the moves in reverse, grieving anew with each piece placement for my dead wife. I had refused to resurrect her. How little did I love her if did not pursue her to rescue her from the land of shades? While playing back each move, I felt as though I was shoveling fresh dirt upon my poor wife's grave and sealing her away for all eternity.

Unbidden images of monstrous horrors began to break the surface of my grief, and I knew that the djinn, servant of whoever commanded it, still did not wish to be forced back into imprisonment. Its rage flared the room with red violence, and in my mind I could see death and destruction imposed over the chess pieces. My hand began to shake as though I were afflicted with the palsy. The djinn wanted to be free to serve and dispense power to please its master. But I had sent its new master away. Dr. Dee had turned its power in on itself by causing it to be both captor and prison guard with his endlessly looping chess command.

I took a deep breath and steeled myself. The djinn forced terrifying images into my consciousness, and I could scarcely see the chessboard through the flapping of leathery wings and the sounds of teeth shattering bone. The light spilling out from the egg crackled and seethed with a destructive, angry energy. I kept my eyes averted.

As I reached for the next piece, I heard an agitated buzzing noise, as though the djinn had released thousands of malignant bees into the room. I focused my eyes on the chessboard and called on every bit of discipline I possessed to concentrate on completing the reverse move order of the game to seal closed the Egg again. But beyond the peripheral cone of my vision I could not help but notice pinpoints of pulsating blue-black light that flashed purple explosions. It seemed as though the reality of the room about me was soon to shatter into a million pieces. There was, I began to understand, very little time for me to complete the move reversal and return the djinn to its prison. But my vision was wavering and cold arms of fear wrapped themselves around my chest and began to squeeze the air from my lungs.

I remembered my Abilene, and her flawless face supplanted the terrors that filled my mind. Once again, I could concentrate. I followed Morphy's move list backward at a more rapid pace. And yet, when I had arrived again at the first move of the game, I found myself sobbing once more. I felt no sense of triumph. Was I indeed doing the right thing? Was it unnatural for a man to so grieve for his lost loved one that he risks damnation?

At that instant I realized the hideous djinn did not value any person's life. To the creature, returning my wife to the living held no importance. It was using my anguish as a tool of manipulation as Professor Pickett had attempted to do.

I grasped the last chess piece and forced it down onto the board as I had plunged the knife into the professor's heart.

The djinn's light began to fade, but an inner compulsion to glimpse this being that had caused me such misery gripped me, and I stole a furtive glance at its disappearing glow just as the Egg closed up again completely. The realization of what I had done horrified me.

With a shudder, I took the andiron and began the systematic destruction of the chess board and then the Turk itself. After the board was reduced to pieces, I smashed apart the cabinet and reduced the cables and gears to scrap. In an almost hypnotic trance I struck the hideous puppet-face over and over again until I at last came to my senses. One blood red stone eye rolled away across the floor.

I escaped the estate and the city of Arkham under the cover of darkness that night and journeyed south. My final act before leaving was to set fire to the Pickett estate.

ꟾN Chains Lighter Than Air

by Nghi Vo

IT WAS THE NINETEENTH CENTURY, the age of the iron horse and of dirigibles that ruled the sky while submarines prowled the sea floor. It was the nineteenth century, and humanity stood on the brink of the aether.

It was the nineteenth century, and people still barred their doors with rowan. Most hospitals tied an iron coin around the ankles of new babies to keep them from turning changeling.

Preiss, whose scars still ached when it was cold, was painfully aware that he was designing an airship with no trace of iron in its elegant lines and streamlined bulkheads.

୧୨୫୦

On the morning of June 14th, 1894, the HMA *Titania* set out for her maiden voyage from Cornwallis Airfield, two hours south of Chicago. The airship was set to refuel in New York, and after that she would push on across the Atlantic, making landfall at Prince Albert Airfield by the morning of June 28[th.]

She made it to New York without incident but when Preiss went to oversee the refueling, he was stopped on the asphalt by a pair of guardsmen.

"Sorry, sir, but at the moment, no civilians are allowed on the ground. The refueling will be handed by crown technicians."

"What? But why?"

The guard looked at Preiss balefully, and he knew that his accent had slipped again. He had been in the Americas for almost eight years and the colonial drawl leaked into his speech when he wasn't thinking about it.

"Troubles with the indenture reformers again, sir. Senior Engineer MacLauren says you'll be refueled and set for launch by nightfall."

He had to be content with that, and though his nerves were still a tangle of wire and grit, he knew that the crown technicians wouldn't fumble things. The HMA *Titania* was the third of the Olympus-class airships to take to the sky, and though she was the largest by almost 200 feet, her sisters, the HMA *Hippolyta* and the HMA *Cressida* were already well known in the airways.

From the men's dining room on the fourth level, he caught glimpses of the crown technicians dodging underneath the ship.

As he watched, he saw the crown technicians scatter and for a moment, he couldn't tell what had caused it. Then the asphalt was crowded with angry, shouting people. Some of them wore the yellow vests of city indenture workers, but the rest blended into a furious, howling swarm.

They hit the side of the ship, causing a barely perceptible shudder, and then then they were pounding on it.

"Down with indenture!"

"Free rights for all!"

"Better a slave's collar than an indenture's contract!" Priess was pushed to the window as the passengers came to the window to stare. They were three stories above the heads of the rioters, and he was glad that there were no windows on the third class decks. They might pound on the hull, but they were wasting their time.

As if to prove his words, the guardsmen arrived on the scene wielding hoses and blasting the crowd with water. Chanted slogans turned to shouts of pain and the rioters were driven back. One or two had been hit directly with the hoses and lay unconscious on the asphalt. The guardsmen moved to arrest them and it was over. The crowd that trapped Priess against the window started to dissipate.

"Hope they lock 'em up for the night," one African gentleman remarked to no one in particular.

"Make it longer and maybe they'll think twice before trying it again," suggested another. There were a few isolated chuckles, but they sounded strained to Preiss.

"Your coffee, sir."

Preiss had forgotten that he had ordered coffee. The waiter who offered it to him smiled blandly. Preiss found himself staring at the tattoos on the back of the waiter's hand. They were the twin stars of the Starline Company, which owned the *Titania*.

"Sir?"

"Um, yes?"

"Are you all right?"

"Yes. Yes, I'm fine, thank you."

∞

He was the one who had given the ship its name. For the first year or so of planning, it was called the *Portia*, but when the primary investor who had suggested the name pulled out, the decision was made to change it.

Preiss wasn't even supposed to be at that meeting. He had had an armful of designs that required approval, and found himself in a conference room full of angry men. The name of a ship was a serious thing, and he had been waiting patiently until someone pointed at him and demanded a suggestion.

"Why, Her Majesty's Airship *Titania*," he said in surprise, and his surprise was genuine. The words fell out of his mouth like live fish, and once out, there was no calling them back.

The investors loved the name and adopted it immediately. The Portia became the *Titania*, and soon the press caught wind of it. She was not the largest airship to take to the sky, but her romance and her elegance were unquestioned. By the final year, the Chicago papers were full of pictures of her bronze and purple cloth sides and the tall mullioned windows of her observation deck.

The first time Preiss saw the name *Titania* in print, he walked out of the frigid, arid offices of the Starline Company and bought a bottle of anise liqueur. He took it up to his apartment and drank steadily, taking one licorice swallow after another. Preiss was not a drinker, and instead of passing out, he became violently ill.

"Idiot," he muttered, curled up in a miserable lump on his bed. "Idiot, idiot."

The anise liqueur was a poor choice. It reminded him of the twisted overgrown gardens of Faerie, where all paths led precisely nowhere. Once he had become lost in the queen's gardens. He wandered the narrow trails, nearly drugged with the smell of safflower and lotus, but unwilling to cry for help. One of the seneschals had found him, and he still remembered its sharp fanged mouth opening to smile at him.

After he rose from his bed, head still throbbing and stomach in total revolt, Preiss forced himself to put it out of his mind. He needed steady hands and a steady mind for his work, and he gave himself over to it He let the airship's clean lines drive away the sinuous labyrinths of the fae gardens.

Every day, he found something new to love in the *Titania's* grace and form. Every night, he woke up terrified.

CRISO

The *Titania* departed New York's Tudor Airfield at dusk. Preiss joined the crowd on the observation deck to watch the New World's tall buildings drop away into the sunset. From where he stood, he could see the copper statue of Winged Victory standing tall in the harbor, wings spread and sword raised.

The observation deck was formal dress only, and Preiss tugged uncomfortably at the collar of his shirt. He missed the days when he could stand alone in the observation deck. Now, surrounded by the elite of the New World and the Old, he wondered where the engineers were. There were serious men from the Lakota Territories who knew the ship as well as he did, and that pair of sisters from Phoenix who were responsible for nearly every piece of glass on board. They might have had their hands over every bit of the airship, but they could never afford the observation deck.

A waiter offered him a glass of champagne, and Preiss was too distracted to refuse.

He drank the champagne and the band struck up a pleasant song. Preiss found himself nodding along to it.

"Do you know what they're playing?" he asked the waiter.

"Mendelssohn's *Fairy March*," the young man said. He spoke with all the assurance of a music student, and Preiss wondered if he had been one, once.

Preiss smiled weakly. He wanted to laugh at his own nervousness, but he didn't dare. Instead, he drained the glass and handed it back to the waiter.

No, there were ways of getting into the air no matter how poor you were, he thought, glancing at the back of the waiter's hand.

His parents called it his sabbatical, when he had disappeared from Yale on his twenty-second birthday. He returned- he was returned- precisely one year later, and since then, they had tried very hard to pretend that he was never gone at all.

His father told him he was lucky to have parents who were so wealthy and teachers who were so patient. Preiss knew he was lucky in those those things, but they were like drops of water against the sea.

He was lucky that they hadn't given him marble hands or a tongue that spoke only truth. He was lucky that he could breathe air instead of water and he was lucky that they had not crippled him in one of the frenzied dances that happened every dark moon. He had known plenty who were.

Preiss was lucky that he had returned at all. He had known plenty who had not.

The deck was crowded full of talking, happy people, and he knew that he must have looked terrible there. His tie had come undone, and he knew that his hair, now that it was starting to dry, was sticking up into cowlicks. Suddenly he grew cold, and the red streaks of the sunset looked bloody.

Preiss pulled himself into a corner like a wounded cat, shaking and terrified. Sometimes, he was sure that he had brought an illness with him, some slippery Faerie virus that lived in his blood, underneath his skin. Sometimes it would seize his tongue and keep him from speaking and sometimes it would prick his arms and legs with icy cold needles. It wasn't an illness, though, it was fear, and he looked around wildly.

The music had changed, and there was discordant quality underneath the smooth notes, a harsh ridge of sound that the people around him couldn't seem to hear.

"Please, he said, tugging the sleeve of a man passing by. Through strange coincidence, he realized it was the same man that had offered him champagne a few minutes before and now that he looked, he could see that it was the same waiter that had asked after his health during the refueling.

"What are they playing now?" There were words falling out of his mouth again, and he swallowed hard, hearing a dry click in his throat.

"Tchaikovsky's *Swan Maiden*, sir." The waiter paused for a moment, watching Priess warily. Preiss realized that the man must have barely cleared his teens. In the Americas, you only needed to be fifteen to sell yourself into indenture and the waiter, who he had accosted twice now, looked a small handful of years older than that.

"Sir, are you you all right?"

Preiss could feel a ghastly smile on his face, and he wondered why the young man simply did not take his champagne elsewhere.

"What if I'm not?" he found himself asking. In another world, he would have been shocked at his unruly tongue, but now he just wanted to hear what the waiter would say.

"Would you care to step into the corridor here, sir? You look like you could use a little air."

"That's presumptuous," Preiss said shakily, even as he complied. "I might speak with the overseer about you."

"You don't even know my name," the waiter said peacefully.

Preiss sat down on one of the small sculpted aluminum benches in the corridor, and the waiter found a glass of water to push into his hand. He drank it in slow sips, loosening his tie beyond repair, and glanced up at the other man.

"I don't," he admitted. "Know your name, I mean. Will you tell it to me?"

The waiter grinned at him, and now up close, he looked less like one out of a dozen waiters and more like a real person.

"That depends, are you going to report me to the overseer?"

Preiss shook his head, attempting a smile of his own and the waiter picked up his tray again.

"My name's Lachlan," he said. "Give me a call if you need anything else."

It was less a suggestion than an order, and Preiss was amused until he realized how very much he liked receiving orders.

He shook his head but Lachlan was already gone. Preiss knew the name of the man who was captaining the vessel, but he was not sure that he could recognize him on sight. The waiter, though, he could recognize the waiter.

⋘⋙

Preiss was sick the night of the ball. His head pounded, and when he looked into the mirror, he was momentarily sure that it was not his own face he saw. He blinked before he screamed, and then he recognized himself. The face in the mirror was thin and drawn, with lavender circles under eyes that seemed leached of all color.

Preiss washed his face harder than he needed to, welcoming the shock of the cold water. He dressed quickly, and when he glanced out the porthole, he was obliquely terrified to find a sea of stars that seemed closer than they should have been.

He got himself to the ballroom somehow. For the two nights, ever since they had left New York, he had become convinced that the ship was pitching and rolling like a steamer in a storm. The ship flew true; he was the unsteady one, and he knew it. He forced himself to keep his hands at his side, rather than reaching for the walls, and when the footman opened the door to the ballroom for him, he walked in instead of bolting. He had done harder things, but at the moment, he couldn't remember them.

The lights of the ballroom were too bright, and the chandeliers reflected thousands of dagger-point glints around the room. It wasn't crowded yet, but it was only nine o'clock and people were still filing in.

Everywhere he looked there were fleshy, red faces, and people talking and laughing. Their mouths and eyes were terribly dark to him, as if they had been painted on with kohl and carmine. There was no depth to anything, and Preiss broke out into a cold sweat.

The music changed too quickly, and Preiss wanted hold his head in his hands. He couldn't see the musicians and suddenly he thought that they weren't there at all, that the music was coming from the ship itself.

It was a brief lapse in reason that frightened him badly and Preiss groped for something real.

"What are they playing now?" he said uneasily, looking around for the waiter he knew would be there. The music was sweet but nervous, and he felt as stretched as a violin string.

"Why, they're playing Purcell's *Fairy Queen*, James. Calm yourself."

Her skin was colorless and transparent. He could make out the fine tracery of blue veins at her temples and her hands, and Priess knew that if he touched her, he would find her cold. She barely came up to his chin, but he stepped back as if struck. He knew her eyes, lapis flecked with gold, and he knew her strength.

"Your Majesty ..."

"Why are you so surprised that I am here, James? You named your wonderful airship after me."

She tapped her long, gold-capped nails against the stem of her wine glass, making it chime, and her thin lips were pressed into a firm line. No human born could read her unless she let them, and Preiss broke into a cold sweat.

It had been ten years since he had seen her, ten years since he had woken cold and lost in the Black Hills of the Lakota Territory. He never thought about his lost year, or at least, he told himself that he never did, but now he knew it for a lie. She was in his blood and she was in his breath; if she told him to stop his heartbeat, he would have stopped it for her.

Preiss kept his hands at his side and stood as firmly as he could. His blood drummed in his ears, and when he spoke, he could hear himself, as if from a great distance.

"You ... you do me a great honor, ma'am. I ..."

"You are terrified," she said, without a trace of humor.

"I am in love with you," he admitted. "And yes, to love you means to be terrified of you."

She smiled coldly at that, tilting her head to one side in a way that reminded him of a snake.

She had smiled like that before dismissing him from her service. Hours later, he awoke on the cold hillside, naked and unable to speak for nearly a month. Seeing her again, his tongue felt thick and knotted in his mouth.

"You may show me the ship," she said, offering him one thin hand. She was dressed in a traveling gown of black and cream satin, and as he watched, one eye on her fox stole opened slyly, glinting gold at him before closing again.

With the queen of Faerie on his arm, people parted before them. Her hand rested lightly in the crook of his arm, and through the wool of his suit, he could feel the gentlest prick of her long golden nails. They weren't hurting him, not yet, but they brought back memories of those same nails tripping along his spine and digging into his shoulders. He wasn't sure how he was walking in a straight line.

He guided her through the ballroom and took her through the long corridors of first class. They walked through the cramped servants' dorms as well as the third class bunks. No human looked up at the man in the suit or the woman in satin, but Mercutio and Tybalt, the airship cats, purred when she stopped to scratch their chins.

She touched the steering wheel gently, and pressed her hand flat against the furnace, uncaring of the intense heat. She seemed irritated when she realized that no one person could control the ship completely, but the communication system, with its trumpet speakers and carved ivory mouth-pieces, enchanted her.

By the time they gained the observation deck, it was full dark and the stars were coming out. A party of Ottoman businessmen spoke intently in a far corner while a young girl and her governess used the telescope.

The lights were dimmed, and the early starlight gave the queen's face a cold cast. Preiss waited with his heart in his throat as she peered out the tall windows and took her turn at the telescope.

"What a beautiful lady," the girl murmured, as she and her governess departed.

Eventually the Ottoman businessmen departed as well, and Preiss wondered if the observation deck's door had disappeared, for no one else entered.

She stood by the telescope, one hand on the aluminum shaft, watching the stars drift by. She was as still as a statue and Preiss waited. The habit of stillness came back to him. Though he was inclined to fidget with his hands and with his clothes, now he fell into a calm silence. He could have stood there for years, waiting for her to speak.

"She's a wonderful ship," the queen said presently. "But the *Cressida* is faster, and the Lefevre Company's *Marianne* is larger."

"She's more beautiful," Preiss said. Though he was afraid, this he could say with certainty. "No other ship is half so beautiful."

The queen of Faerie smiled, and it was like a storm had broken. Her smile revealed long ivory teeth, but it was warm.

He had only a moment to relax and then she spoke again.

"No ship that bears my name will be ordinary," she said. "I speak for myself, and you speak for the ship, and so I say that you may choose."

Preiss could feel the hair at the back of his neck stand up, and he put down his glass carefully. Choices were the bedrock and seabed of Faerie, and once they were made, they were as immovable as stone.

"Choose, ma'am?"

"Yes." The queen turned to an elegantly curved bulkhead, which was carved resin dyed to look like oak.

"No ship that bears my name, no matter how beautiful, will be ordinary."

"Ordinary-!" He choked back a stutter, and she didn't even glance at him. Instead, she was stroking the bulkhead. It bore her name, it belonged to her.

"She is a beautiful ship, but she will be forgotten in the blink of an eye. Twenty years, a hundred, and it all will be gone."

"It's what mortal things do," Preiss said hesitantly, but she wasn't listening.

"*My* ship will be remembered," the queen said, placing both hands on the brass rail and leaning closer to the glass. The fox head on her shoulder stirred, winking at Preiss before closing its amber eyes again.

"My ship may be a great mystery or a great disaster. Choose."

"The mystery ..." he said slowly. "A disappearance?"

She smiled at him, almost coy.

"Yes."

Her smile grew marginally sharper, and against his will, he remembered nights spent enraptured by stars that swam in the sky. It was a real memory of Faerie's moving stars, but just as real was the feeling of carved ironwood hooks digging into his skin, tethering him in place. They healed his skin and made it whole the next day, but it did not make him forget that they had torn it.

"Tell me more about my choice," he said. He was stalling, and her smile told him that she knew it, but she took another sip from her champagne and continued.

"There is a storm up ahead. It's blowing from the north and moving fast. It's small but its violence will rip through this beautiful ship like a whip through thin silk."

The image was shockingly clear. He imagined the ship slashed in two by driving gales, and a thousand tan parachutes drifting towards the freezing black Atlantic.

"Tell me ..." Preiss swallowed hard. "Tell me what you would do with this ship, then."

Her smile turned dreamy. She opened her hands wide and he could see the blue runes tattooed on her palms. He couldn't read them but he knew that one stood for death and the other stood for life.

"There is a field on the banks of the Asp River, where the ground is open and where the treetops are lapped with light. I would moor my ship there with cobweb ropes and crew her with the spider people who came from the dying woods. It would be a palace, a jewel hung up in Faerie's sky and all who see it would gasp at its beauty and its craft." As she spoke, he could see it. In Faerie's strange clear air, every line would be distinct and far cleaner than it could ever be on earth. The colors would be sharper and the spider people, gray-bodied and bristle-limbed, would crawl over the hull and the envelope, spinning orbs of delicate art that would be shattered and lost forever when the airship flew.

"You would fly her, wouldn't you?" he asked suddenly. "She's meant to be flown."

"Yes, of course, James," the queen said reassuringly. "She is far too beautiful to rest anchored."

He could have said that he was bewitched by the idea, that her upturned face and the cold light that turned her skin to marble seduced him. It was her ship after all. Whether it was the faery queen's whisper that prompted him to name it after her and seal its fate or some shadow on his own heart, he had named for her.

It was on the tip of his tongue to agree wholeheartedly, ironwood hooks and all, but then he thought of stars. It was not the swimming stars of Faery that entered his mind, or the ones that he could see from the observation deck. Instead he thought of the twin stars of the Starline Company, tattooed into the back of Lachlan's hand, and he found himself shaking his head.

He spoke for the ship, and suddenly Preiss realized that it did not mean he spoke for the people on board as well. He might have, and they would have all been lost to Faerie for a hundred years, or a thousand, or forever. Some of them would even have thanked him, and that made him turn cold inside.

"The ship is yours," he said slowly. "I named her for you and gave her to you, I know that now. I would rather see it whole and gone from this world than dashed to pieces in the storm."

She didn't smile, and the fox head on her shoulder opened both eyes to look at him intently.

"Not the people," he forced himself to say. "I haven't given them to you and I won't. You can get their service on your own, if the thought pleases you, but they won't come to it through me."

It came perilously close to insolence, and he braced himself what would come next.

"You pose me a pretty puzzle, James," she said coldly. "Take the ship but leave the people. Shall I draw the ship to Faery and see if they can dance on the clouds?"

"You promised me a choice," he said, daring to be a little brave, a little longer. "I've chosen a mystery, not a disaster."

It was all he could say, and he bowed his head. Some habits of obedience could not be broken, and some he would not have wanted broken at all.

She was gone before he could raise his eyes and somewhere, he heard a gate close against him forever.

CஓௐD

The morning of June 18th dawned bright and clear, and the watchmen and sailors of the RMS *Carpathia* couldn't say for certain when better than one thousand people appeared on the deck. Some of them were in evening wear and still dancing, and the orchestra was finishing up In the Shadows. There were people sleeping underneath blankets, finishing a throw of dice and in one case, kissing behind the lifeboats.

Third Officer McKinnon later told *The Times*, that they looked like ghosts at first, too intent on pastimes and passions from previous lives to notice the living.

"Of course," he said wryly, "that was before the yelling started."

People started shouting and some of them started crying. Those who had lost family members soon found them again and started to ask what had happened. There was no trace of the HMA *Titania*, either in the air or floating in the water. No trace would ever be found.

Preiss walked among the startled people, skirting families and stepping over a few heavy sleepers who had yet to wake up. There was a babble of languages on the deck, and Preiss could hear the Colonial drawl, the crisp accent of Queen's English, and other languages that he thought might have been Arabic and Hindi. He saw Lachlan in a group of waiters, looking around and exclaiming at their circumstances.

He stepped up to the rail, and looked over the broad expanse of water. The Atlantic was a perfect glassy gray, and no matter how hard he stared into the ocean, no faces stared back. No long arms reached up for him.

Somewhere, the HMA *Titania* was docking in a misty clearing. She would be crewed by the spider people from the dying wood, and she would travel high into the aether, buoyed by Faerie magics and lighter than air.

Preiss stared up into the empty dawn sky and knew, with relief and a longing that he refused to name, that she would fly without him.

THE UNICYCLIST'S FATE

by Michael J. DeLuca

MICHAEL, THE UNICYCLIST, pedaled furiously along the crowded pier, threading the needle through his rivals. La Bella Linda waved from the rail of the great skyscraper ship; her broad hat, tilted like the rings of a planet off-kilter, spilled its sooty plume into the threatening November sky as though she too were powered by mighty coal. The crowd of young men who'd come to vie for her attention sighed and shouted, "Sing for us! Sing!"

And for them—a faceless crowd, neither old friends nor recent lovers—she obliged. Parting her lips, Linda let out a storm of singed-angelic notes to battle the noise of the port and the city. Michael's heart, though it ached, knew Linda's song could never lose. But in the pit of his gut—his center of balance—he rooted for the city.

A steel beam slipped from the shoulders of a quartet of dockworkers enervated by the furnace-vent of regret that was La Bella Linda's lungs. Michael knew what they suffered; only instinct, polished skill, and the calluses of time kept him alert. He dove to avoid the great weight crashing down, tumbled over gouged tar, and was up again, racing.

A wild-haired old man stepped into Michael's path, a silver dollar pressed between thumb and finger, his lined face intent, strangely unaffected by the sadness of Linda's voice. Was he made of iron, that he preferred a Unicyclist to a Siren? Michael orbited past him, fast and low, though his pockets were empty and that coin as much as he might earn in a day.

As the ship's great horn sounded the final boarding call, passengers pressed at the foot of the gangway—a line of skirts and suited shoulders, hands cupped to ears to catch the song. Michael gripped the unicycle's seat and pulled it from beneath him, stumbling to a halt. His shin stung hot where he'd scraped it on the pier.

Roped handrails led up along the gangway to the deck: a schoolboy trick, old hat. He couldn't win her back with tricks—but he could reach her. Springing the wheel loose from the fork, he deflated the tire, yanked it from the rim and looped it round his neck. He reattached the frame, then settled the empty rim atop the handrail. With a running start and a leg up from a piling, he pedaled along the gangway like a tightrope acrobat, hopping over hands and support poles, crossing high above the gray, cold river.

He tried to think of something he could say to her.

As he neared the ocean liner's flank, a stately woman reached across the rope to Linda, hands clasped in supplication or in rapture, her bulk obstructing his path, oblivious to his approach. He backpedaled too fast—morning's fog had left the rope slick. The wheel slipped from beneath him. The woman gasped.

Linda's voice died away against the thrum and echo of the city.

He could have milked it, played the fall for her pity, but he couldn't have lived with it. He caught himself with one hand, balanced upside-down atop the rope, the other gripping the unicycle's frame. He used his momentum to launch into a spring and was rightwise again in a moment.

The woman who had nearly killed him swooned and had to be caught by a man behind her. Michael sped past, planted a hand on the railing of the ship and vaulted flat-footed onto the mezzanine deck.

A few scattered voices cheered him from the pier below: children, that goggle-eyed old man—those who'd never known love, the easily impressed. But the crowd was with La Bella Linda: his antics had caused her to break off her song, and devastation rolled in to thicken the fog.

Surrounded by crestfallen admirers, Linda stood rigid in dark heels and soot-colored cashmere, familiar and distant, lips pressed to hold back those heart-stinging notes.

"Don't go," he said.

"You know I must," she told him, her low voice, rough, and tarnished in a way her songs were not. "The clubs and theatres of Rio, Moscow, Paris—my career is there, across the oceans. My future."

"Then take me with you." It was all he had to offer. She'd heard it all before.

Her lips quirked expressively, giving away her careful poise. "Your art and mine ... we're not in the same league anymore. Look around. You risk your life, perform your greatest feat, people laugh, they're astonished—but that's it. I open my mouth, and they feel weak."

"You know I worked as hard as you to achieve what I have."

She shook her head, plume wagging gracelessly like an alley cat's tail, betraying her elegant clothes, evoking her past with Michael: a street corner, a scuffed hat without a plume spilling coins over concrete. "You worked harder than anyone. But you never had as far to go."

Two burly deckhands jostled into view, eyes on Michael—but they halted at the sight of her.

She reached a gloved hand to the dirty tire about his neck; at her touch it turned to lead, dragging him down. He looked at his battered, worn-thin saddle shoes, his trousers, knees threadbare, his clownish waistcoat and pinned sleeves.

"How could you come with me?" she asked. "You can't even afford a ticket."

"I love you," he said, and let himself be hauled away.

CXƏ৪D

The great ship's engines thrummed, the smoke from its stacks mingled with November clouds and its horn sounded low as they tossed him onto the pier. No one offered him a hand. The crowd watched his Bella Linda and the great ship that bore her, under the guidance of the tugs, breaking in a churn of white water across the dark river toward the bay.

Then someone was stooping over him — the wild-haired old man. The same intentness filled his crinkled eyes as he raised something in a fist overhead — not a coin this time, but a brick.

It swung down. Sparks burst inside Michael's skull.

CXƏ৪D

He woke on a cot in a dim concrete room; rain hissed against a corrugated roof, and his head pulsed with electric pain. The floor was cold. Against the wall, cleaned and polished, its tire replaced and inflated, leaned the unicycle.

He clutched for it, pressed it to him, hating it with all his being.

He could have been some other kind of athlete, any kind. A dancer — a cyclist, even — and Linda's life might never have outstripped his. He had chosen the art of a street-performer, she that of a muse.

He jammed the wheel down, climbed astride the seat and moved his feet smoothly from the cold floor to the pedals. It was a cramped room, windowless, with a single door. He circled it three times with the precision of a clock. He spun to the wall, pedaled towards it and up, then tucked, gripping the seat between his thighs, and flung himself into a backflip.

He landed half an inch from the opposite wall and came to a halt where he'd begun.

Balance — that struggle to resist on three planes an insurmountable force — once had occupied every mote of his attention. Now it was second nature, useless — if it couldn't help him to forget.

He raised the unicycle to smash it against the concrete.

"Bravo!" The wild-haired old man stood in the doorway, eyes shining.

Michael interposed the unicycle between them, a clumsy weapon. "You can't keep me here."

The old man backed away into a shadowed space where an otherworldly light flickered across his crinkled features, shifting from ice-white to golden. "It won't be me that keeps you here."

Michael peered cautiously past him into the room beyond. Beneath a broad, arched ceiling of tin rattled by rain, a toothed, hollow disk — like a bicycle gear, only immense — hovered above the floor. The disk wobbled and spun about no discernible axis, as though unacquainted with the influence of such laws as gravity, inertia, centripetal force. Tentacles of furred lightning, blinding one moment, black the next, reached from it in all directions, exploring the limits of its space like sentient fingers. And in the center of the disk, illuminated only piecemeal, a flash and afterimage at a time, there was a void in the shape of a human form.

The broken heart of the Unicyclist stirred for this strange machine, drawn to it as though by magnetism. "What is it?" he whispered.

The old man's eager eyes flickered with reflected light. "For lack of a better term, call it an *aerostat* — a device for manipulating the electromagnetic field generated by the earth's atmosphere, in order to achieve flight without the need for lift or propulsion, or indeed an engine of any kind.

At least, that's what I've come to believe in the years I have observed it."

The old man caught him by the shoulder. "Careful!" Michael realized his legs had taken two steps towards the aerostat of their own volition. "The paraelectric discharges won't harm you, but the movements of the disk are unpredictable to say the least. Look here." He tugged at his collar, revealing an ugly scar across his collarbone, telltale of a badly-healed break. He turned his left wrist, revealing another; the two smallest fingers of the same hand were crooked. "There's more, in places modesty prevents my sharing."

"Who are you?" said Michael. "Where did you find this?"

"A Harbor Rescue pilot—retired. Nicholas Eyck is my name. On a misty night like this one, eleven years ago, I saw the aerostat crash into the sound. Dispatch wouldn't believe me when I told them. Nor did anyone show interest in attempting a salvage. So I financed my own. I found it empty—no one inside, no sign of any body or bones—but still flashing and spinning and sending out feelers of fire under eighty feet of murk. I called in a favor from a friend who captains a tug—and here it is. Here it has been."

Now Michael thought he recognized that driven look in the old man's eye. Learning the unicycle, he'd had scrapes and lumps of his own, twice knocked himself out on a curb—tough nothing so hard as that brick. He rubbed his head. "And since then—eleven years—you've been trying to fly it?"

"Eight years," Eyck corrected. "Took that long to learn my lesson. In a rescue plane, I could rely on instruments—altimeter, airspeed, artificial horizon. Even in deep fog, I knew which way was up. The aerostat requires its pilot carry that ability within him—and other talents, no doubt; I never made it far enough to understand. When my broken bones began to ache when it rained, I realized one more fall might kill me, and I'd never have the skill to master it. That's when I started looking for someone who did."

"After all that work? You devoted your life to it—and then you just gave up?"

Eyck frowned. "You've never had to give up something you loved? Then you're lucky. I suffered for the decision, believe me—but in the end, it was the best thing for me."

The aerostat called to Michael, crackling tendrils beckoning. What did he stand to lose? A few scrapes, bruises, broken bones. Nothing he hadn't suffered. Nothing like what he was suffering now. And, if he were lucky, he could lose *himself* within it—forget his utter mastery of a worthless craft, the dead-end career he'd thought he lived for. The love he'd sabotaged.

He shook her from his head to focus on the aerostat. He tried to discern a pattern to its complex, tumbling motion, to understand its sudden changes in orientation and speed. There had to be a pattern.

He stepped free of Eyck's protective hand. "I understand the risks," he said.

The old man's eyes moistened.

A pseudopod of electrostatic lightning reached out to meet Michael's approach. He flinched away, but the charge engulfed him, moving too swiftly to see. Searing pain coursed from the goose-egg on his skull, and he doubled over, clutching at his head. Behind his closed eyes, lightning. Linda, dismayed by the last words he'd ever speak to her.

"Sorry about the brick," called Eyck. "You wouldn't take my money. I didn't know what else to do."

The pain receded, and when he was able to straighten, Michael found that the tendril of energy had left him unharmed. "I don't do what I do for the money," he said.

Eyck sighed. "That's how I knew I had to bring you here."

Michael rehearsed the motions in his head—leap, grab the rim of the disk as it passed, let the motion of it carry him above the void, and release. That was assuming he could grasp the pattern sufficiently to anticipate it, or at least to react. Assuming his muscles would continue to obey the laws of motion once he had come into contact with the disk. Assuming he could even maintain a grip on its surface.

The unicycle had been impossible to rationalize or to prepare for on any intellectual level. To learn, he'd had to jump in, to try and fail. Wasn't it the same with everything? Even with love.

The disk reversed direction. He threw himself forward, groping for purchase along one of the broad teeth. The worn soles of his shoes scrabbled uselessly against its smooth surface. He remained in contact for a span of three heartbeats, then found himself in free-fall, trying desperately to guess which way was up.

He knew how to fail; he had done it enough. He tucked his chin against his chest, threw his elbows up around his head, palms out, and took the floor with his left shoulder, rolling.

Eyck's face, wrinkled with concern, interrupted the play of static lightning on the ceiling. "Never seen it done from this perspective. It looks ... " He breathed. "Exhilarating."

Michael smiled wryly. "It hurts."

The rain thickened, thudding against the hangar's corrugated roof. The aerostat crackled. Somewhere out on the Atlantic, Linda would be checking into her stateroom, the deck rocking gently beneath her, some dedicated admirer helpfully spinning an umbrella to shake off the rain.

Thinking of her hurt far worse.

It wasn't working. He couldn't forget.

He picked himself up and went at it again.

CछƁ

After many failed attempts, he sat on the floor, body bruised, joints loose and aching, breathing hard. He'd thrown off his shoes and his shirt in hopes of gaining better traction on the surface of the disk; all it had done was leave his skin vulnerable to the scrape of concrete when he fell. The aerostat corkscrewed and crackled, unchanged by his efforts, unchangeable. His stomach growled.

Eyck brought water, a tin of canned tuna and a biscuit that might have been baked before the war. He hunkered down beside Michael on a wooden chair, knees popping. He massaged the joints. "Storm coming," he muttered.

Michael sopped fish oil with the biscuit. "You live like this? Alone?"

"Not here. A cottage, inland, on the marsh. Alone, yes."

Linda's cabin aboard the skyscraper ship would be rocking with the swells. Could she sleep? "Were you ever in love, Eyck?"

"Of course—but it's been a long time. People change. Everything changes. The trick is to change along with it—like the aerostat." As they watched, the aerostat momentarily swelled, forking intricately in a hundred directions at once. "In all the years I've known it, I've never once seen it go still. When I start to regret, I try to remember that."

"Is that what I have to look forward to?" Perpetual motion. Broken bones and loneliness interrupted only by the chaotic exuberance of an alien machine. He shoved the biscuit whole into his mouth. It stuck in his throat; he coughed and drank deeply.

Eyck thumped his back vigorously. "No, Michael. Your fate will be different, because you'll learn to use it: to fly it, and who knows what else. You will."

"What makes you so sure? You spent eight years."

"You're already closer than I ever got. I'll tell you the secret of it: the aerostat operates by interacting with electromagnetic fields. Every living thing generates such a field, but not many can manipulate it with such innate athleticism and ease as a truly gifted human being. That's how you will gain control—by making the machine's electrostatic power into an extension of your own."

"How can you know that if you've never flown it?"

"Haven't you noticed? It reacts to our presence, our movements—changes its rotation, casts fire in our direction. We're a part of the field that controls it. "

A lightning-flash—a real one, from the storm constricting over the Atlantic—poured livid light through the windows of the hangar, momentarily drowning the ethereal discharges of the machine. Michael washed down the last lump of biscuit and got up to try again.

CBEO

Over the next hours, it seemed easier, the falls less jarring, the aerostat's motion more familiar, more like his own. Finally, whether by the inspiration of the old man's words or dumb luck, he leapt, took hold, the disk's precession carried him with watchwork-smoothness to the aphelion of the sphere, and he dropped with uncanny ease into the void within.

Unseen forces caught him, cushioned him. The paraelectric discharges lessened briefly, then redoubled. All over his body, hairs stood out from the skin.

Eyck was shouting something, hopping with excitement, waving his arms as though signaling in semaphore, warning gestures Michael couldn't understand. He worried Eyck's heart might seize from joy—this was what the old man lived for.

It wasn't so different from the posture required astride a unicycle—save that now, instead of three planes, those on which he must find balance were infinite. In the pit of his stomach, his center of gravity held perfectly still, and he found he could freely shift his body, orienting himself as he chose, while the world, strobed with lightnings, whipped insanely about that stationary point. The trick, he realized, would be to extend the same control to the motion of the disk.

In the moments before the aerostat ripped like a claw through the sealed door of the hangar into the storm and darkness, it dawned on him that the elation of success, however fleeting, had granted an escape from grief.

☙❧

Weathered-steel heavens and spent-charcoal sea wheeled like the colors of a barber pole, streaked by the rain-starred lights of the city, of ships scattered across the river and the sound. Rain furred Michael's cheeks and chest, vaporized to mist by the paraelectric field. Wind—yes, there was wind too, on all sides at once. He was flying, somewhere between the earth and sky. The universe whirled in free-fall, a rudderless chaos; he alone was fixed within it.

He felt at home.

But that was an illusion. The bruises throbbed, the tender lump ached at the back of his skull where the brick or Linda's dismissal had struck. At any moment, the aerostat might plummet into the sea.

What had detachment gotten him? Freedom from risk, but also from ambition. A false sense of balance, while his whole life slid downhill. What he needed was to fall.

Michael struggled to reorient himself with the world.

He extended his senses beyond the void that cradled him, into the whirling gear of alien iron and the paraelectric storm. Vertigo slammed him. His stomach inverted itself into his throat. He fought to swallow back the bile.

A black spike whirled past him, pursued by its shadow. It came again, closer, a warning red gleam flaring from its peak. A lighthouse—a point of reference by which he might understand everything else. Tucking his knees instinctively, he spun backwards, counter to the disk's rotation, holding the red gleam in his sight. The spiral horizon began to straighten, the mottling of earth and sky to slow.

He hung a hundred feet over the sea, the city lights a blur behind him, the Atlantic and the storm ahead. Below, a spur of the lighthouse island reached into the surf. Lightning flashed, and the paraelectric fingers of the aerostat stretched to greet it, a child's fingers exploring an adult's offered hand.

He drifted, spine bent at an awkward angle, limbs askew, shifting wrists and ankles experimentally in an effort to comprehend the fine manipulation of the fields. He hadn't felt so clumsy in a long time. He started to laugh; if she could see him now ...

With that, his control slipped away, and vertigo rose to swallow him. Lightning fissured the sky. The aerostat shot seaward, crackling and barking back at the storm.

C8⬥80

He fought to a standstill in the middle of a downpour, paraelectric tentacles lighting up the rain. The city lights had disappeared; he forced down panic as he realized he didn't know which way was up.

There—he could make out the dull, reflected glare of the aerostat's discharge on the rain-burred waves, enough to orient himself. Too close. He tried to gain altitude, spinning sideways like a diver in midair. His muscles ached. The wind and the rain were frigid on bare skin. He wondered how long he could last before exhaustion sent him into the sea to drown.

An ocean liner blew its horn, deafening, forlorn, evoking the elemental lungs of La Bella Linda.

It might be her ship. How many liners could be out on the sea on a night like this? None but the biggest. He could fly. He could find it. It might lead him to land. But if he lost control too near a ship ... No. He didn't want to think of it. She didn't want a Unicyclist; he didn't deserve her.

He shook his head to thrust Linda away, and the rush of wind and the hole in his stomach told him he was hurtling forward once again. Closer to the sound of the foghorn or farther, in the dark he couldn't tell.

Then a gap opened in the sheets of rain. A ship's flank loomed out of it, scarred along the waterline with barnacles and the black rubber smears of tugboats. He couldn't react—the aerostat smashed into it headlong, ripping a hole through the iron of its hull with a head-splitting shriek.

He skittered to a stop among wreckage somewhere in its bowels. The light of the paraelectric flares played over black water gouting in through a jagged gap in the hull. Crates of cargo slid across the fast-tilting deck, propelled by the inrushing sea. He strained his ears for the sound of the engines, heard only a long, strangled cough, then the aerostat's ceaseless crackle and the hard rain on the hull. A freighter—not Linda's ship. He'd killed it, knocked out its power. It was sinking.

From the rip in the hull, the foghorn blast came again, deafening, dangerously close. The ocean liner.

If he caused a collision, the freighter's crew would certainly drown. And the other ship—Linda's or not—all those people were at risk.

He'd gotten in here without getting killed—could he get out? Would the aerostat protect him? It hadn't saved its previous pilot eleven years ago. But he had to do something. He shook himself, felt his body over, searching for a mortal wound, a broken leg, a scrap of torn iron impaling him. He was whole.

With a graceless jerk against the control field, he wrenched the aerostat out of the wreckage where it had lodged, aiming for the same hole by which he'd come in. A clang, a teeth-jarring jolt as the disk clipped the ruined ship's hull. He spun out of control, saw an instant's reflection of himself in the face of a wave — a pale revenant, ghost-lit by paraelectric light — then crashed through it.

He fought to a standstill, numb and spluttering. Bile mingled with rain and seawater running over his skin. Salt stung the cuts on his forearms. The ocean liner appeared dead ahead, aimed straight for the foundering freighter. Merry lights blurred from the portholes. There was music — a kit and a stand-up, plunking out a swing groove muffled by the rain. How many clubs had he snuck into on a rainy night in a borrowed jacket, the unicycle stashed in an alley under cans? It couldn't be her ship. It couldn't be.

The aerostat drifted higher, spinning up away from the sea above the great skyscraper ship. The decks were empty, chairs and sun shades lashed against the storm.

This was wrong. The last place he wanted to be. She'd think he had followed her here — that he couldn't let go, couldn't accept her dismissal, couldn't scrape together the remains of his own life. To say nothing of how she'd react at the sight of him trapped inside a ball lightning's heart. Even if it was true — even if the only future left open to him was Eyck's, alone and wounded, wild hope for the fate of an alien machine all that remained to comfort him — she didn't have to know.

The aerostat skewed crazily. He couldn't think like this — couldn't succumb. Not now.

He shoved away all other thoughts, focused on balance, the motions of the disk. He wrested the aerostat into the storm and darkness, set it on a widening orbit of the two ships. There was no other point of reference — no buoy, no feeble lighthouse beam, just the huge, ponderous liner and the darkened freighter, nearly-invisible, sinking fast—but not fast enough.

The few members of the freighter's crew burst from the wheelhouse, loosed a life-raft from its berth and wrestled it sliding wildly across the skewed deck. This was their livelihood. He'd taken it from them. A few of them paused to gape at the glowing thing hovering off their bow; Michael backed off quickly out of sight. They could do nothing to stop a collision—it would take all they had to save themselves.

He circled back to the liner, close this time, as close as he dared, keeping low to the waves to avoid being seen, tendrils of electrostatic lightning caressing the scarred hull and the waves. If he could knock out one of the screws, turn the liner off its course ... He didn't have that kind of control. He'd rend the hull apart as easily as touching it.

Music drifted from an open porthole—percussive bass and a voice like hot lead dipped in bourbon. His muscles turned to jelly. No other voice could strike such a wound. It was her. The aerostat fought against his control.

He concentrated on the fields surrounding him, the heavy iron of the liner like an electromagnetic sink dragging him back, the salts of the sea disruptive and chaotic below. Balance could betray him again at any moment, send him driving through the liner's hull.

Resisting, striving upward, he crossed above the liner's empty pleasure decks towards the bridge. The glow of the aerostat's discharge lit pale fear in the faces of the helmsman and officer. Carefully, compensating with his legs to prevent the aerostat spiraling out of control, he raised a hand and waved. Their eyes bulged from their heads, and the officer reached for the com. Michael rolled backwards, rocketing away from the liner, zigzagging wildly over the black waves until he found the freighter. He traced the spear shape of its keel tipping up from the dark water. He rushed back to the liner.

The helmsman heaved at the tiller; the officer gestured wildly as he shouted into the com. A siren screamed, signaling collision. Ponderously, the immense ship began to shift its course.

Out on deck, the ballroom doors burst open; passengers in eveningwear streamed into the rain, scattering to crowd the rail. A searchlight struck the freighter from the liner's conning tower, illuminating the tossed raft of its crew, the black tear left in its hull by the aerostat, the skewed stern. It was too close, coming on fast. It would drive into the liner's flank.

Michael spun about, dropping into the narrowing canyon between the two ships. He couldn't place his hand against the hull and push — the aerostat encased him like a womb, sealed him off from the world for all purposes except destruction. To accomplish anything at all, he'd have to strike a perfect balance, matching the aerostat's lateral speed, its rate of rotation and angle of approach against the wrecked freighter's vast inertia. With practice — months and months of practice, not a single night — he could master that kind of control.

He had no choice but to try it now.

He pulled back from the freighter until the liner towered behind him, blurred and glistening with light like a city block ready to topple. He breathed slow, steadying his fear, stifling the shakes brought on by the wind and the cold. He launched himself at the freighter's keel.

The aerostat struck at the riveted seam between two plates — the internal field shielded his body from impact, but the shriek of tearing metal was like a drill against his spine. The great, alien bicycle gear of the aerostat caught fast in the freighter's hull. The electrostatic tendrils stuttered and died, their ubiquitous light dimmed to nothing, and he found himself kneeling unsupported on the smooth inner surface of the disc, cold rain drumming on his shoulders, storm wind dragging at his chest. The warning siren of the ocean liner keened in the darkness.

The aerostat's power had seemed unquenchable, drawn from a source not of this earth. In eleven years, Eyck had never once seen the aerostat go still. It had taken Michael only a night to kill it. Like everything else he touched.

Maybe — if he could just start it spinning again?

Grinding his jaw to hold back panic and to keep his teeth from chattering, he slid shivering hands along the curve of the disc. He found a handhold around one of the teeth overhead and pulled himself up. Hanging there with all his weight, he swung forward, then back, trying to wrench the disc free.

The disc teetered backwards; his stomach surged into his chest. With a screech, the aerostat came free from the freighter's hull and fell in darkness towards the waves.

At least when he was dead, he thought fleetingly, he could give up trying to forget.

Then the paraelectric fields coughed sparks, spat fire, and crackled back to life.

Michael tucked himself into a cannonball and rolled heels over head. Hoarse, breathless laughter pushed its way out of his throat as the aerostat swept out of the dive and corkscrewed up into the rain.

The ocean liner's prow sailed past beneath him. A single swell broke between the liner's flank and the freighter's spearlike keel. They slid apart.

The aerostat's incomprehensible engine lit pale the faces of the crowd assembled on the liner's decks, their cheeks glistening with rain, their fine eveningwear clinging drenched to their skin. How must he seem to them? Deathly pale, covered in cuts and bruises, shivering, surrounded by otherworldly light. He scanned their faces for sympathy, pity.

La Bella Linda lingered in the shelter of the ballroom doors, hair plastered to her face, the plumed hat gone, the sopping hem of her green satin dress bunched at her ankles. Her mouth was open. Her tattered, beautiful voice reached him, raised in a disbelieving, grateful cry. She was cheering. And by her voice's insurmountable power, that overwhelming relief spread to the hearts of all who heard it.

In a moment, they all were cheering. Cheering him, Michael. The Unicyclist.

He worried what he could do when they stopped. He hadn't brought a hat to pass for coins.

What could he say to them, to Linda? Nothing that would change a thing.

He could follow her now if he wanted. He didn't need a ticket. He could fly.

Could a man inside a sphere of lightning sneak into a dance club in a borrowed jacket? If he could, would her fans even notice he was there?

He made a bow inside the aerostat's womb, compensating awkwardly for the shift in his magnetic field with a swanlike gesture of his arms. The crowd laughed—then gasped, as his legs spun up behind him against his intent and the aerostat dipped, sending forth feelers of power to prick their out-stretched hands. He overcompensated, sending the aerostat hurtling backwards into waves and darkness until he could see nothing else.

What was it Eyck had said? Everything changed, and the best that anyone could do was try to go with it.

He knew what he should do. Let Linda go on her way. Let her live. Let the aerostat take him where it would.

He was lost, somewhere in the midst of the Atlantic. He barely knew which way was up, let alone which way was home. If he didn't follow Linda, let the great ship lead him, if not home, then at least to the safety of some foreign shore, what could he do? Below, the black waves crashed, offering forgetfulness. Overhead, there was the rain, the clouds beyond.

How did ship captains find their way in the dark? They used the stars. This storm couldn't go on forever.

What did he have to lose?

He tucked into a roll and let the aerostat carry him to the heavens.

Iron And Brass, Blood And Bone

by Alma Alexander

Body

THERE ARE MOMENTS I LOOK BACK over the events that have brought me to this point, and I can look at them quite dispassionately, from a distance, analytically, as though they happened to somebody else entirely and not to me.

I remember clearly the sort of person I was. I was mild, and polite, and dedicated; I was near-sighted, with round wire-framed spectacles, and I always tried to hide my lanky height by walking a little hunched over, with my shoulders sloped inward and my hands wrapped anxiously around each other before me. I worked long hours in the back room of the lawyer's office, dealing with contracts and inheritances and judgments, keeping the accounts. The lawyer, my employer, had a lavish office out front, all decked out in leather and dark wood; he would receive clients there and take on cases, and then he would turn the details over to me to write up. I was the only other employee there, other than the woman who came in mornings to clean the offices and make the first pot of tea (anything of that kind, later in the day, that was my responsibility too). I was paid barely enough to make the rent and to keep from starving, but I was mild and polite and dedicated, I didn't deserve more, I never asked.

The lawyer didn't know about my monster, the creature I came home to and dedicated long hours of painstaking work to. The lawyer never knew that I was capable of independent thought or original invention, that I could ever conceive of, let alone build, the mechanical man which I put together over weeks and months during long nights lit by lamp and by candle, poring over every wire, every connection, every tiny detail.

The reason? Because I wanted to. Because I could. Because I believed–with all the passion that I was capable of mustering–that I would be the one who would find the mystery of what makes a thing alive — that I would be the one who would provide that divine spark that animated my mechanical man, and make him live. I had never thought beyond that moment, not really — I was just dedicated to the idea of that one instant when I would see my creature look at me, and see me, and recognize me as the nearest thing it could have conceived of as his God.

He was a thing of beauty, my mechanical man. I never really gave him a proper name, but I thought of him as Ludo — why that, more than anything else, I do not know. But his body was iron, and his legs were iron, and his arms were iron, but his hands and his feet and his head were golden brass. I gave him two glass eyes. I even contemplated providing him with a head of hair, with a wig I could have purchased a few shops down the street from where I worked and which I passed every day, but I finally dismissed that idea — he was perfect enough as he was, Ludo, with his shining brass pate and his blank eyes.

He was almost done, almost, when I ran out of materials late one night — twelve more rivets I needed. Just twelve. And he would be complete. But I was all out, and it was late, and at any rate I would not get paid for another week—and in that time he would have to sit there unfinished, Ludo, just a pile of scrap metal until I could complete him and start the real work, that of giving him life and motion.

It was well past midnight that I rose, frustrated, and put on my hat and coat, and stalked out into the foggy gas-lighted streets, walking aimlessly, blundering along the cobbled alleys without a destination in mind, too hyped and upset to sleep.

I must have taken a turn somewhere into an unfamiliar part of town because I found myself hesitating before a shop—lighted, and, it looked like, open, even at this hour. There was something coming out of a vent on the side of the house that the shop occupied the front of--smoke, or steam, something white that mingled with the fog—it smelled vaguely of hot metal, and something else, something chemical, sulphuric perhaps, certainly acrid enough to make me catch my breath and cough. But more than that, the windows of the shop made me stop and stare.

It was a machine works.

They had, perhaps, the rivets I needed—the last twelve.

They were closed—they had to be closed—it was well past midnight—but it was like a miracle laid out before me. I needed something and God had provided; there it was, the very thing, right in front of me, right then .

I pushed open the door, and a bell jangled somewhere in the back. Very soon a balding man with a pencil moustache and a pair of thin, elegant eyebrows pushed aside a curtain hanging over an alcove and stepped into the shop.

"Good evening," he said.

"Rivets," I said, after a beat of silence.

"Indeed." He pulled open a drawer behind the shop counter and pulled out a box, putting it softly on top of the counter and pushing it toward me with one long, white, bony finger. "Will these do, sir?"

I looked. Inside the box, there were twelve rivets.

Exactly the kind I needed. Exactly the number I needed.

"How much?" I managed, through a mouth that had gone suddenly, inexplicably dry. I was afraid—I did not know why I was afraid—I was exhilarated, and suddenly flooded with ecstasy, with a heady excitement.

"Thirty silver pennies," he said.

I gave him a sharp look; he gazed back at me out of a pair of limpid, pale blue eyes, one of those eyebrows arching over like a delicate dark caterpillar.

"Too much," I said at last, after a long pause. Which had told him far more than I, perhaps, had intended.

But he responded instantly, without hesitation.

"I'll take a down payment," he said, "or in kind …"

"In kind? Rivets?"

"Let us just say that I am perfectly willing to let you take these with you through that door, right now. And I will defer the payment."

"How do you know that I won't just take them and never return?" I muttered.

He smiled, and some part of me shivered in terror at that smile.

"Oh, I will be paid," he said.

I thought of Ludo, sitting propped up in the corner of my bedroom, slumped over, his brass hands between his iron knees, his head lolling without support for lack of these very rivets.

I thought hard.

"I'll take them," I heard myself say.

And I took them. And walked away. I don't remember looking back, but somehow I knew that the lights had gone out the moment I had stepped outside that small, strange shop—that it had never really existed, except for the small box of rivets in my pocket. The world was empty and sleeping--all except for

me, and for my Ludo, who would wake once I hurried home
with the last small thing I needed to finish him …

SOUL

*He remembers that night — but he remembers it as if it was
a story that was once told to him. He remembers it as though
he watched it happen, floating above the streets like a crow,
watching the hunched man with the box of twelve rivets in
his pocket hurry home through the dank fog in the early hours
of that morning.*

*I remember the rest of it, when he returned home, and took
the rivets out of that pocket, and began to work.*

I remember, because that was the beginning of me.

*It is not given to many to remember the moment of their own
birth, but I do. It was slow; it came by painful degrees; it came
rivet by rivet, a little bit at a time, and I could feel it slipping
into me, dripping into me, oozing down the wires and pooling
in the glass eyes out of which I could suddenly see. With every
rivet, a bit of him, into me. With every rivet, a little piece of
his soul. Until, at last, it was all done, and all twelve of those
accursed things in place and tightened, and I was all soul, and
he was none at all — and the sky was lightening in the east
already. He would need to be at work soon, very soon.*

*He should have been too tired. He should have fallen onto
the bed in an exhausted heap, fully dressed, and slept the sleep
of the dead. But he was not. He stood gazing at me where I
sat at his workbench, giving me a dispassionate and apprising
look as though I was a piece of merchandise that he was con-
templating buying and weighing the money bag in his hand as
he appeared to find me, on some level, wanting. But he had no
real time for anything more, not right then. The work was done
here. The final rivets were in place. I was finished — I, Ludo,*

was finished. At least the form of me was. The rest would have to wait on his other obligations and responsibilities.

He left me there in the cold, pale morning light. Alone.

He didn't know that I could think and feel. Not then. Not yet. But already he would not have cared.

The hours crawled by—and at first I sat as he had left me, without moving, because that was what he appeared to expect me to do. But he had no reason to think of me as anything other than a doll, a mechanical thing without life—and I was no longer that. Not with all of his soul animating my iron-and-brass body. When I moved, the first time, it was in every bit as mechanical and graceless a manner as he might have expected—but even though he had made my brass feet a little too small I found a way to stand, and then to balance myself upright, and then to take a step. It had not occurred to him to dress me—I was just a metal man—but something had passed into me with the soul he had transferred there with those rivets he had found in the night, and I felt the need. His clothes fit me badly, too tight in some places, too loose in others, too short in sleeve and leg, leaving long naked vistas of iron wrist and iron ankle—but I was dressed, eventually, in a pair of his older and shabbier breeches, and a frayed shirt with a hole at the elbow which he had been thinking about discarding; these things I did not think he would miss, but I also took a waistcoat, although it did not fit me well, which he would probably want to take back when he returned. But it felt proper, to be dressed in an acceptable manner, even though I had no watch fob to tuck into the waistcoat pocket as would have been correct. But I didn't need to tell the time, after all.

I was empty, except for feeling and instinct. I looked out of the window and the streets were strange to me, unfamiliar—I carried his soul, not his memories. The tiny set of rooms he rented—bedroom, small parlor he had turned into the workshop where he had built me, a nook of a kitchen which contained *very little by way of sustenance — I explored it all as though it was new to me, which it was. I had been born here, but there was nothing here that I, myself, knew — I took in the details, the faded wallpaper, the brazier in the bricked-in fireplace, the narrow single bed in the bedroom which had not been slept in that night and was still neatly made, the scattered tools on a small bench in the corner ... the empty rivet box.*

I understood it first, the bargain that he had made. I was the receptacle of a soul that was sold, already no longer the property of my creator. Those last twelve rivets — the ones that he had so desperately needed for me to live — had cost him his own salvation.

He knew nothing of it yet. But he would. He would. And I was afraid of what he would do when he found out.

Oddly, I was never afraid of what he could do to me. Perhaps I already understood more than I knew--and I knew far more than he did ...

BODY

Work was strangely different that morning, the morning after I had finished Ludo and left him sitting there in the shop. I arrived early as I always did, despite the sleepless night, there long before the lawyer got to the office, making sure everything was in order for his first client. Then I went back to my room and started on my own work, which was never done--the moment I made any headway, a new pile would be deposited on my desk for me to deal with. Usually, that was just ... the way things were. But that day, it was different.

I worked mechanically, at first. I had been doing this job for twelve years, would be thirteen years come that February; I could do it with my eyes closed. I didn't have to think, so I didn't think, and the paperwork was dealt with methodically, tidily, efficiently, as always.

But then ... then I heard the cleaning lady leave, and then the lawyer left for a court date.

And I got up ... and left my desk ... and went into the lawyer's office.

I had never done this before. This office was not for the likes of me; I had only been in there to deliver some important paper, or to receive a swift, last-minute instruction if required—always with the lawyer present, often sitting there behind his desk with his horsehair wig still on, smelling of cologne and old leather and dry justice. But now ... I was in there alone, and it was as though I was seeing it for the first time. The high, arched windows, the plush curtains, the shelves lined with thick, dusty books, the large desk inlaid with red leather which was almost hidden beneath an untidy pile of papers and files. I actually went over, pushed some of the files out of the way, brushed my fingers against the leather. It felt good.

Outside, the streets were gray under cloudy skies. People looked cold, hunched against the wind, hands tucked into the sleeves of their coats and their collars up around their ears. Carriages drawn by black horses, with liveried coachmen up on the high seat, passed busily by underneath my gaze; I could hear the faint sounds of hooves on cobbles through the closed windows.

It looked as though it might snow.

There was no color outside, other than black and white and gray. Nothing at all. The world had turned monochrome.

The red leather on the desk. That was the only color in the world.

I stood at the window, staring at the desk. I could not take my eyes off that red leather. Red leather. Red leather. It had ... some strange subliminal meaning. Red. Leather. Red.

There was red, later, too. When I found myself looking down at the lawyer's body, at my feet. Red pooling around him, from the gash in his neck … dripping from the knife I held between the thumb and forefinger of my right hand.

I held it as though I did not know how it had got there, finding myself gazing upon it — at first, at least — with a measure of astonishment. I wondered why I had killed him, and could not remember.

It did not matter. Not one little bit. I wiped the knife on the curtains, tucked it away into the lawyer's own leather satchel, and walked out of there without looking back. It was as though I was walking out of an illustration, a two-dimensional thing, an etching from some book, not my reality for the last dozen years. The lawyer's office was already forgotten, gone, behind me, over. I knew I would not go back there again. The satchel, besides the knife, contained what money there had been in the lawyer's safe — I knew the combination, of course. They would find him, and the empty safe, and they would find me gone, and they would begin to hunt for me — but I could not find it in me to care.

I came home … to Ludo, standing in the middle of the parlor.

I didn't think I had given it a voice, or even intended to attempt to do so — but somehow, it had one. A flat, metallic one, befitting the flat, metallic mouth out of which it came — but a voice, nonetheless.

"What," Ludo asked inflectionlessly, "have you done?"

I shrugged. "Everybody dies," I said, "eventually."

"You have killed."

"Yes," I agreed. Without any guilt, or shame. It was a simple fact, it was the truth. And inside of me, there was a vast and glassy emptiness, nothing at all for any emotion to cling to or survive.

My insides … were *his* insides, the empty tin man I had made. And yet …

SOUL

… and yet, he contained me. And I contained him. He was the man, the human, the blood and the flesh and the bone and the sinew, with the muscles in his face which he could move to make himself smile or frown, with eyes that could weep, with a voice that could scream. I was the brass and the iron, doomed never to express an emotion — I could not move the metal skin on my face, or clench my hands into fists, or howl with rage or with pain.

He could do all these things — and would never do any of them again.

I could never do any of these things, but carried every painful urge to try, and was doomed to fail forever more, for as long as I existed.

He looked at me and if it was still possible for him to feel any emotion at all, he hated me. I looked at him and I adored him, and I pitied him, and I loved him. He was my creator, my God; he was me. I was him.

"I could destroy you," he said at last, after a long silence.

"No," I said. "You cannot."

And he knew it for truth.

"What if I die?" he asked.

"You cannot," I said. "Not while I live."

"And you will live … forever?"

"I do not know. But some day this body that you have given me will fail. Some day, the bill for those rivets will come due."

We were tied together now, he and I.

He could not die — because there was no longer a place for him in either Heaven or Hell — because I carried his soul, and I would not be admitted into either of those places. I, who had never lived. I, who would carry all his guilt and all his pain, from here on, into eternity.

"What do you plan to do," I asked, my voice still flat, without

the inflection of inquiry, but he understood it as a question.

"Well, I no longer have a job," he said. "I guess, if I need money to live, I will have to get it some other way."

"You will kill again."

He smiled, a little, but his eyes were cold, cold, cold—colder than my glass ones.

"I will kill," he said equably. "And why not? Who among us deserves to live so much that another must give way? I have needs—and I will meet them however I am able. And the beauty of it is ..."

He stared at me, and I knew that he knew, and that I was lost.

The beauty of it ... for him ... was that he would feel nothing, when he killed. Nothing at all. I would feel it, all of it, everything, every ounce of anguish and fear and pain and moral recoil. His hand would wield the knife and the soul which he no longer carried would pay the price for it.

"I will be your conscience," I said.

His smile was a thing of terror. "I have none," he said.

And so it began. The shadows gathered around him, and swallowed him. He remained ageless, stuck forevermore at the hour in which he had poured his soul into me. Within a few years they had stopped looking at him when they sought the man he had once been—because logic and common sense told those who hunted him that the killer they were looking for must have aged as the years passed and now looked different. They no longer hunted the younger man whose features he continued to wear, whom he remained.

He lived well enough—he dabbled in things occasionally, sometimes picking up a transient occupation when it amused him to do so. For a while he even worked as a lawyer, out of the offices where he had once clerked—and he had learned enough law that none suspected a thing, until he grew tired of it all and simply walked away. He became a merchant, a doctor—even, for a little while when it became necessary to remove to the country when the heat got too close to him after a killing spree, in a grim mockery of all that was holy, a soul-less priest in a rural parish where the poor came to him for succor and advice. He found that he excelled at sermons and speeches. He became a politician, several times, in several different incarnations, and he was good at it. But sooner or later he would kill again because he could, and the stain of it slipped off him like water off oiled brass, and came to me.

I have no memory of the details of his crimes. He carries the memories, not me. I sleep, in a way that I sleep, and on the mornings after the nights that he has killed I wake to a day of agony and recrimination—because the guilt comes home, to me. He kills, he spills blood, and he walks away from it all—he can tell you the names and the places, all of it, he remembers it all in detail, but he does not care about it. That is my burden. My anguish. The tin man with the glass-goggle eyes who follows him when he moves lodgings—sometimes he tries to give me the slip but I always know where he is, how could I not, and if he moves and leaves me behind I simply wrap myself in a cloak and trudge after him, slowly, on my too-small brass feet on the dark roads that lie between places, and I always find him. He never drives me away—when I turn up and take my place in his new home he simply carries right on doing whatever he was doing, as though it was the most ordinary thing in the world that I should be there. I had always been there. I always would be.

BODY

I sometimes wonder what would happen if my brass-and-iron shadow followed me into a shop that wasn't there, that shop I never found again to pay my dues for the twelve rivets

I had got there on a foggy midnight in the city, so long ago now. What would happen if he came into that room and I was there, and that devil also, the one who had sold me those rivets—I was still not sure about the ultimate price, but I did not really care, not any more–and if he stood there, my metal man, Ludo, with my soul behind those goggle eyes that I had given him. What would the devil take? Him? Me?

He has done nothing—nothing, except carry the guilt.

It is my hands that drip and reek.

And I don't care. And he does.

I wonder what would happen. Would he offer himself? To the Devil? To God?

Does he belong to either of them?

Do I? …

SOUL

I wondered if it had an end. If some day something would happen to me, and the soul was free. Would that be the day he paid that final bill, would I — his soul— watch his physical body crumble into the dust that it should have been long ago, and then be taken, after all? The devil can wait. He has an eternity.

So do we, him and I, as things stand. Unless things change for one of us. Unless one of us makes things change.

I questioned my own beliefs — which were partly his, and partly forged out of my own metal. Was I — Ludo — the metal man — insane to even ponder the idea of salvation? It could not possibly affect me. I could not go to Heaven or Hell, after all.

But "I" was that soul I carried within me. And it was black with sin.

He would probably never again set foot inside a church, ask for forgiveness — because he no longer knew how to ask, because he no longer needed it. And I, who knew, who did, well . . .

. . . Forgive me, Father, for I have sinned . . .

I said those words. I meant them. If I had had the tears, I would have wept over them. If I had had a real heart it would have broken in two. But although I now carry all the emotion that it was ever given to my human creator, I lacked the basic means to express any at all. There were no tears. There was no inflexion to my voice when I spoke, hidden behind the curtains in my half of the old wooden confessional — nothing that would indicate true penitence. I said those words flatly, because I had no choice to do otherwise. But I, who felt every agony and every anguish now, could not show it — and he, who suffered none of it at all any more, would never again do so himself. Broken, both of us. Damaged. Wounded.

Sold.

Alive, but dead.

Dead, but existing.

The priest in the other half of the confessional heard the voice that asked for forgiveness. The flat and metallic voice. The voice that was so wrong. He had leapt from his seat, flung back the red plush curtain, saw me sitting there--machine, iron and brass and glass. He saw none of what was inside of me because I had no means to share it other than in plain words and those words he would never believe from me. He shouted, and screamed, and clung to his crucifix, and damned me (as though I could be damned) to everlasting Hell for heresy and for daring to profane the holy sacrament which was, as he said repeatedly, ". . . only for true men who hold a soul that God Himself gave them!"

And then, with surprising strength and determination, he was done with words, done with anathemas; he had said what needed to be said. It was time to do, now — he reached in with both hands, hauled me out of the confessional, pushed me *staggering down the aisle, all the way out to the front door, all the way out, down the steps that led out from the main portico, into a pile onto the path below.*

I felt struts snap, something shatter.

I did not care. It did not hurt. That which was inside of me did, and that I could not heal, ever again.

Ever again.

Only for men who possessed God's gift of a soul . . .

Little did he know but that it was that very soul which I took into the church and tried to cleanse. But the priest that drove me away did not know, could not know, could not possibly have understood. All he had to give in response to my presence was fear, and fury, and holy righteousness.

And yet . . . what he felt . . . what he did . . . it was the right thing to do.

He broke me that night. For all that I was made out of iron and brass I was a fragile enough construct; when he threw me down those stairs, he smashed things--essential things — and I knew that Ludo was done. The monster was done, the metal body was twisted and snapped, there were wires and connectors that were split, there were bolts that were sheared. I would not get up again, I would not follow the man whose soul I carried within me again.

They would find me here, where the priest had thrown me down.

The priest would tell them what had happened, what he had done, where to look. They will call me an abomination or a saint, but they will destroy me, they will destroy this body of iron and brass that had been a secret for so long.

I was right when I had believed that we would have immortality, he and I, the body and the soul and the metal man who carried it — so long as we existed, together. But perhaps salvation lay in the simple fact that it could not endure forever.

Immortality seems to have lasted a little shorter than its usual promised span. This I knew — I knew, as I lay there, dying.

They would free this tortured soul — and perhaps, if it … if I … could cling to holy ground, to these hallowed stones, when they send the earthly remains of me to the scrap heap … perhaps it will be well. Iron and brass, expiating the soul of flesh and blood and sinew and bone.

I wonder if I will see him again. If I will ever again look into my own eyes.

⚬⚬⚬

There were two headlines in the newspapers that week.

One was the strange case of the metal monster who had tried to confess his sins to a parish priest.

The other was the body of a very, very old man which was found in a back street of the city. His hair was down to a few white wisps on his head, his face deeply furrowed, and his expression seemed to indicate that he had perhaps died of a stroke — because one half of his face was smiling, and the other had the corner of the mouth turned down. There were even traces of tears on the cheek of that other, anguished, side. As though … as though half of him had wept.

There was nothing to connect the two things.

Nothing, except that the metal man was oddly … unfinished.

And the old man in the street had a box of twelve twisted rivets in the pocket of his coat.

The Trouble
with Bombs

by Jay Caselberg

THE DIN WAS TREMENDOUS and I had to lean in to hear what Herr Krupp was telling me. All around us, the clanging and bangs, hammering, the sound of hollow pipes hitting the ground, the smell of oiled metal in the air, echoed through the vast factory space. The workers leaned over their pieces, barely able to shout to each other above the cacophony.

"You are telling me, Herr Krupp, that you have over 20,000 workers here?"

"Yes, Herr Major Bitfeld, it is as you say." His eyes gleamed behind his small round glasses, full of the pride of his family's and his own achievement. Of course, it had been his father that had first established their operation, but since then, it had grown and grown. I looked down from the platform where we stood together, scanning the vast array of half-assembled and nearly completed weapons, artillery, all of it, at least in this particular section. I knew in other areas of the Krupp establishment the fabrication extended to other metals and products, but here, it was the big guns for which they were so famous. Of course, Essen had always been a center of industry, but its glory today had much to do with this man and his father before him. Weapons had been forged here for more than two hundred years, but it was only in this century that the city had grown to true industrial greatness.

"Herr Krupp," I said, leaning in to him. "Perhaps there is somewhere a little quieter, where we can discuss the particular problem we come to you with."

The man's curled moustache spread with his smile and then he laughed out loud. "Herr Major, there is nowhere quiet. Everywhere is the sounds of our production. It is as music to me, sir." He smoothed the ends of his moustache, making sure of its curl. "Come, come. Follow me. You have seen enough of the works, I think."

I smoothed down the front of my dark blue coat and followed along, considering, and I was not sure that Krupp was the man to satisfy the challenge that the Generalmajor had set me. Prince Friedrich Karl had decided to take Metz, a decision that I could only applaud. It was a fine strategic location, fortified, strong, and the French under Bazaine had made it their own. But, the Prince, unfortunately, had special requirements, and he wanted it done quickly. Had I not, in fact, seen Metz for myself, I might not understand, but I had seen that gem in the landscape and it was easy to understand his sentiments. Who was I, a mere Major, to question the wants of the Prince and his advisors or that of my superior?

"We will take Metz," the Generalmajor had informed me. "But we will do so, without damage."

Did he not know that this was a war?

CRSO

Krupp was accommodating, but I feared, only within the bounds of his own imagination. His specialty was artillery, and we had been experiencing great strides in the campaigns as a result of the superior nature of their devices.

"And, I am sure, Herr Major, we can come up with something to suit your needs. Why, look at the success we have already had with the French balloons. It is our newer guns which have cut their lines of communication, no?"

That much was true. The French had been using balloons as couriers, and the Krupp artillery had taken them down on more than one occasion to give us advantage.

He leaned forward in his chair, spreading his hands. "You see?"

"I do see, Herr Krupp," I told him. "But the nature of this problem is slightly different. We do not want to blow things up. We do not want to punch holes in the side of that glorious cathedral. Just think of the cost. What about the Saint-Pierre-aux-Nonnaians Basilica? Why, it is the oldest church in France, one of the oldest in Europe. It was once a Roman spa. The Saint-Arnulf Abbey. Itis the necropolis of Charlemagne himself! You nsee? Thr traditions, the history, all of this is dear to the Prince's heart. The city is not the problem. It is the French who occupy it."

Krupp sank back into his chair, nodding slowly, his lips pursed in thought. "Yes," he said finally. "It as an interesting challenge."

The silence between us stretched, broken only by the ever-present clashes and clangs of the production works surrounding us.

"Let me take this challenge, Herr Major," he said at last. "I have the best craftsmen, the finest mechanical minds in Europe. Our products are of the highest quality. Surely, if I cannot solve your problem, then no one can!"

He stood, his hands thrust into his pockets, rocking back and forth on his heels. "Yes, yes, we will solve this."

As I also stood, he placed a hand upon my back and steered me to the door. "We will send word," he said. "A few days, no more."

I stepped out of his offices and into the fields of frantic activity and noise, workers rushing and pushing carts and carriages between buildings, banging and crashing all about, not at all sure that in those few days my quest would be fulfilled. The smell of the works, the smokestacks, lent a hard taste to the atmosphere, a pall within the air, not unlike a battlefield itself. I returned, somewhat downhearted to my billet to await Herr Krupp's response.

☙

Though I had suspected it might be more, it was a mere four days before a messenger arrived with a summons to the Krupp-Werke. I was to meet with Herr Friedrich Krupp at his offices as soon as possible. Without further ado, I donned my coat and headed out for the works.

When I arrived, Herr Krupp seemed immensely pleased with himself and he beamed at me, smoothing the ends of his handsome moustache with a flourish as he welcomed me.

"Herr Major, I believe we have some good news for you," he said. "Come with me, if you would. We must go to a particular workshop."

As he led me through the grounds, seemingly oblivious to the cacophony all around us, there was a spring in his step. A small building projected from the end of a larger construction, as if it had been thrown there as an afterthought, its windows dusty, I presumed from the works itself, but making it impossible to hazard what might lie inside. Krupp opened the door and stood back to let me enter, following behind and quickly closing the door behind himself.

It took a few moments for my mind to make sense of the jumble that lay cluttered before me in piles and on benches, stacked in corners and on shelves, all made harder to distinguish by the smoky light filtering through the dust covered panes. Despite the confusion, regardless of the dust all around us outside this obvious workshop, the place seemed spotless. There were coils of gleaming wire, springs, pipes, and countless bits and pieces that I could barely guess their function or purpose.

I was still trying to absorb it all and make sense of it when Krupp spoke from behind me.

"Herr Major, allow me to introduce Herr Ewertz, our little magician here at the Krupp-Werke."

For a moment, I was further confused. Herr Krupp seemed to be introducing me to an empty, if cluttered room. Then, from behind a stacked and jumbled shelf there was a brief cough, a clearing of the throat and a little man emerged, sporting a long brown coat, pockets stuffed with bits and pieces, his hair thinning atop his small round head and a pair of thick round lenses affixed to his face. These were no normal spectacles, because they were some sort of contrivance, brass, multiple different layers of different sizes affixed to the corners. His eyes appeared magnified by the array of glass, peering at me and blinking, seeming to take up much of his face. Then, as if suddenly realizing, he flipped back a group of the lenses from each eye, diminishing the apparent largeness, leaving him with a single layer in front of his gaze. The lenses that he had pushed out of the way stuck out above each side of his face, looking like some strangely fashioned brass and crystal insect antennae. He blinked at me again, and then rubbed his hands before him.

"Ewertz, this is Herr Major Bitfeld, the source of our little commission. I am sure he will be highly interested in what you have come up with."

Ewertz dipped his head and stepped back, motioning for me to approach the bench and shelves which had previously concealed him. I stepped forward, rounding the edge to confront a lengthy bench space, covered with scraps of drawings, tools and various objects, metal, wood, other substances that I could not divine. One thing was certain; it did not seem that there was anything that constituted a solution to my problem.

Krupp stepped over to join us, an enigmatic half smile upon his lips, his eyes glinting.

"I do not …" I started, looking back at him, confused, but he held up a hand to still me.

"Herr Ewertz?"

The little man cleared his throat. "It has taken some work and some thought. Oh yes. But I believe we may have what you need." When he spoke, his voice was high and reedy, just as I might have expected from one with such a diminutive frame. He waved his hand at a spherical metal object in the center of what appeared to be a scattering of cogs and wheels such as one might find in the inner workings of a clock. When I leaned over to peer more closely, the fist-sized globe was seamed with tiny lines etched across its surface. Was this some sort of new, tiny, explosive device?

"Forgive me, Herr Ewertz, but I still do not see …"

The little man stepped forward, flipped down his lenses, then tapped twice on the top of the sphere. In the next moment, a strange whirring issued from the object. One by one, the seams broke apart, extended, stretched out from the body, for that was what it had become. Another small section extended from the front, and then the main body started to … separate … no, it was lengthening, becoming thinner at the center. I stepped back, aghast. This was no new little bomb. Sitting in the middle of the bench, rocking slightly and continuing to whirr, was nothing less than a metal spider—a large metal spider. I could not suppress an involuntary shiver. The creatures naturally invoke a feeling of dread. I made to take a step forward to get a closer look, but Ewertz thrust out an arm to stop me.

"Do not get too close, Herr Major. Not while it is active. You see it seeks out the warmth of a human body. Although it is not yet primed, it could still damage you." He tapped the gently whirring spider at a particular spot on its body, and the beast subsided to the bench. Ewertz lifted it and turned it upside down, drew it closer to me so I could inspect it in greater detail. Below, the mechanical arachnid was a marvel of engineering detail. Small joints, tiny holes, and in front, instead of multiple eyes, there were just two, with some small jewel like thing affixed above. Twin silver fangs extended from the front of the head, and I could see the tiny hollows running up their center.

"Yes, yes," said Ewertz, following my gaze. "That is where the venom is delivered. Ingenious, no? And that, in the middle of the body, that is where you wind them up."

"What do you mean, wind them up?"

"Well, they are driven by clockwork mechanisms, by a series of springs inside the body. They will function till the power winds down, just like a clock. The poison reservoir is contained within the head. It will deliver a lethal dose as required. It acts within mere minutes."

I quickly took a step back.

"No, no," said Ewertz. "This one has not yet been filled. There is no need to worry." He grinned, showing big teeth.

I decided I had already cultivated somewhat of a dislike for this little man, brilliant though he might be.

"All right, Herr Ewertz, I understand the principle. So, we infect the city of Metz with these things and they will assassinate anyone whose range they come into, is that what you are telling me? They need to be primed and wound and simply delivered, and they will do the required work. Anyone who comes into contact with them will die a rapid death."

"Exactly so!"

"And how do they find the population, those indoors for example?"

He grinned again. "Just like a normal spider, they climb walls, they creep through windows, they clamber down chimneys, always seeking the body heat they so desire."

I considered. "But how long?"

"Once they are fully wound and primed, they will operate for more than an hour; each one, scuttling hither and thither, till their reservoirs are depleted or they simply wind down." He moved the beast in his hand around before him in demonstration and I could not but wrinkle my lips with distaste and lean back from the little man's display. He saw my expression and replaced the bronzed beast back on the bench, tapped the carapace precisely in a particular spot and one by one, the legs retracted, the head and fangs drew back into the body, the whole widened, became rounder until such time as the faintly edged bronze sphere sat inert in its place.

I was thinking hard by now. Certainly the contraption would serve as a solution to part of the problem, but I was not yet convinced.

"Herr Krupp, Herr Ewertz, I understand the utility of the device, but I have one doubt. What precisely is the intended means of delivery? We cannot simply walk into the French barracks and deposit the devices. Regardless of the threat of capture, any man transporting them would be a potential subject of their attentions, no? Certainly, we expect casualties; this is war, but there are limits even there."

There was a lengthy pause and Ewertz avoided my eyes. Finally he sighed and stood up from the bench. One by one, he flipped back the lenses covering his eyes.

"There, you have hit upon the sole thing that has been standing in the way of finalizing our solution." He rubbed the back of his neck. "At first, you know, I was playing with the idea of a web spinning mechanism, but the size of the reservoir at the rear could not be large enough to accommodate the needed solution. A device cannot secrete material in the same way as a living beast can. Then we considered, perhaps, a longer, or even a short range delivery shell — something that could be fired into the city, not with an explosive charge, but something that would release a load of the devices upon impact or not."

"Herr Ewertz," I said. "That defeats my purpose entirely. Were we to hurl missiles into the city, the required number would surely cause great damage to buildings and structure, whether packed with explosives or not. No, that will not do. That will not do at all! You are wasting my time."

Krupp held up a placating hand. "No Herr Major, we have just not yet solved the problem. Herr Ewertz, please continue."

The little man nodded. "So, we considered our latest artilleries. The French balloons. We have the height and the range. If we could release them far enough above the city, they could fly, suspended by a sail, or a small balloon … drift down into the city …" He was demonstrating with his hands again.

Even I could see the failure of his reasoning. "The weather, the prevailing wind, the sheer numbers, the accuracy, all of these would stand in the way of a successful outcome." His words though, had triggered something in my thoughts. I turned away from him, thinking, as the thought took shape. The French balloons. I turned back to face them both.

"Perhaps …"

"Yes?" Ewertz could clearly see my brain working. "Yes, what is it?"

"We need a delivery mechanism. We need to be able to guarantee maximum effect in about three specific areas in the city. Being able to direct where the devices are dropped." I paused for a moment, still thinking through. Both their faces reflected eagerness, but I was not done yet. I ignored their expressions, letting them wait. "We could use something like the French courier balloons, but something more directed. If we were to hover low enough over the city, surely we would draw fire. There would have to be protection. Somewhere between …" I paused again, testing the concept. "Somewhere between the delivery shells you were talking about, Herr Ewertz, and the French balloons. A combination of both. But it would have to be armored. It would need to take fire from guns below. They would surely try to shoot us down, just in the same way that we have continued to take down their messengers." There, I had said it—"us." I knew then that I would be in the vanguard of what we were about to do, what I was planning for the Krupp-Werke and a select number of our troops. It seemed that I was in the right place, after all. If I needed armor, then Krupp was the place to provide it.

"Do you think, Herr Krupp that your factory can provide what we need? We need something light, so it can be suspended from a large enough balloon. It needs to be shielded, but light, but still able to resist fire. We need to be able to maneuver. What we need is a ship, but a ship of the air. And in its hold we can store the devices, ready, primed, that we can drop when close enough at several different points throughout the city, so, at least three individual compartments that can be sprung open below the vessel at separate times, large enough to contain a quantity of these devices."

Krupp was clearly seeing my vision, because his eyes were gleaming. "Yes, yes!" he said. "Ewertz?"

The little man was nodding enthusiastically and rubbing his long, thin hands together. "Yes, yes, Herr Krupp. We will have to make some refinements though." He reached out to gently stroke the side of his little brass beast. "Just one or two. But I can see it already. Yes. Yes."

"Then, Herr Krupp," I said. "I will leave you once more and await your messenger once again."

Though I was not entirely confident, I thought that now, there was some chance for the mission I was tasked with. Perhaps …

I was beginning to despair entirely when another entire week passed and I had received no word. Time was running out and I knew that if I did not come up with a solution, then we would be forced to revert to the old standard tactics of laying siege and waiting for the enemy to break. The Generalmajor would not be pleased, and it would reflect badly on my record, I was sure. Finally, however, my wait was rewarded.

C8&0

Krupp lent some of his men for the transport from Essen to the boundaries of the French territory close enough to Metz to serve our purposes. The best way to test the vessels, of course, was to fly them, and so we did. First, a few brief voyages around the Krupp-Werke themselves and then, further afield. The ships, I had to admit, performed magnificently. Despite the metal cladding, it was fair to say, the paired vessels, simply soared. The vast dark gray balloons, long, unlike those contrivances used by the French, billowed above the ship body, simulating storm clouds, changing shape with the varying winds. It was then that I decided I would name the "Donner" and "Blitzen," names to instill fear and terror. Herr Krupp and I christened them together. I had to admit, my trepidation had been stilled. Ewertz and Krupp had more than exceeded my demands. The long hull, clad with the lightest metal, had been treated in such a way that the body was a dull blue-gray and would merge quite well into the billowing cloud shape above. At a distance, it would be hard for an observer to identify the vessels for what they were, to mark them as anything other than a rapidly moving pair of storm clouds. And storm clouds they would be for the French garrison at Metz! The lightning they would deliver was a lightning of a mechanical sort, like nothing they had ever seen before. I was pleased, and I shook the hands of both Krupp and Ewertz with gratitude.

Each vessel was duly loaded, their spring loaded compartments filled with fist-sized bronze spheres, primed and ready for their task. To be honest, I was amazed at the amount Krupp had been able to accomplish in such a short time, but with the number of workers he boasted, perhaps I should not have been so surprised.

All the checks were made, and I, along with the borrowed Krupp men sailed off above the factories and in to the skies to seek my destiny.

We brought both *Donner* and *Blitzen* to earth not far from our agreed mustering point. I then spent some hours, explaining to the Generalmajor the operations of the vessels and those of their poisonous cargo. As he gazed up at the vast balloons, vaguely stirring and rippling in the breeze, I could see the clear look of awe upon his face. Three times I was forced to go over the intended operations as his gaze kept being drawn upward. I could only hope that the French, once they worked out what was above them would be similarly enraptured, that it would draw them out of their buildings, fingers pointing at these strange visions in the sky above them, and then, before they realized what was happening to them, it would be too late. Ewertz's little mechanisms would be upon them.

When I could drag his attention back to the matter at hand, the Generalmajor seemed pleased, if doubtful. A naturally formal man, he did little to praise my action, but enforced the need for speed. Donner and Blitzen were large and obvious. We could not afford the word to get out, some idle talk from the troops, the passing French spy. We would launch on the morning of the following day and no later. Our path was set.

I spent a restless night, my mind spinning with my own doubts and I was awake well before first light. I dressed carefully and slowly, my attention turned inward. As I stepped from my tent into a damp empty field, empty except for the two grand outputs of Krupp's endeavors, the dim light made them even more ominous, the large bladders turned black rather than grey. I stared up at them considering, sucking at my teeth. As the first, early light crept above the horizon, the faint illumination painted their undersides, making them look like large clouds pregnant with lightning. Now, more than ever, their names were sealed. Sucking in a deep breath and holding it, I turned away and strode off to rouse my men. We were ready!

One by one, my crew clambered up the ropes and on to the deck. The chief started the machinery that further inflated the bag above till it was at the point of straining. All around me, men worked, straining at ropes, undoing knots, and below me the smell of well oiled mechanisms floated up through the morning air. Beneath my feet, the machine thrummed and whirred and above, I could sense, rather than see, the giant bag straining at it edges. First at the left, and then to the right, ropes were cast off. Before us lay the city of Metz. Beside us, slowly creeping into the air, sat Blitzen keeping pace. I sensed rather than felt the motion as we gained more elevation. Then behind me, the rotor that gave the whole forward motion kicked into life.

Stationed toward the front of the deck, I had a few of my own men, bearing weapons, just in case some of our enemy were startled into life. From our vantage, I was certain they could give a good accounting, picking them off if necessary. For, although the French were surely familiar with balloons, they had seen nothing like those that were descending upon them now.

We fairly whisked across the ground, the breeze at our back, pushing us on to our target. The wind flapped at my cloak and brushed around my moustache. I narrowed my eyes, peering forward into the distance, straining for our destination. A short while later, it was there, dreaming in the morning light that glowed behind, turning the distant yellow walls of the great cathedral dusky. The river snaked silver in the predawn light and now, truly, I could see the magnifiicence and the beauty that this city held, why the Prince had no desire to bring it to harm, because it was a gem upon the landscape, filled not only with history, but promise. We had no choice but to make it our own.

As we neared, we could already tell that the city was quiet—too early for most of the population to be stirring. I stepped forward, positioning myself next to the three large levers that would release out deadly cargo, not once, but thrice upon this gleaming city. I glanced to the side, checking that the other ship's captain stood in readiness, and was satisfied to see him similarly positioned. One of my own men, it was, because I simply could not pass a task of such importance to Krupp's men who flew with us.

A sudden gust of wind buffeted us, and I reached out to steady myself, feeling a deep shudder run through the vessel. Nervously, I looked all around us, feeling the vibration continue far longer than I thought it should, but I quickly turned my attention back to front, because we were nearing our prize. I gestured to the men to start bringing us lower, and waved to our sister ship to do the same. We would need to be almost level with the buildings to have the most success when we released. So close now. Together, as designed, the ships started to drift lower.

Suddenly, there was a loud scream from the front of the deck, and a motion. One of Krupp's men dropped, and then beside him another. All in that instant, I saw it. The entire front of the deck was alive with motion, golden scuttling, flashing in the sun's first rays. Another man to the side tore at his neck and cast something from him. Another brushed desperately at the front of his coat. In that awful moment, I realized what was happening. The entire ship was alive with Ewertz's mechanical beasts. Something had brought them to life!

I scrambled backwards, looking desperately for some protection. After all, I had just seen what these things could do. Before me, shapes moved along the deck closer and closer, driving me in desperation to the rear of our vessel. I barely had time to think, but I had but one choice, and with a cry, I leapt from the back of the ship, falling, crashing to the ground below. I felt my leg break, snap as if it was kindling, and pain washed through me. As I grimaced I barely had time to watch as the two vast airships sank majestically towards the city, their great dark bags flapping lazily in the wind. Lower, lower they sank, heading right for the city's center. And then I could see no more, for the pain had taken me and dark blackness poured over me.

Our troops must have found me there, because I was transported, semi-conscious, incoherent on a stretcher away from the place where I had fallen.

Despite everything, despite everything I had planned, it appeared in the end, we had failed.

It was only later that I learned the truth, as one of my fellow wounded recounted to me how *Donner* and *Blitzen* had fallen, how they had crashed into the city, causing some, but not vast damage and how the mechanical beasts had escaped, scuttling through the city and doing their work after all. Metz, it seemed, was ours and the French no more.

The Generalmajor had visited me in my tent, congratulating me for the success, but deep within I knew it was far, far from the truth.

CR80

As I lay there on the cot, my mind full of despair, I could only berate myself. Despite myself, I spoke my words aloud. Perhaps it was the pain.

"I cannot believe that we did what we did, that we attempted such a thing. It was mere nature that brought us undone. The wind. Nothing more. That I thought I could be successful ..." I paused. "I am surely insane!" I cried.

The young, pale medical orderly with the persistent cough looked at me with an intense gaze through his round spectacles. He could hardly have helped hearing my outburst.

"I think not, Herr Major," he said.

"Pfah!" I said, still disgusted with myself.

"Herr Major," said the young man. "Insanity in individuals is something rare — but in groups, parties, nations and ages, it is the rule. That much I have observed. Just look around us. Look at what we have wrought."

I frowned, caught by his words, caught by his intensity, and I held that piercing gaze.

"What is your name?" I asked him after a moment, wondering at such observations coming from a mere medical orderly. Perhaps it was nothing more than battlefield philosophy, but the young man's words had struck a chord.

"Friedrich, Herr Major."

"Friedrich. Friedrich what?"

"Nietzsche, Herr Major. Friedrich Nietzsche."

It seemed unlikely that I would see or hear from this young man again, but one never knew. "Well, Herr Nietzsche, I thank you for your ministrations as well as your observation."

Seeming, for a moment or two to consider a response, in the end, he simply turned and ducked out of the tent, his cough following in his wake. As I sank back on my cot with a grimace, I thought perhaps there was something to what this intense young man had said. There was a kind of insanity in what we had done, what we all had done. Perhaps there was some kernel of wisdom in his words, after all. Time would tell. Certainly, it was something to consider, something to tease apart at leisure. But such ponderings would keep for now. I had achieved what I had been tasked with, though not in the way I had intended, and it seemed I would bear its legacy for some time to come. Not only was there the battle, but also, it seemed likely, that I would leave this place with a pronounced limp that would be sure to remind me for the rest of my days.

Soon, I would have more business with Herr Krupp. And while I was there, perhaps Herr Krupp's little man Ewertz could come up with some clever device to aid my walking—something artful, something shiny, strong and metallic. Certainly, he had the skill. All he would have to ensure was that it worked properly this time.

Taking Flight

by E. G. Gaddess

FEB 17, 1945. Carolinia Independence Day.
At a plantation along the Cooper River, near Charleston,
Carolinia.

"HUDDY!"

Huddy shuddered at the bellow but kept running. In all her sixteen years she'd never heard Mr. Willoughby bellow like that. It was loud enough to crack her ears. She'd known he'd be mad at her running, maybe even spitting mad, especially since he'd been trying to catch her alone so he could check up her skirts.

She'd expected him to be busy with the holiday celebrations. The whole house had been out on the lawn. The Carolinia celebration banners were flying, a pig was roasting on the outdoor pit, and Mrs. Willoughby had brought out the huckleberry wine for all the womenfolk to drink. Mr. Willoughby had stood and smiled at it all behind the long white goatee he wore. Jacob said he wore it to hide his saggy jowls.

Like Mr. Willoughby, all the buckruh were dressed like they were going to church, with white linen shirts and trousers, and wide straw hats to keep their cheeks from burning. They arrived in fancy wagons that used steam, imported from up north, where folks like Huddy were free. Huddy had never seen such things before and Jacob had teased her for staring.

They had been told they could have the afternoon off if all their chores got done. Huddy'd been working so hard, she hadn't heard Mr. Willoughby come up behind her until she'd felt him grab her arms and lift her skirt.

She'd kicked him, hurt him. She'd meant to, but if he caught her, she'd never tell no one that truth.

When he went down, doubled over and yelling, she'd run for the river. She'd thought—maybe—he'd think she'd done gone and drowned, but he'd spied her pushing through the short yaupons and into the woods.

Her wet skirts slapped at her legs and slowed her down but the water felt good against the chigger bites. She slipped in her hard-soled boots; they were wet and soppy from the sprint through the bog. The boots were loose; half the buttons were lost. She stubbed the toe that stuck out of the hole, but didn't make a noise of pain. She didn't have the breath left in her lungs for it.

She had to run. She just had to.

She wished she could fly. Fly like the hen harriers from their aeries in the swamp that bordered the Miller Plantation, fly north with them when they left for the summer. Fly away, high in the sky, where Mr. Willoughby couldn't catch her and check under her skirt.

A rusted, barbed-wire fence was just ahead, marking the boundary of Willoughby Plantation. If she could make it to the other side, Mr. Willoughby might have to stop. He'd need permission to cross onto someone else's land. He'd need to find a gate or a stile through the fence and the dogs couldn't climb over.

Huddy paused. Her lungs hurt to bursting. She looked right, she looked left. A live oak tree, gnarled and half rotted, probably over a hundred years old, bent over the fence.

Huddy ran to the tree and grabbed a branch. It cracked under her weight, but she didn't stop. The tree smelled old, of rot and animal droppings. She pulled herself up, up, up into the tree, scrambling with hands and feet and knees. The bark was rough, and its sharp ridges cut into her skin. There'd be blood, she knew, but there had been blood before. Lots more blood.

She was glad Mama had cut her hair short for the summer. Short so that the little black curls were tight to her head and couldn't catch in the branches that grabbed at her, tore her shirt and skirt.

Huddy crawled out on the branch, dangled over the other side and dropped. Her skirts pouffed and she bent her knees when she landed. Just like Jacob had taught her to jump off the big rock next to the girls' sleeping shanty.

The branch came with her. She let it fall. It broke on the ground, showing innards made holey by termites. Huddy ran again, brushing bugs from her hands and arms, lifting her brown cotton skirt and single petticoat up over her scraped knees. This was no time to worry about lady-like manners.

Ahead, between the trees, Huddy could see a dark, metal building, green from wet and weather. It was arched, with a large sliding door, sitting open, on the end. Huddy ran to the building, not bothering to worry about who owned it or if they might be inside, and ducked behind a wooden crate. She eased herself between two of the massive boxes, creeping deeper into the dark.

The building smelled of coal and fresh wood and something metallic and hot, like the forge at the smithy.

"Huddy! I'm not gonna warn you again. I'm loosin' the dogs!" Mr. Willoughby hadn't bothered getting permission. Maybe he already had an agreement with the landowner. Maybe he just didn't care. Mr. Willoughby didn't often care to obey the rules. Not that there were many for him to obey. In Carolinia, the ruling class made the rules, and the rules were made for slaves–like Mama and Huddy and Jacob.

In Carolinia, a slave couldn't own property, not even their clothes. Mama always lamented that a slave didn't even have the right to raise a chile. Huddy and Jacob belonged to Mr. Willoughby, not Mama, and he decided what they were called. Mr. Willoughby called her Huddy; Mama named her Thandiwe.

Huddy pushed farther back into the hidey-hole. The dogs growled and barked. She imagined them straining against their leads, rearing up on two legs, foam dripping from their jowls.

She'd been feeding those dogs for months now, putting water in the trough and sneaking bits from the kitchen for them. They didn't bark at her anymore, they didn't snap or bite when she picked up a dish. Some even let her pet them when no one else was looking.

"Here they come!"

The warning was followed by the scrabble of paws on gravel. The dogs barked and growled, yelped and howled.

Huddy held her breath. Bile burned in her throat. She swallowed it down. She braced herself against the crates, wincing when a splinter wedged itself into her arm where her yellow blouse was torn. She wore a yellow blouse to show that she worked with the animals. Jacob wore yellow, too. A green blouse meant you worked in the fields. Black meant you worked in the iron shop. Not many girls worked in the iron shop. Mama got to wear white since she worked up at the big house.

Huddy's never been into the big house. But Mama had told her about a contraption from the north that played music when you put steam in a reservoir. Huddy'd heard a lot about the north. About steam cars, and factories with jobs, and gas lights that turned on by themselves. That's why she'd been making plans.

The pack grew closer. Noses nudged against crates and

debris. One dog stopped and howled. They were desperate on the hunt, probably hungry and crazed into a frenzy.

Huddy had watched Mr. Willoughby dangle a carcass over the dog's pen, dripping fresh blood into the faces of the slavering hounds. He'd have one of the boys throw rocks and another swing a switch at them, making them mad with pain and hunger.

Then he'd let them loose in an field enclosure baited with a deer or fox. The dogs would shred the animal when it was caught, tearing at even their litter mates for a scrap of meat.

But Huddy had been planning for months, ever since she'd been given the task of weaning the last litter of hounds, then graduated to feeding and watering the older ones. Mr. Willoughby always let the hounds loose when someone ran off, so she'd known she had to make ready.

Huddy could hear the snuffles and snorts of the dogs; they weaved through the maze of crates, moving steadily closer in a chaotic, four-legged mass.

"Hie! Hie!" Huddy winced. Mr. Willoughby had Jacob running the dogs.

One of the dogs found her. Huddy pressed back and braced against the floor. The dog hunkered down, barring her only escape, head down, hackles raised, fur standing straight up from its back. It growled a low, deep rumble from its chest.

Huddy swallowed and stretched back.

The dog sniffed the air and whined.

"Good boy. Good boy." Huddy reached out a quivering hand. The dog growled again, weaker though. It was in its throat instead of its chest. "That's my good, little man."

The dog stretched out and sniffed her hand, licked her fingers with a dry tongue. The dog's fur was matted and smelled of swamp and poop and old blood.

"Poor baby. Big ol' buckruh hain't given you nothing, has

he?" Huddy reached her fingers out to scratch behind the dog's ear.

The dog cocked its head, pushing it into her hand. It whined again.

Huddy sighed and dipped the fingers of her other hand into her pocket, pulling out a bit of jerky she'd saved from breakfast. She held it out to the dog, who snatched it away and gulped it down, not even bothering to chew.

"S'all I got, boy."

The dog licked her cheek and backed away.

Huddy sat on the cold floor. She still couldn't relax. Another dog could always find her. One that wouldn't recognize her, that wouldn't accept a bit of jerky in trade for leaving her alone.

Huddy thought the prayer Mama had taught her. She didn't dare speak it aloud, even in a whisper.

"Oi. You there! What are you doing?"

"Looking for a runaway."

"In my hangar?"

"That what this is?"

Huddy didn't recognize the voice that spoke to Mr. Willoughby. It didn't have the same drawl that Mr. Willoughby and the other buckruh's had.

"Yes. And you, sir, are trespassing."

"Trespassing?"

"Indeed. Please leave before I summon the authorities."

Huddy licked her lips. She wanted to look out, to see the buckruh who spoke such to Mr. Willoughby. He had to be a buckruh; no one that wasn't spoke like that to the master and got away with it.

"Do you know who I am?"

"No. And frankly, I do not care to."

"Why, I oughta-"

A frantic barking in the distance stopped Mr. Willoughby.

"It be one the dog's, Mista Willoughby." Jacob's voice sounded close.

"Probably found that damn, girl. Let's get going. I want to see her caught."

"Yes, sirrah. I'll get the rest the dogs, sirrah."

"You do that Jacob. Then catch up."

"Yes, sirrah."

The dull thud of running feet and the sharp clop of horse hooves signaled that Mr. Willoughby was leaving. Huddy wasn't safe yet. There were still dogs. And Jacob. And the owner of the other voice.

"Shh."

Huddy snapped her head up.

Jacob held one finger to his full burgundy lips. "I be leading the dogs away. Keep running." He dropped a small sack on the ground.

Huddy nodded.

Jacob disappeared, whistling for the dogs.

Their claws clicked on the floor. They weren't running. Their frenzy had abated with the departure of Mr. Willoughby. She reached for the sack and opened it, reaching one hand to feel around. There was a small piece of cheese coated in wax, a couple of biscuits wrapped in a linen hankie, and a bottle of ginger beer: Jacob's lunch. He'd saved it for her.

Tears pricked at the back of her eyes, but Huddy couldn't afford to cry. Not yet. She was still a dead girl if she couldn't make it across the northern border into Neo-Virginia. That border was still a hundred or more miles away, across plantations owned by men just like Mr. Willoughby.

Huddy sagged to the floor. She'd never make it. Mama'd be mad at her for nothing.

A metallic tick-tick-tick pricked at Huddy's ears. She'd never heard such a sound before. The dogs and Jacob were gone. What would it hurt to take a peek?

Huddy edged herself up the side of the crate, stretching on tiptoe to see over the ragged wood of the top edge. Near the wide door stood a tall, dark-haired buckruh in brown pants and jacket, with tall, shiny black boots. Huddy could tell he was a buckruh by the pale skin of his neck. He had short metal tubes on a band around his head. The ends looked a bit like the spy glass Mr. Willoughby used to spy on the plantation across the river. He cranked a large brass wheel near the door.

A shaft of light cut through the dark: The roof was splitting.

Huddy crouched down again, eyes wide, looking up at the ever increasing wedge of open sky. It grew, until the whole ceiling was gone, and only the purple-blue of dusk could be seen above.

"Dumaka. Bring them out."

"Yes, sir."

Huddy sucked in a breath and held it. What was the buckruh bringing out? More dogs?

The squeal of nail pulling from wood echoed in the edges of the hangar, where the retracted ceiling bunched and still offered shadows.

"Hurry. There's not much time."

Scuffling feet crossed the hangar. Followed by another squeal of nail and more scuffling.

Huddy peeked out again.

The open ceiling let enough light in for her to see what looked like a great black egg reaching up to where the ceiling ought to be. An egg with fins—or maybe wings, smooth like the bats that lived in the attic of the big house.

The bottom of the black egg looked like a basket. Huddy knew it wasn't a basket, but that was all she knew to compare it to. It looked woven, like the wicker baskets used to collect tobacco. The opposite end had what looked like one of Mrs. Willoughby's new ceiling fans that ran on steam from the furnace, steam that flowed through pipes that Jacob had helped install in the big house.

Outside the basket, metal canisters, like those on Mr. Willoughby's steam tram that took folks out to the fields, were strapped to the sides.

Huddy had never seen the like before. It looked like a fat fish from the river, only with extra fins.

A line of twenty folks, their skin ranging from caramel to hazel-black, crossed the room, leading from opened crates to the "basket." Some folks wore shoes, some had dirty feet. The men wore pants, most rolled to the knees. The women wore skirts or dresses. Children clutched each other. All the clothing was ragged and thin with age. They all held a rolled piece of paper in one hand, holding it out like a ticket, like they were boarding the steam train to Savannah.

Huddy had only gone once by train to Savannah, with Mrs. Willoughby, to help keep watch on the little ones. Mrs. Willoughby had kept hold of Huddy's ticket; she hadn't trusted her enough not to trade it in for a ticket somewhere else. But that was illegal. Colored girls weren't allowed to buy a ticket, so how would she ever be able to trade it?

A young man, his own skin just as dark as Huddy's, stood to the side of the front of the line, gathering the slips of paper and waving folks through a door and into the basket.

The folks hurried up a small ramp made of the same material. They were smiling.

Huddy crept forward. Why were they smiling?

The young man looked up. His eyes were gray - buckruh eyes. But his hair was tiny knots, just like Huddy's, and his lips were full like Jacob's.

Huddy started back, but he waved her ahead. "C'mon. Times a wastin'."

Huddy stepped forward and looked around. She took a place at the end of the line, using the toes of her good boot to scratch her calf, staring at the nape of the neck of the old woman in front of her. The woman was shorter than Huddy and old enough to have wrinkles in her neck. There were scars, too. Burns from the looks of it. The woman was nearly bald, only tufts of wispy white stuck up in random spots.

Huddy shuffled forward, hands knotted and clenched, Jacob's lunch sack dangling from her left wrist. She didn't have a paper.

When she got to the front, the young man held out a hand and Huddy shook her head, unclenching her empty hands to show him. She looked at the ground. Her big toe poked through the hole, still bleeding from the tree. Miss Mandy had grown out of the boots last year. It didn't matter that Huddy's feet were already bigger than Miss Mandy's. At least she had a pair of shoes.

The young man nudged her. He wore shiny new boots. Huddy could see her reflection in the smooth toes.

Huddy looked up at him and backed away.

He grabbed her arm.

Huddy flinched and ducked her head.

"S'okay. There's room." The young man whispered and pulled her forward. "Just don't tell anyone."

Huddy stared into the buckruh-gray eyes just level above hers. His skin was unmarked, unscarred, smooth and clear.

"Okay."

"My name's Dumaka."

"Mine's Thandiwe, but I'm called Huddy."

Dumaka smiled, showing solid white teeth. "Go on. Get inside. We'll be leaving in a few minutes."

Huddy stepped up the ramp. People stood inside, some holding hands, some hugging each other. Some were crying. But everyone was still smiling.

Huddy wedged herself next to the wall, behind the old

woman with the wrinkled neck. The woman grinned, her teeth a bright spot in the dim light.

"We almost there Sugapie."

Huddy nodded and smiled.

"It be worth it. It be worth it in the end." The woman rocked, smiling, her eyes focused on something Huddy couldn't see. She hummed under her breath. Huddy recognized the tune, but didn't know the words.

Maybe it was one of the forbidden songs.

Mama had told her about the forbidden songs, and hummed some to her, in the dark at night, after she'd had a bad dream. But no one could sing the words. It was illegal for a black person to sing those songs. Huddy thought maybe no one remembered them anymore.

"We'll be able to sing when we get there. We all will." The woman leaned toward to Huddy. "Do you know the words?"

Huddy shook her head.

"Don't matter. Knowing the words won't matter when we get there."

The woman hummed again and Huddy listened to the tune. She swayed to the humming, engrossed in the vibration. It echoed inside her.

It *was* one of Mama's songs.

Dumaka jumped up the ramp and cranked a handle. The ramp pulled up and swallowed the opening. Huddy heard a click and the old woman stopped humming. They were in the dark, only slivers of light bending through the woven fibers.

"We'll need to stay quiet. It's best if we sit down and don't move around much. It's almost dark."

The old woman clutched at Huddy and Huddy kept herself steady while the woman sat down. Then Huddy sat, too, tucking her legs under her skirts, staying close.

"Thandiwe?"

"I be here." Huddy whispered.

"Just making sure."

Huddy felt someone sit next to her, a warm body in soft fabric.

"It's just me." Dumaka smelled clean, like the soap Mama used in the laundry up at the big house. Mama's hands, wrinkled and red from the hot water, always smelled like that soap. Like lemon and lavender. Like home.

It was quiet in the dark, only the sound of breathing and an occasional cough breaking it. It was warm in the basket, the exhale of breath making it warmer yet. Huddy let her eyes drift closed, and leaned her head on the old woman's shoulder.

"Sleep chile. I'll watch over ye."

Huddy snuggled down.

She thought about floating down the Cooper River, heading out to sea. She'd be in a basket, like Moses, in Mama's favorite story from the church. Mama couldn't read, so the reverend never wasted a Bible on her, but Mama had listened hard to the stories, and recited them to Jacob and Huddy.

Huddy liked the story of the baby in the rushes. She imagined the rushes to be like giant feathers growing from the ground, but Mama said they were probably more like the thin, reedy grass that grew near the duck pond.

Huddy thought feathers would be nicer than the reeds. The other chillun liked to pull up the reeds and swipe at her legs when she washed in the river, leaving thin red welts down her thighs. They stopped the day Jacob caught them at it and picked them up and threw them into the middle of the river. He'd had to go in after one of them that got caught in the current and almost drowned.

Mama had been furious and was ready to beat on Jacob, until Huddy pulled up her skirt and showed Mama her leg. Then Mama had wept and held Jacob and Huddy tight to her, sobbing.

She could see Jacob and Mama, standing on the other side of the Cooper, smiling and waving at her. She waved back, and looked for a way to cross. But the current was too swift, the water too deep, the river too wide.

She'd never get to them.

"Here we go."

The whisper, direct to her ear, tickled Huddy awake and she realized she'd been resting against Dumaka instead of the old woman. She had his arm hugged to her chest, her head resting on the broad surety of his shoulder. She grabbed for something and found a warm hand waiting. The fingers were long and trim and strong.

It was Dumaka's hand. He wove his fingers through hers and squeezed.

The basket moved. Huddy heard a dull roar, like the fire in the smithy after the bellows and the basket lifted off the ground.

Huddy's stomach lurched.

"It's okay." Dumaka whispered again.

Others whispered, too, the sound a quiet surge that spread through the basket. Bodies shifted and squirmed, following the whisper, a ripple of movement that made the basket rock.

"Don't move!" Dumaka's sharp command only made them more restless, and the basket rocked sharper. It edged back down, bumping the ground.

"We won't get up if you don't stop moving." Dumaka's hand tightened on Huddy's.

The old woman started to hum again. Folks listened and the whispers stilled and the shifting bodies rested. Others hummed, joined in, keeping the sound low. The sounds melded together, like the choir at church.

The melody seeped inside Huddy, soothed the jumping of her heart, and slowed the rush of her blood. Huddy hummed, too. Softly, because she had never hummed it herself, only listened to Mama.

Dumaka didn't hum. But he didn't tell them to stop. His grip on Huddy's hand loosened and he relaxed.

They rose, higher and higher, until Huddy knew they had to be above the trees, where the harriers flew. Then, Huddy heard a new noise. A thup, thup, thup, like a hound's tail against the ground when she came with its supper.

"That's the propeller." Dumaka's voice was warm in her ear.

"Propeller?"

"What looks like a fan, on the end."

Huddy smiled. Dumaka couldn't see it though, so she squeezed his hand. He squeezed hers back.

Everyone hummed, the propeller keeping time behind the music.

They hummed for hours. They hummed when the last sliver of light through the cracks faded and they were left in closed blackness. They hummed when the wind picked up and rocked the basket and they clutched at each other, not caring who it was beside them. They hummed when the fire-roar from above grew louder to make them climb, and softened to let them drift back down.

When one song ended, someone started another, taking a turn to lead. Some songs Huddy recognized, but most she didn't. She listened, taking them into her heart, memorizing them as best she could. She wanted a new song to hum to Mama if she ever saw her again.

Huddy didn't notice the when the basket descended. She'd been trying to hum along with a new song, to imprint the sounds into her soul.

Dumaka shifted and leaned forward, letting go of her hand. Huddy turned her head in the dark. She couldn't see him, but she could feel him there, solid and warm.

"We're landing."

His announcement stopped the humming. The dark made the quiet louder, harder. Huddy thought some folks might be holding their breath; she knew she was.

Huddy tensed and forced the air from her lungs, taking in new air slow, to keep it quiet. Where were they landing? She really should have asked, but she'd been too relieved to be leaving Mr. Willoughby and his dogs behind.

"Ooh. We be singing now." The old woman next to Huddy took a deep breath and started her song. She didn't hum this time. No, this time, the she sang the words.

> *The sun be setting, setting,*
> *over the way hill.*
> *It be gone to faraway sands.*
> *But it be climbing, climbing,*
> *by the early morn,*
> *Giving its light to our lands.*
> *The sun be shining, shining,*
> *bright up in the sky*
> *The sun be guiding with its hand.*
> *Setting and climbing,*
> *Shining and guiding*
> *God's Son be watching over our lands.*

When she started through again, others sang with her, some singing higher, some lower, the words building them up. Huddy felt lighter, like she could float away without the basket.

The flame roared and the basket jerked. The flame roared again and the basket swayed.

They kept singing though. Nothing stopped their song.

The basket bounced, once, twice; the third time it hit the ground hard enough that Huddy was knocked over into Dumaka and the old woman fell over into Huddy.

But still, they sang.

With a final hard landing, the basket stopped and the roar sizzled and faded to nothing. The only sound left was the song.

Dumaka stood and slowly cranked on the wheel that let the ramp down. The tick-tick-tick was a soft, back rhythm, keeping time. The ramp lowered. It was still dark, but there were smells that reminded Huddy of the coal used to light the tobacco dryer. An acrid scent that would burn her nostrils and make her throat dry and raspy.

Huddy waited until everyone else had filed out, still singing. They sang loud, the sound carrying outside the basket. They clapped and stomped with the song, they danced and hollered and let loose the joy of the words.

Huddy stood and stepped out. Dumaka stood to the side, talking to the buckruh in the brown suit and high boots. The buckruh nodded at whatever Dumaka said and glanced in Huddy's direction.

Then he patted Dumaka on the shoulder and strode toward Huddy. Dumaka followed, his hands in fisted balls by his thighs, his lips pressed tight together, made thin.

"You are Thandiwe?"

Huddy nodded.

"You were the runaway the dogs were after?"

Huddy nodded again and looked down, covering the bloody, peeping toe with her other foot.

"Well then, welcome to Neo-Virginia!"

Huddy looked up at the buckruh then looked around. Mama had told stories about the country to the north, of how a black man or a black woman could get a job and be paid, could buy their own clothes and food with that money. Could have a child together, raise that child, and see that child to have children of its own.

Neo-Virginia was beautiful. They stood in the midst of a grand meadow, the grass green and clipped short. The meadow smelled like the back hay field on the plantation, just after the hay was cut; when the hay was still green and laying long on the ground. Orange-pink light lit the horizon above the ragged tree line, spreading upward, chasing the dusky purple of night from the sky.

Huddy looked behind her. The basket looked smaller in the open meadow. In the light, Huddy could make out wooden blades on the other side of the basket. The fans were turning slowly, pushing the basket forward while the ropes to the ground held it still.

Dumaka pointed at the metal canisters. "There's helium in them. It's lighter than air and gets pushed into the balloon and we rise up."

Huddy looked at Dumaka. "We truly floated here?"

He nodded and smiled and took her hand. "She doesn't make a lot of noise. No one ever sees us up in the sky at night, and no one ever hears us, either."

Huddy smiled back and linked their fingers.

The buckruh in brown nodded. "Spectacular, ain't it?"

"Spek-ta-ku-lar." Huddy wasn't certain of the meaning of the word, but it sounded right for something so wonderful.

"I'm Dr. M." The buckruh held out one hand.

Huddy stared a moment, and a nudge from Dumaka's elbow had her taking the hand in her own. Dr. M pumped it up and down.

"Got a place to go?"

Huddy shook her head.

Dr. M glanced around her to Dumaka and grinned. "Well, there's always something to do at my house. I'm sure I can find a job for you."

Dumaka bowed to Dr. M, then took Huddy's hand and led her forward.

What Huddy thought was a steam train wasn't. It looked like a train car from behind, except it didn't set on tracks, and the front looked like a wagon, only Huddy had never seen the likes of what was hitched to the front: Gleaming metal horses, four of them in two pairs. They stood, unmoving, on four metal legs, with metal heads. They had no mane or tail, and you could see some of their inner workings; the gears and levers and rods.

"Let's get in. We're still close to the border." Dumaka handed her up into the front. "You can sit up with me."

"Where's Dr. M going?"

"He's got to take the dirigible on to the aerodrome. No one can know that we landed here first."

Huddy nodded. Dumaka made sure everyone was inside then pushed a lever. The hiss of steam pushing through pipes filled the air. Dumaka pushed another lever and wound a crank and the metal horses' heads came up and bobbed once. Another level and they moved forward, sixteen legs in perfect time, like a marching line of soldiers.

The machine lurched forward then settled into a smooth surge, surge, surge, not unlike the steam train to Savannah. Only the train to Savannah didn't have gleaming metal horses that beat a rhythm on the ground with metal hooves.

Someone laughed in the back and another song started.

Huddy smiled and settled back. Dumaka grinned at her. "You'll like working for Dr. M. He hires a lot of people he brings up from Carolinia. Gets them trained up for something better. There's jobs in the city."

Huddy leaned forward. "Really?"

Dumaka nodded.

"And are there balloons and metal horses?" Huddy pointed to the steeds in front of them.

Dumaka laughed. "Yes. And more, much more."

Huddy wondered at that. She hadn't heard stories about metal horses. She wondered about Dumaka. "Are you training?"

Dumaka shook his head. "I'm all trained up. I help Dr. M."

"Help him do what?"

"Bring folks up from Carolinia."

"Oh." Huddy thought, watching the light dapple over the metal rumps of the horses. "I think I'd like to do that, too."

Dumaka smiled and reached for her hand, squeezing it and not letting go. "I thought you might."

An Urchin, an Adventureman

by Eric Del Carlo

THE PORT'S SKY BREATHED LIKE BELLOWS, never so roaringly as when a big one was coming in. This, Socko heard and saw with pressure on his eardrums and eyes raised to the purple twilight, was a battleship, enormous, puffed up. It looked like a great ruffled bird, only it hovered and was slow, stately in its progress; and it sounded like ... well, something that growled in a nightmare.

He grinned up at it, thrilled, even with his palms clapped over his ears and eyes narrowed like they couldn't take in the whole size of the thing all at once. These ships were new. Hawke class. Not Hawk, like he used to think, but *Hawke*, a name, an old admiral of sea boats, somebody the lime-os wanted to remember. Socko was proud to know the distinction, that Hawke meant person, not bird. He didn't flap about it much to the others, though. Didn't want the razz for it. But he hoarded up little bits of knowing like that, kept them in his head.

These newer Hawkes were better armed and had a longer range, and this one must be coming back from massacring christophers in the West.

But there wasn't time to gawk, wasn't even time for the look up and the grin that he had already indulged in. A chum, passing, shoved him; too hard, and Socko went off-balance

and turned to give it right back, to find Linc mouthing
"Come on" at him. It was easy to read the words, dark lips
on bright teeth. He liked Linc. He didn't want to shove
him back, not least because Linc was bigger, a 'mancipate's
son strong from the family line that went back to the hell
of Carolina fields. That war was long over. That war had put
the nation back together.

But all *that* had done was make it so that the lime-os
could swallow it whole again. Least, that was how it looked
to Socko.

He followed Linc and the others. A big ship coming in
made a good time for the gag. The port was always busy,
always lit up and rumbling, but a battleship alighting put
a frenzy into things. Lots of distractions. He and the half
dozen other flashes scurried along the shadow of a brick
wall. An automatonic had built the wall, you could tell.
Every brick laid exactly the same, the mortar smooth and
not sloppy anywhere.

Loosely grilled vents, ducts—those were friends to flashes,
because the guards didn't know to watch such tiny entries.
They had eyes, probably, for bomb-throwers, for people who
called themselves Uprisers. Socko had met some of these, or at
least been in earshot when they mouthed stupidly about how
they would take the nation back from the lime-os. If those
people ever saw the port the way the flashes did—up close,
with a good gander at the ships and their weaponry—they
would know the Uprising they had in mind was never going
to come. Not that way. Maybe not any way at all.

Socko stayed aware of the descending Hawke as he and
his chums ducked into the grate, through the wall, and past
other obstacles, hurrying low and quick. The port's field had
a great paved oval at its center, and around it were quarters,
administrative buildings, stores. But it was all an ongoing
chaos, with uniformed people making to and fro. Mechanics,

administrators, support staff—and of course the guards. But the flashes could and did flit from shadow to shadow, making deeper way into the site.

Discarded equipment moldered at the outer edges. It was incredible what the lime-os threw away, and sometimes the flashes—Socko's band or other crews—scavenged here. There was pressed steel, belts of rubber, panes of unbreakable glass. (*Unbreakable* glass!) Smuggle that gear out and the nearby town's black market would snatch it up. You'd get jingle for your pocket. But tonight's gag was something else, something more.

By well-coordinated bursts of speed and hiding when they should, they made toward the motor pool.

The port crackled with lightning—or that was how it felt. It got under your skin, made your nose itch. Rubberized wire lay everywhere, connecting to the soaring light stanchions and to the many buildings. Everything hummed. Everything was alive with the fantastic machineries of the lime-os.

They were so ... different. They had gotten out ahead, like there was a race on, one involving the building of better mechanisms; and the men from across the ocean were winning the race. No imagining otherwise.

It was so easy, though, to think of them as devils or angels, as creatures who could bring terror from the skies. Just ask the christophers in the West, if you could understand their savage talk, and they'd say, surely, that the battleships and those adventuremen who manned the skyborne vessels were evil spirits.

But Socko knew better. He knew more. He had paid attention and absorbed the details. The adventuremen were men, lime-os or not, fabulous engines and weapons or not. They had simply—well, not *simply*—advanced the mechanical sciences. That those scientific miracles seemed to have come all at once, like some magical pot boiling over, probably wasn't right either. But that was how it looked, from this side of the ocean anyway, in this land being reclaimed by the irresistible lime-o war machine.

These United States hadn't lasted even a hundred years.

The flashes slipped among the motorcoaches. The vehicles, unattended, stood in rows. As the armed ships menaced the sky, these ground carriages were a terror to the land. They too were weaponed, and their sides plated with metal, making them relentless. War crafts. They could resist bullets. They could even—Socko had seen—withstand the fiery splatter of alcohol bombs, and keep right on rolling. What could Uprisers do against that might?

It wasn't Socko's worry. The gag was on.

Working fast, working quiet, the flashes uncapped the fuel tubs on the undersides of the coaches, stuck in their hoses, and starting sucking.

The Hawke battleship was down. The vast roar eased.

Socko wanted to see the adventuremen disembark.

His jug was filling steadily with the precious propellent. This, better than anything, the black market paid for. He didn't know what they used it for—lamp oil? It didn't matter. He was a flash, and he needed the money so he could eat, so he could have a life. Motherless and fatherless, it was all on him. Survive. Figure out a way.

But right now he wished desperately to catch a look at the adventuremen, the ones just back. You could hate and admire the lime-os all at once. What he couldn't do, though, was try to explain that fact to any of his fellows. They'd do more than give the razz for that.

The fuel continued to flow. The smell was strong. It would take minutes. Socko, deciding, rolled out from beneath the armored motorcoach. Bad idea and he knew it, giving up this cover; but this was already a bad idea, risking himself for a look. He was going to do it anyway.

He stepped over Linc's legs poking out from under his vehicle and got to the low wall enclosing the motor pool. He needed to go further. Moving like a whisper, like a shadow, he went over the wall and hunkered past bales of equipment. The paved oval was ahead, and the Hawke sat dead center on it. The ship gasped and vented white vapor from its boilers. Its inflated body eased as he watched, drooping a little. Its blazing lights started to wink out.

Above, though it was hard to tell with all the lights, the twilight was edging into night.

He found his vantage, the nearest he dared get, crouching invisibly. Personnel milled about the ship, but still he waited. Until ...

His heart thumped fast in his scrawny chest. His eyes went wide and he was grinning again, mouth stretching so that his cheeks ached. Down from the battleship's belly came the gangway, a smooth lowering with a machine's humming--amazing. The ship was so ... big. But it *flew*. It was a marvel.

And now, the first stirrings from inside the ship, boots appearing on the stepped gangway. The adventuremen, here they—

The hand felt huge. It grabbed his ragged shirt at the back of his neck and lifted. His feet, so suddenly, were dangling. He couldn't see who had seized him.

Tobacco on the breath, oil on his clothes. Mockery and the promise of punishment in the grating voice: "Well well well, an' wot 'ave we got 'ere?"

But still Socko strained to see the adventuremen dismounting their mighty ship. Even though he was caught. Even though his life was now, certainly, over.

CR80

Socko was shivering. He wasn't cold—the room was heated through a grate—and he had been telling himself he wasn't afraid. It seemed better to be stubborn about that than to give in to the fear. Even so, his heart pounded. It felt like he'd been subjected to hours of questions, but probably it hadn't been even a single hour. The two interrogators wore drab uniforms. Port personnel, administrators. Dull men, who spoke in wooden voices, who plainly regarded Socko as an inconvenience, an annoyance. One had slapped him several times while the other tapped a pen atop a sheaf of papers. No inkpot for the pen, like everybody had in the town for their pens, yet the writing tool always wrote, never--somehow--running out of ink.

They had wanted to know what he was doing at the port, of course. Socko had managed to delay telling them explicitly for several minutes, enough time to let his fellow flashes finish swizzing propellent and get away—he hoped. The first slap he had received had split his lip and loosed the names of his chums. The names wouldn't mean much, though. They weren't *name* names for the most part, just what the flashes called each other. After all, "Socko" wasn't any kind of Christian name.

"Gutter snipes," sniffed one of the interrogators.

"Street Arabs," snotted his pal.

After that the questioning expanded dramatically, but it all had the sound of routine, like everybody who got caught doing something bad got asked these same extreme questions. The two men wanted him to tell them all about the Uprising. Or, really, about the Upris*ers*—any that Socko might know personally.

"There ain't any Upriser folk I know," he said. He was slapped, asked again, and said it again, because what else could he say? Nobody gave up Uprisers. It just wasn't done.

But as the hour started to dwindle, one of the questioners—the pen-tapper, not the slapper—asked in an offhand way, "How did you manage to get yourself captured? You were siphoning, you say, yet you were apprehended well away from the motor pool ..."

So Socko told them. "I wanted to see the adventuremen coming off that ship."

"Why?" asked the man, staying his more hostile colleague with a gesture as that man, annoyed, took a step toward Socko.

Socko couldn't think of a good lie. "Because they're"—he groped through dozens of words, finding only one that was close—"... beautiful."

A short time later the men, following a whispered exchange which Socko couldn't overhear, left him sitting in the chair alone in the windowless room.

Then came the snap of the doorknob, and a figure entered, and those bone-rattling shivers Socko had been suffering all this time vanished, completely and at once.

"So. You wished to see me, did you, my lad?"

Socko went goggle-eyed. His jaw fell, and he gaped. Where before his heart had pounded, now he wasn't sure it hadn't stopped, frozen, stunned.

An adventureman had come. He entered the room and pushed shut the door behind him, and looked at Socko.

"I've the wrong room?"

His voice had a lilt; it wasn't dull. How easily the man moved, how suave he seemed just standing there, looking down at Socko. But it was, of course, the man's appearance that captivated him. It was his dress, his look, that announced so boldly that *here* was an adventureman.

"N-n-n-no, sir," Socko managed; then, determined not to stammer his n's again: "Not the wrong room, sir."

His boots were supple leather, brown, a smooth shade of it. They reached to his knees, where his trousers bunched a bit; dark green piping against beige, the weave of the fabric visible. A belt, heavy and black and elaborately buckled, held up the trousers and was strung with numerous pouches, each bearing a shiny silver clasp and containing the Lord knew what and all the more intriguing for it. His shirt was stiff gray cotton, its buttons headed with pearl, it looked like; collar like a bird's folded wings and decorated with insignia. A waistcoat over the shirt, the same beige as the trousers but embroidered with a sea boat's anchors. The coat which draped his high trim shoulders was long, a different tougher kind of leather, with straps here and there, most dangling loose. Gloves on the hands, snug, revealing the metal device—a machine, an actual small *machine*—blinking with light strapped onto his left wrist.

And the headgear—the leather cap, the fleeced earflaps, and of course the goggles. There had to be goggles. Riding up on his forehead, the lenses as dark as smoke, rimmed with grooved brass.

Then there was the face of the man, mustachioed and those mustaches waxed, his blue eyes as lovely as any girl's, the easy play of the jaw, the cheekbones, the twinkling look he was giving Socko.

Yet for all the splendor of the adventureman's raiment, he also appeared ... used. Somewhat disheveled. Sweat stained the collar. There was stubble on his chin, a redness edging those blue eyes. The uniform not just freshly put on. This man, then, was back soon from his work. This was an adventure-man just off that Hawke battleship that had so entranced Socko earlier.

"Not wrong, then," he said with that same ease and confidence. A joke. He knew this was the right room, this man who didn't walk into a wrong room, not ever. "Well, lad. Perhaps you will do me the courtesy of telling me your name."

Socko's cheek and lip still smarted vaguely from when the man had slapped him, but that didn't matter, not at all. He sprang to his feet, stood rigid and with barely the breath in him to blurt, "Socko, sir!"

Amusement danced in blue, red-rimmed eyes, but it wasn't cruel amusement, not ridicule. "That's a fine name, lad. Socko. I wonder how you came to earn it." He wasn't asking outright, though. "Any objection were I to sit with you for a time?"

That one was explicitly a question, and Socko, still standing, gestured exaggeratedly at the two empty chairs the interrogators had left behind. When the adventureman sat in one, the tails of his coat spilling about him and trailing buckles to the floor, it was his turn to gesture, so to put Socko back in his own chair. Socko sat down, still astounded by this turn of events.

"My name is Edwin. Someone told me you wanted to see me. Is that true?"

Socko's mind raced. How unreal this all felt, like a frantic dream that was going to break apart any moment. "I—" he started, and felt the stammer ready to grab hold of that *I* and repeat it endlessly. He forced a normal breath into his lungs, then let it go without hurrying it. "I did not ask to see you, sir. I'm sorry. Somebody's made a mistake."

"Oh?" The adventureman—Edwin—sagged back in his chair. The hard wood creaked, but he made it look comfortable. "You didn't, then, steal onto this rather restricted military post in order to see ... someone like me? How disappointing. I must admit, Socko, I would have found that rather flattering." He lifted, then dropped, his shoulders in an easy shrug. His accent was purring, easy-going, not harsh like some of the lime-os.

Edwin was fitting a thin long black cigarette into a holder.

Socko said, "I did want to see someone, uh, like you, sir. That's true." These words came easier. He was starting to feel a strange new calm, like he was borrowing it from this man who had such a relaxed manner.

Edwin set the holder between his teeth. It looked like ivory. Instead of a matchstick, he produced something from a pocket, a small brass thing whose top he flipped back with his thumb and—too quickly to follow—somehow got it to ignite a perfect yellow flame. He touched the cigarette's tip and snapped shut the device and pocketed it again, more amazing than any conjurer's trick.

This time, Socko made a real effort not to gape.

"How old are you, Socko?"

"Twelve years come November, sir."

"Where do you imagine you shall be, when November arrives?"

Socko had no idea; he couldn't—and wouldn't let himself—think beyond this room for now.

Edwin blew trails of sweet-smelling smoke. He didn't press for a reply, but asked, "What is it you fancy I do, Socko?"

"You're ... you travel—up there." He pointed to the ceiling, past it.

"That's correct. And how do I manage that?"

It was the way some adults talked, the kinder ones, when they were trying to help a youngster think something through for himself. "In the ships."

"Yes," said Edwin.

"The new Hawke class battleship."

Edwin's blue eyes opened wider, and his eyebrows—blond—rose a little. His mustaches moved as he worked the ivory holder in his teeth. "How"—his voice had lowered—"do you know that?"

Socko shrugged, consciously trying to imitate the casual roll of the man's shoulders earlier. "I ask. I listen. People in uniforms say things in the town."

Edwin nodded slowly. "I would wager they do, those loose tongues on leave. So. I travel in the skies, aboard a ship. What do I do up there?"

This was a test, which was different from the questions the two drably dressed interrogators had asked. Edwin—could he really think of this man as *Edwin*?—was taking him seriously, expecting smart answers. Socko didn't want to disappoint him. "You go to the West."

"Yes, you can tell that much from our departure vector. What do I do in the West?"

"Kill christophers."

Edwin paused, blinking. "Christophers?"

The wrong word. Socko hurried to fix it. "Indians, I mean."

The man was still puzzling over it. "Christophers?" he asked again.

"Christopher Columbus. Long time ago. Thought they'd be Indians here like he had come to India. He was wrong, though." Socko remembered that much from the little schooling he'd gotten.

Edwin puffed his cigarette and said to himself, "The Colonial vernacular. How charming." He tapped away a bit of ash. "It seems, however, you don't truly understand."

He had disappointed this man, which was unthinkable to Socko. He wanted desperately to please him, to win his approval. He would say the right thing, do anything.

"B-b-but"—he bit his lip, right where it was split, to stop the stammering—"*but* I want to understand. Sir. Please."

Edwin regarded him through the accumulating bluish smoke.

"Very well. Perhaps a new perspective is in order for you."

CʒꙄꙄ

The adventureman led him, gloved hand on his shoulder, out of the room, out of the building, onto the field. Edwin, it seemed, needed only to speak his wishes to send obedient personnel scurrying into action.

The hand never left Socko's bony shoulder, not until they stood at the claw-like metal feet of a comparatively smallish craft. Windows gleamed blackly; brass fittings blazed. The shape was sleek, elegant, yet the thing was the size of a house back in the town. Steam seethed into the great canvas pouches mounted on the flanks. Edwin indicated the rungs of a ladder.

"Up with you, lad. Don't touch anything." He ground the end of the cigarette under his horseshoe-shaped heel and pocketed the ivory holder.

Socko put a hand to the ladder, looking up into light and mystery, thinking with frantic wonder that this couldn't possibly be happening, not really. But Edwin gave the seat of his raggedy britches a soft swat, and Socko went up.

It was small inside, with tight slanted walls that were brightened with a dizzying array of lights. He almost reached out for one of the nodes before remembering Edwin's warning. Seconds later boots hit the rungs, ascending.

"Forward. To the seats. That's a lad." The bigger man stooped his way through the interior but made it look graceful, like he was intimately familiar with such cramped accommodations.

Socko found a padded bench at what he figured out was the fore of the craft. Windows that had appeared black from outside were now, somehow, transparent. He could see through, see the whole of the port. The bench faced a mind-boggling arrangement of switches, levers and devices he couldn't guess at.

"I must apologize for resorting to this little scout flit," Edwin said, swinging himself nimbly onto the bench alongside Socko. His coat's buckles rattled on the corrugated metal flooring. "But prepping the big boats is a chore. Besides, this will be more ... private."

Socko did not now shiver, nor was his heart pounding madly. He felt instead elevated to a sublime state, almost like being in a happy dream that felt fantastically real. He was without pain or fear. More, it felt like he would never know either of those unhappy states ever again. He was on the cusp of something great here, the fulfillment of young lifetime of wondering about the crafts which dominated the sky.

Gloved fingers were setting dials, snapping switches. The speed and ease spoke of this man's nonchalant intimacy with such a wondrous machine. The boiler moaned with life somewhere behind them, and steam continued to heave into the inflatable sacs strung across the ship's hull. After a moment Edwin looked sidelong. His mustaches drew up like wings as he smiled.

"Grab hold. There's always that first jolt."

Socko seized a bar, padded just like the bench, before him and hung on with whitened knuckles as the craft jerked with a sharp amazing force. A roar grew under them, around them. It was so different from hearing the engines from without, bellowing through the night. Being inside, it was like the growl of a dog when your head was laid against its side. It was a powerful consuming sound, and it shook through him, but that only made Socko feel a part of it.

His eyes flashed toward the windows, edged with silver and fixed with fat-headed screws. The port was dropping away! A great fabulous vertigo whirled through his skull, even though he knew exactly what was happening. His gut churned, but he would not be sick. He wouldn't dare.

Edwin's light touch on the levers made for an easy rising. Up they went, with the earth opening wider and larger beneath, spreading out to an infinite land mass. It was a darkened landscape, to be sure, but the port shone brightly and its light bled out over the surrounding terrain. Socko picked out the road to town. He even saw vehicles on it. How like tiny toys they looked, though he knew they were neither small nor harmless. The tips of treetops swayed in the night. They were above these. They were truly where once only birds flew. Finally he could see the rustic pile of the town itself miles away, so puny, and so dim compared to the port.

They turned slowly, maintaining a level, the craft's advanced inner workings rumbling. Socko, enraptured by the vista, didn't even turn to look when Edwin started to speak.

"Socko, my lad, we do more than ... kill christophers, as you said earlier. We, all of us"—peripherally he caught the edge of Edwin's wide gesture taking in the whole port below and maybe much more than that—"want what is best. We love this land. That is why we are so eager to have it back. We see your people living in such squalor. Such ... such backwardness. We have sciences which improve life everywhere we go. As we speak here, in this little vessel, the world is changing. Being made over. Advancing, all due to our auspices. A nation at a time we bring the peoples of this entire world under our order. We shall go on doing so until there are *no* nations, none, save the one, the Crown!"

His voice had grown impassioned. Socko finally did look away from the majestic, slowly wheeling view.

Edwin caught himself and let out a chuckle. "So, you are twelve this November. That is a fine age. Did you know that we recruit a junior corps? We even have leave to take numbers from indigenous populations—that is, people who live in these lands we come to. We find their native knowledge useful. Sometimes. When they are cooperative."

The vision flashed with sudden force into Socko's mind, reinforced by the fact that he was already up here. But he also saw himself in some version of Edwin's garb. He would be smart and suave, boots on the gangway's steps, going up into the belly of the battleship. Welcomed among the others who manned the craft, treated kindly, affectionately, every man like an uncle. He would be given responsibilities. He would help, in small ways, with the running of the vessel. He could learn these complex controls, if he was taught. His was an eager mind. One day, through effort, he would even become an—

The adventureman pressed a recessed stud, and a pearl-bright light activated over a small brass plaque etched with TRANSVOX, a word Socko didn't know. A strange crackling sound followed. Edwin then reached a hand over to brush a lock of Socko's matted dark hair away from an eye. It was the hand with the winking device strapped to his wrist. That light shone in Socko's eye as the gloved fingers gently tucked the hair behind his ear. "Now, lad. Tell me what you know about the people in that town of yours. The ones who call themselves Uprisers. Half of New York is on fire because of their ilk, and we don't want that out here. Say their names clearly into that grille there. Tell me what you know ... and you shall belong truly to these skies."

The leathery fingertips grazed his cheek as he started to dredge up the names of everyone he had ever overheard saying anything favorable about the Uprising. They were mostly people he didn't like. He spoke faster and faster as the hand continued to stroke his face, until he was just repeating names. When the gloved thumb hooked softly into the corner of his mouth, Socko tried to keep on speaking but couldn't.

☙❧

He was back in the windowless room. The men with the pens and paper didn't come again.

There were things he couldn't remember, recent things, and those gaps had a strange substance to them. But he did recall climbing down a metal ladder. Edwin already stood at the bottom, waiting impatiently. He worked at a catch on his left wrist and tossed something underhand to Socko. Somebody, probably Edwin himself, had said the word "chronomaton" to him, which he supposed was what the device, cased in copper and faced with crystal, was called. He had studied the thing doggedly for a while. It didn't have hands like a clock, but he deduced that the lighted numbers indicated the passing time. He didn't know why he had this amazing gadget, why no one had taken it back from him. Why would the adventureman just give him such a thing? What had he done for Edwin to deserve it?

Nothing. He had done *nothing* for him.

Socko held onto the wrist machine and watched time passing.

The door of the windowless room was, of course, soundly locked. After quite a while, when something like a numbed panic overcame him and he had to do something, Socko went to work on the heating grate, thinking there must be a duct beyond. But the screws were recessed each into their wells and held the frame tightly, and anyway, he couldn't figure out how to shut off the gas. Finally, he sobbed himself to sleep on the floor, feeling nothing, remembering only confused images and the sensation of leathery fingers moving strangely.

In the morning, two men, a different pair than before, came and put him into a carriage. Socko presumed the so-called Uprisers in the town who he had named — he remembered doing that — had been captured by now. He wondered if his own name had been mentioned during the course of the roundup. He wondered what consequences awaited him. No one said anything to him about a junior corps. He didn't see Edwin or any other adventureman on the field. He didn't want to see them. The fascination was gone. He didn't care anything about sky vessels anymore either, and didn't know why that was.

This conveyance was not one of the armor-plated motorcoaches he and his chums had swizzed last night, but a flimsy motorized thing. Still, the speed amazed him. Just a few years ago he had never seen a wagon that wasn't horse-drawn. Then the lime-os had come — or come *back*, really. And they had brought so many machines, so many products of the new sciences. No one would ever defeat them, he knew, not ever again.

The two men in drab uniforms put him out on the road halfway to town. He had trees on his one side, brambly Kentucky hills on the other. He had the chronomaton strapped awkwardly to his bony wrist. He saw now that a dial on the incredible device also functioned as a compass.

But Socko, alone there on the morning road, had nowhere to go.

FLIGHT OF THE PEGASUS

by Darin Kennedy

WE STAND, THE DOCTOR AND I, below the buckle of his ship at the precipice of Bellerophon Tower. The wind is so powerful, I fear I may be flung into nothingness and rejoin the teeming masses below at a velocity I'd rather not consider. The cycling of the hard steam engines vibrates the entire deck and leaves my teeth shaking in their sockets. So close are we to the heat coming off the ship's dual motor assembly that I've sweated straight through my uniform. The days when the ambient temperature was a concern for me seem a distant memory since the hard steam experiment left me, as Professor Lydon likes to say, "augmented." At the present moment, however, I feel as if I'm swimming inside my long leather duster. Still, the fact that Doctor Bellerophon stands perfectly comfortable, unprotected from the elements in the dead of winter at the highest point in the city exemplifies the power inherent in his vessel.

Or, as he calls it, his magnum opus.

From the street below, the *Pegasus* appeared an enormous barracuda, its gleaming silver mass floating on air currents above the barbed hook of Bellerophon Tower. Now that I am close enough to touch the massive dirigible's rough outer hull, the comparison could not be more apt. The surface of the ship is made up of countless scales, all lined geometrically in an endless repeating pattern in an effort to, as the Doctor explained, maximize speed.

Two words that are music to my ears.

Bellerophon has busied himself for nearly twenty minutes making minute adjustments to the various gears and cogs of one of the rotor assemblies. I'm not certain which impresses me more, this brief look into the workings of the good Doctor's mechanical masterpiece, or the expert way the man manipulates the tools of his trade. It's akin to observing a watchmaker reassemble a timepiece in the midst of a raging cyclone. Still, the day is growing short.

"Doctor Bellerophon, I truly appreciate your allowing me to inspect the ship prior to finalizing our arrangement, but may I ask how much longer we might expect to be up here?"

"Quiet, lad." Flavored with that unplaceable–Eastern European?–accent, his shouts are barely audible above the howling wind and pulsating engines. "I'm close, but I need my ears as much as my eyes for this part of the sequence."

I quietly beg his pardon, though the buffeting winds steal the words from my lips even as they pull the moisture from my eyes. I remember the gift Bellerophon gave me before we entered the steamlift at the skyscraper's base and pull the brushed leather bag from the pocket of my jump pants. Within rests a pair of goggles the likes of which I've never seen before today, the left lens green and the right lens a deep red. He claims they are the height of optical technology. His words echo in my mind.

"You'll never see the world the same way again, lad."

Bellerophon's confidence has worked many wonders today, not the least of which is my very presence atop his building. To say I am not fond of heights is to say that Napoleon was less than successful during his last tour of Russia. Even the strength and resiliency granted me by Professor Lydon's hard steam infusion doesn't help me with this particular anxiety.

I press the goggles over my eyes and pull the leather strap tight around my short-cropped hair even as a rogue wind tears their bag from my grasp. Opening my eyes, I realize Bellerophon understands as well as I the art of understatement. Though the sky remains overcast as the afternoon wanes, I find I can see everything across the city as brightly as if the sun beat down from directly above. Perhaps even more miraculous, somehow the heat and steam coming off the engines don't fog the lenses.

"There." Bellerophon clasps his hands together. "Finished." He slams the panel shut and beckons me to follow him back to the control area within the gondola. The door hisses as it slides open, the sound repeating as the door closes behind us.

I tap one of the dials by the door as the needle within moves from red to black. "Air tight?" I ask as I slide the goggles into my pants' front pocket.

"A necessity. This ship can go to altitude like none other on the planet." He presses a button on the console to his left and a doorway to my rear slides open. "Your coat, Captain Carruthers?"

I slip out of my full-length russet duster, fashioned of the highest quality leather the great Republic of Texas can produce, and hang it in the closet. Bellerophon loses himself in his machine for the third time since we stepped off the tower's steamlift, so I take advantage of the moment to absorb my surroundings. I've shared a meal or two with Edison and visited the home of Nikola Tesla half a dozen times—a shame those two are no longer on speaking terms—but neither of them possesses anything like the feast of technology that Bellerophon now has at his fingertips. Watching the man flit from this gauge to that lever to an apparently unrelated set of switches is like watching a skilled dancer on the stage. His every motion purposeful, there is no doubt in my mind that I am watching a master at work, doing what he does best.

After a few minutes, I interrupt the not quite uncomfortable silence. "So, Doctor, is there anything on this ship you can't control with the flick of a switch?"

"Just one thing, Captain." He strokes his chin as he takes my measure. "Just one." Another button, another sliding panel. "Brandy?"

We retire to a compartment near the rear of the gondola, a space clearly set up to entertain guests. A plush couch covered in purple velvet interlaced with gold thread takes up three quarters of the circular room's circumference. Above our heads, a chandelier made up of hundreds of miniature lamps fills the room with muted light. The wood paneling is mahogany, and unless I miss my guess, the inlaid decorations are crafted from ivory.

"This ship of yours is a marvel, Doctor Bellerophon." I run my fingers along one of the winged horses carved in relief into the dark wood of the wall behind our heads. "How does one afford such extravagance?"

"My mother, even in death, is now and ever will be remembered for her kindness, but in matters of business, no one in history holds a candle to my father. When my parents passed, they left a fortune to their only child, a fortune that I've doubled again and again in the years since. I wish to propel mankind into this next century, and in doing so, have created many a wondrous thing. The many patents I have in place guarantee that my research may continue ad infinitum. Those goggles you wear, for instance. Your military ordered five thousand pairs just last week. Part of Washington's Billion Dollar Congress on which papers worldwide continue to rant." He thumps the side of his glass, the tone clear and true. "I understand Harrison is outfitting your soldiers as best he can, but I can only imagine the backlash if the average American taxpayer knew where their hard-earned money was going."

"These inventions: the goggles, the steamlift, this ship, they all come from your mind?"

"I didn't earn the title of Doctor by working in the mines, Captain."

"And in what field is your doctorate, sir?"

"The products of my qualifications exist all around you." He strokes the large monographed B at the center of the console. "I don't suspect you'd have come aboard if you had any doubts as to my abilities."

"Fair enough, though I must ask one other question. It's nagged at me since I first heard your name."

Bellerophon's lips spread wide in a mischievous grin. "Ask."

"I've taken more than my fair share of courses in the Classics over the years. You named your ship the *Pegasus* and call yourself Bellerophon, yet you bear no resemblance to any Greek I've ever met and your accent is anything but."

He chuckles, looking at me through his bushy gray eyebrows. "You, lad, claim the title of Captain, yet you have no ship. You wear a uniform, yet you have never served in the military. And trust that I scrutinized your background before you set the first foot in my building. Would it surprise you to learn that the Carruthers of Pittsburgh, Pennsylvania you claim as family have apparently never heard of you?" He draws close and whispers in my ear, the scent of whiskey on his breath overpowering at this proximity. "You have your affectations, lad, and I have mine."

"My pardon, sir. I meant no offense. As my employers never cease to remind me, secrets usually exist for a purpose." I glance out the circular window at the clouds rushing by. "Perhaps we should get down to business."

Bellerophon drains his glass and sets it on a ledge above his head. "Very well, Captain. State your proposal."

I finish off my own brandy and set my glass next to his. "I've been sent to arrange, shall we say, transportation to a rather remote location."

Bellerophon lets out a deep hearty laugh. "I had gathered you were going to say something like that. Most come to the tower to avail themselves of our fine dining and other delights. Your area of interest was," he glances around the room, "a bit loftier."

"I've never been chastised for subtlety." I endeavor to remain collected, though my fidgeting fingers find Bellerophon's goggles in my pocket. "Tell me, sir. What do you know of Herr Klaus Behringer?"

For the first time since our initial meeting, any sense of cordiality leaves Bellerophon's voice. "Behringer?" He loosens his tie and unbuttons his starched white shirt. "You mean the man who left me with this?" He pulls open his shirt to reveal an oddity that threatens to take my breath. Not to mention Bellerophon's, in a much more literal sense.

The left side of the Doctor's chest appears normal for the most part, rising and falling with his every breath. The right side, however, is anything but. The "skin" overlying his chest fashioned of some form of translucent membrane, he bears ribs of iron while the "lung" that pumps in his chest appears like the center portion of an accordion. As the strange breathing apparatus expands and contracts in his chest, a cold glare transforms Bellerophon's visage.

"Tell me your wishes, Carruthers," he says. "This just became personal."

"Herr Behringer, late of Berlin, has reportedly moved his base of operations to somewhere on the Yucatan peninsula near the Chichen Itza ruins. Exactly what he plans is unclear, but what is more than clear is that if he succeeds, people will suffer."

"And you plan to stop him."

"You're not the only one who owes Behringer a blood debt." My heart races as Jane's delicate face fills my memory; her skin so pale, the blood coursing from the corner of her mouth as red as the roses she used to prune every spring, her body but one of the hundreds littering the site of the Eiffel Tower explosion.

Bellerophon raises an eyebrow. "It would seem that each of us has lost a part of ourselves to this madman. What would you have me do?"

I produce a letter from the front cargo pocket of my uniform. "The President sends his regards."

Bellerophon studies the paper, then looks up at me confused. "And where is this 'elite unit' Harrison wishes me to convey to the other end of the world?"

I study the floor for a moment, then meet Bellerophon's gaze. "You're looking at him."

"You?"

"Me."

"Fascinating. One man alone against the Butcher of Berlin?"

"Fear not for my safety, Doctor. I am far more than I appear."

Bellerophon's studying gaze fades into a whimsical smile. "Then we have more in common than even I suspected." He pours himself another brandy. "Does your Commander in Chief have a proposed timetable for this expedition?"

"As soon as possible. Our intelligence is limited at best, and every passing day is an opportunity for Behringer to escape our net. Can you assemble your crew by morning? As the letter states, you will be more than well compensated."

"My crew?" Again, Bellerophon laughs. "Your intelligence is indeed limited."

We return to the control room. He presses another button and a hatch in the ceiling opens, revealing a spiral staircase that descends from above to meet the floor between us. Bellerophon takes the first couple of stairs. "Shall we?"

I follow him up into the belly of the metal sky whale. "Even the smallest of dirigibles requires a crew, Doctor. You have indeed created a technological marvel here, but without men, how can you possibly—"

The words catch in my throat as the reason behind Bellerophon's mischievous grin becomes apparent. Between the two nearest aircells and atop a pipe that no doubt conveys the hard steam from one end of the ship to the other comes a strange form. The metal torso branches into three articulated arms and supports a triangular head, the single lens at its center resembling an enormous glass eye. On each side of the head, curved rods tap against metal plates in a strange rhythmic pattern. One side, then the other, back and forth, again and again. I focus for a moment and realize why the taps sound so familiar.

"Yes, Captain Carruthers. It's Morse code. To run such an advanced ship, my crew must be synchronized beyond the capabilities of mere men. Therefore, I created something better. Sixty of these three-armed automatons circulate through my ship, obeying my every command, a crew of loyal, infallible, indefatigable metal servants. I ask you, who better to service my *Pegasus* of steel than three score steel satyrs?"

I run my fingers across the "face" of the satyr, the metal smooth as satin and warm. Strangest of all, I would all but swear the thing shuddered at my touch.

"What have you created here, Doctor? It's almost as if these things are alive."

"Not alive, per se, but they do think."

"Think?"

"More or less. They are designed with an intricate mechanism of magnets and electrical condensers that allow them to obey simple commands. Each one performs only its particular assigned task, but as a unified whole, they allow me to control this ship from the comfort of the bridge. In fact, once I've decided upon a course, the satyrs take over. It's quite an efficient mode of travel, I assure you."

"And they're under your control?"

"Observe." Bellerophon raises a panel on the rail where a curved rod similar to the satyrs' horns is hidden. He taps out a quick message in Morse, I believe the letters R-T-R-T, and the metal dwarf on wheels moves back into the bowels of the ship.

"They present themselves at my whim, retreat when I wish them gone, and make flying this ship as simple as the manipulation of a few buttons and dials."

"Fascinating, though a wise man told me once about the folly of putting too much trust in the wonders of technology."

"Wise," Bellerophon cracks, "or fearful?" He closes the panel and turns to face me, a mad gleam in his eye. "This is the future, Carruthers. Our future. We can embrace it, or we can be left behind. The world will not care."

Bellerophon and I descend the spiral staircase and reconvene in the gondola control room. A quick glance at the panels reveals one large area with sixty well-demarcated control buttons. Mapped out on a scale drawing of the airship, it becomes quickly apparent how Bellerophon is able to fly the ship from the relative comfort of this space. Every role usually performed by a human crewmember has been filled by one of the satyrs. Most of the tasks even have a built-in redundancy of effort, making the flying of this ship practically foolproof.

"How long did this marvel take to assemble?" I ask. "Your ship and its many metal denizens seem quite the miracle."

"It is the work of a lifetime, Captain." With a wry smile, he gestures to the controls. "Would you care to earn your title and take the *Pegasus* out for a short expedition?"

"I'm not certain I'm qualified to —"

"Nonsense." Bellerophon manipulates a complex series of buttons, switches and levers. The floor beneath me shifts slightly and a quick glance out the window reveals we have disengaged from the docking station and are floating up and away from the Tower. The good Doctor steps away from the wheel. "Now, take the controls."

I hesitate for a moment, then brush my fingers along the smooth wood of the wheel, the only thing in the entire control room that seems old and familiar. No sooner do I touch the controls, however, than a metallic clang sounds from starboard and the ship lists to one side.

"What did I do?" I curse the hint of fear in my voice.

"Nothing." His eyes filled with alarm, Bellerophon grabs a handle in the ceiling above his head. "I have yet to engage the controls."

I cling to the wheel's smooth mahogany, the previously level gondola off at least ten degrees, and do my best to remain on my feet. Without warning the ship lists even further as the sound of rending metal fills the air.

"We're under attack," Bellerophon shouts, his wide-eyed gaze focused across my shoulder. "Do you see it?"

"Do I see what?" A quick glance back reveals the answer to my question.

Outside the control room's starboard window, which is suddenly below me, I see what appears to be an enormous metal creature, or at least a part of such a monster. Protruding from either side of a metallic oval, a pair of pincer-like legs moves with clock-like accuracy. I crane my neck to peer out the next window and see more of the thing. Its many-sectioned tail encircles the tip of Bellerophon's tower, like the rear third of some impossibly huge steel centipede. Unless I miss my guess, that means the thing's monstrous head lies imbedded in the side of Bellerophon's ship.

A ship that currently floats a hundred stories above a crowded city street.

I wrap my arm through the wheel. "What in God's name is that thing?"

"Behringer." Bellerophon glares at me. "Who besides your immediate superiors knew you were meeting me today?"

"No one. I received my orders from the President himself and came alone."

His eyes flash with anger. "It would appear that is not the case, Captain."

The ship lists again as a pair of metallic mandibles pierce the starboard wall, the two barbed tips folding together and apart like a child cutting paper with scissors. Bellerophon does his best to hold on, but as the weight of his metallic parts gets the better of him, he begins to slide toward the metal monster. I shoot my hand out as he falls past me and catch his wrist a split second before he falls out of reach and into the waiting maw of the steel centipede.

"I've got you." Though the strength granted me by the hard steam experiment allows me to hold on to Bellerophon, I can't help but notice he easily has the heft of three large men.

"That equipment in your chest weighs a ton," I manage to grunt.

"And yet you hold me aloft with one arm." He brings his other hand around to clasp my wrist. "There truly is more to you than meets the eye."

"We can discuss that later if we make it through this." I glance back at the opening to the gondola's entertainment room. "Can you get that door open?"

He shoots out a foot, flips a switch, and the door slides open. Before he can utter a word, I use every ounce of strength in my arm to hurl him toward the open doorway. Gravity does the rest. As the door closes with a click, I turn my full attention on the metal monster that stands poised to rip me, Bellerophon and the *Pegasus* from the sky.

Like a worm invading a hollowed out apple, its head is now halfway through the fuselage, its slashing jaws ripping through the wall even as it moves in fits and spurts for the very spot where I stand.

"Fine. You want me, you metal horror, you've got me." Releasing the wheel, I launch myself at the head of the centipede. As I suspected, the thing is a simple automaton and doesn't respond to my approach. I feel the hard steam coarse through my arteries as I dodge the thing's scissor teeth and land a blow with my boot to the top of its head. Far more successful than I intended, the strike dislodges the centipede's head and a moment later, we're both outside the ship.

I fall through open air, hands grasping at nothing as they seek anything that might stop my fall. The giant mechanical centipede encircling the tip of Bellerophon's tower brings my earlier metaphor of tower as hook and airship as fish full circle, though I ponder momentarily if at any time in history before today the worm has been the one to draw first blood.

With nothing but a hundred stories of open space between me and what is sure to be a most gruesome death, I am saved by a miracle.

If being impaled counts as being saved.

As if in anger at being thwarted in its quest to bring down the *Pegasus*, the centipede arches its long segmented back, and one of its hundred flailing arms pierces my left shoulder. Fixed somewhere between my collarbone and ribcage, the fully articulated limb continues to flex and extend, its hinged joint mere inches from my lung. The pain is like ice and hot coal at once, and it takes every ounce of self-control in me not to scream out in agony. I grip the thing's arm in my right hand and with all the strength I can muster pull myself off the still-moving leg. The searing pain almost renders me unconscious.

With my left arm hanging like meat at my side, I hoist myself up and wrap my legs around the centipede's metal carapace.

"Heal, dammit. Heal." I scream at the wound in my shoulder, as if the steam-powered cells making up my body can hear. My mind flashes back to my first encounter with the steam. How the scorching gas nearly flayed the skin from my bones. How everyone else that participated in the experiment died on the spot. How I nearly perished from my wounds.

How for weeks I wish I had.

The centipede achieves a new equilibrium and makes another go at the . From my current vantage hanging from one of its rear legs, all I can do is watch. The warmth and tingling I feel when my tissue knits begins in earnest, but I'm afraid it may be too late to save the *Pegasus*. Or Bellerophon. Or me, for that matter.

Then, it comes to me, the simple realization that the creature trying to kill me is actually my salvation, whether it likes it or not. As my father used to say, "one man's trash is another man's treasure," or in this instance: one man's metal worm with a hundred arms is another man's metal ladder with a hundred rungs.

After my dead left arm leads to a couple of close calls, I discover a one-armed method that allows me to climb what must be the most flexible ladder in existence. Fortunately, the centipede has become relatively still, its head again buried in the side of Bellerophon's ship. Within minutes, I arrive at the segment directly behind the head.

I peer down between the two armored segments and note the various gears and cables running the thing. Muttering a quick prayer, I dive my hand into the breach. My fingers find the teeth of one of the gears and I bring all the strength in my good arm to bear against the turning axle. The smell of searing flesh fills the air as the friction burns away the skin of my hand and fingers. Without warning, the centipede rips itself from the side of the ship and rears its head and mandibles back in what would appear to any observer a concerted effort to rip me in half. If I didn't know better, I'd swear the thing was alive and that I just grabbed its spinal cord, though it's far more likely a failsafe to prevent tampering.

Whoever designed this thing is a genius.

"Hold on, Carruthers!" Through the hole in the side of the ship, Bellerophon shouts at me. He holds a wired metallic cone to his mouth that somehow amplifies his voice. "I'll throw you down a rope." He disappears briefly as I continue to dodge the centipede's flailing head and slashing mandibles, then reappears with a coil of rope in his hands. "Catch!"

A knotted cable with a weighted end falls from the gaping hole in the ship and immediately begins to whip back and forth in the wind above the tower. Between the thrashing of the rope and the many-sectioned bronco still bucking beneath me, my odds of survival shrink with every second. Even with my enhanced strength, my uninjured arm can only withstand so much. With each flail of the centipede's length, I feel my fingers give a little. Then, just as I'm about to accept my fate and let go, the centipede freezes in mid-air. Unclear how long that will last, I wrap my legs around the thing's carapace once more and stretch out my hand. The cold rope hits my palm and with all the strength I have remaining, I grab on and don't let go though the fibers running through my hand further tear the flesh from my fingers.

"Got it," I shout. "Now, pull me up before—" I cut off mid-sentence, as I notice Bellerophon's gaze trained on something or someone directly behind me.

"Why thank you, Captain. I feared I would have to obtain the rope myself." This new voice sounds simultaneously muffled and amplified. The German accent, however, is unmistakable.

I jerk my head around to find a tall form standing on the centipede's third segment. The automaton has rigidified into a crude spiral staircase, no doubt in deference to its dark-clad master. Suited head to toe in black, this new player in the game is masked, the smoked oval lenses betraying nothing about the face behind the facade. A heavy suede coat trails to just past his knees, barely concealing the sword at his side, and meets the top of a pair of cuffed boots whose leather is only outshone by the silver buckles at each ankle.

"Behringer," I grunt through gritted teeth. A cold realization chills me far more than the gusting winds that threaten to send me into oblivion. "I should have known it would be you."

He lets out a deep chuckle. "Both strong and insightful, Captain. No wonder the President chose you to represent him today. Not that either will do you much good."

"What do you want?"

"The same as you, Carruthers." He draws a black rapier from the scabbard at his side. "We both seek the *Pegasus*, though while you had hoped Bellerophon's creation might allow you to finally exact what you must see as long overdue revenge, I merely wish to deprive you and the good Doctor of this technological marvel and return home in the fastest airship on the planet."

"Not happening." I do my best to keep any emotion from my face, though I'm baffled at how he knows who I am, and even more at how he somehow knows I have a personal stake in all of this. "You'll have to go through me to get this ship."

"As you wish." Behringer clicks a button on his sword's hilt. "Say hello to your lady love for me, will you?"

A spark of electricity arcs from the rapier's tip to the centipede's body, sending a shock up my arm and through my chest. My fingers ignore my internal pleas and release the rope which Behringer quickly grasps with his free hand. I begin to slide and only a reflexive grab with my good hand onto one of the centipede's legs keeps me from falling.

"You won't get far, you madman." I try to stall as feeling continues to return to my left arm. "Only Bellerophon can fly this thing, and he may be the only person on the planet who hates you as much as I do."

"He's right," Bellerophon shouts. "I'd die before taking you so much as across the street."

Again, Behringer laughs. "Oh, my dear Doctor, I believe you'll be more than happy to take me wherever I would like to go." He points the tip of his rapier at Bellerophon. "That is, if you value your daughter's continued breathing."

"Bellerophon has no daughter." At least none I was briefed on. I crane my neck around to peer up into the Doctor's face and whatever bravery was there previously has been replaced with abject terror. It would seem my intelligence may again be a bit flawed.

"What have you done to Ariadne?" Bellerophon screams.

"Nothing as yet." Behringer ties the rope to one of the centipede's legs, then pulls a small device from a pocket of his waistcoat and flips it open like a wallet. "However, a simple flick of this switch and the man I have had watching her will, shall we say, stop merely watching."

I expect Bellerophon to blanche further, but instead he rallies. "Your man should be careful, Behringer. My daughter, like me, is far more than she appears."

"Noble posturing, old man." Behringer leaps across me onto the head of the centipede, then scales the knotted rope like a trained circus performer and steps past the Doctor into the ravaged gondola. "But you and I both know there's one thing you never gamble on, and that's your family." He draws close to Bellerophon, his whispered voice amplified by the Doctor's device. "Or whatever's left of it."

"We can protect her, Bellerophon." I raise my left arm as best I can, my fingers trembling as I gesture in Behringer's direction. "Don't listen to this lunatic."

"Ah, Captain Carruthers, what to do with you?" I imagine a wicked smile behind Behringer's mask. "I did rather enjoy watching you fight my metal monstrosity. Perhaps you've earned a break from all this action." He slides his rapier back into its scabbard and pulls yet another object from his coat, this one resembling a pistol grip with multiple triggers. "Enjoy the next three minutes."

He squeezes the largest trigger and the centipede becomes flaccid beneath me. A screeching sound fills the air as the automaton's tail dislodges from the top of the tower and before I can pull another breath, the steel monstrosity falls, taking me with it.

Perhaps, after everything, my earlier prediction about an encounter with the teeming masses below wasn't that far off the mark.

The windows of Bellerophon Tower fly past, each faster than the one before. I hold on with my one good arm, though I feel the tissue in my left shoulder growing warmer by the second. The steam is healing me, but I'm afraid it's too little, too late.

We're halfway to the street below before I regain the use of my left arm. Though I no longer have to wrestle with the metal monster, I may as well be holding onto a dead locomotive.

Except, train engines don't bend.

With what little strength that has returned to my healing left arm, I pull Bellerophon's goggles from the pouch at my belt and slide them onto my face. Everything lights up as if it were mid-summer, allowing me to scan the architecture for anything that might save me. Within seconds, I spy what it is I'm looking for.

Gargoyles. One at each corner of the building. A few stories above the crowded streets below and coming up fast.

I release the death grip on the carapace of the thing's second section and push off, allowing myself to slide to the tail of the beast. Knowing I'll only have one shot at saving myself, I wait until the last possible moment and with the last vestiges of muscle in my good right arm, I jerk the tail section of the centipede upwards. Like a bullwhip, the centipede straightens for a moment, and its head and mandible jam between the gargoyle's pedestal and the corner of the building. At the other end of the makeshift whip and still under gravity's influence, I hurtle past the leering stone creature. Gripping the final segment of the centipede with every ounce of strength the steam allows, I squeeze my eyes closed and brace for collision. My body comes to an abrupt stop and a swath of pain rips across my chest as my arm threatens to come away from my shoulder. In the end, however, that final impact, that horrible moment of pain followed by the sweetest of releases, doesn't come.

A part of me bigger than I'd like to admit is disappointed.

I open my eyes to find my feet no more than inches above the cobblestone sidewalk. I release the steel edge of the centipede's tail and fall to the ground. My arm feels as if it's been ripped from its socket, but my fingers still number ten and somehow I'm still breathing.

I glance up in time to see Bellerophon's ship disappear behind the skyline to the east. I take some cold comfort in the fact that Behringer must believe me dead, but it doesn't change the fact that with the *Pegasus* gone, I have no way of getting at him without forging my way through the brutal Mayaztec Republic or braving the swarm of pirates that patrol the Yucatan Gulf. Back to Square One, I suppose, a place with which I am intimately familiar.

"Hey, Mister." A little girl breaks away from her mother and bravely runs to my side. "Are you okay?"

"Not yet." I use my still-healing left arm to push myself up off the ground, as it's now my right that hangs like so much dead weight, and stagger to a stand. I can already feel the bones and tendons on that side starting to knit, but it's going to be a long, painful day. "But I will be."

"How did you do it?" She points up at the side of the skyscraper where the remains of the centipede hang like some enormous metal carcass. "How did you survive? How did you beat that … that monster?"

"The steam, punkin'." I take the girl's hand and return her to her mother. "It's the steam."

GRINDSTONE

by Jay Lake

BLOOD ALWAYS RUSTS the springs in my hand. Other people's blood, to be specific.

It's cold up here on the fly deck where I am cleaning my weapons. There is nothing around us but empty sky, stretching to the horizons and beyond. The good airship *Entwhistle* is two days and more from the nearest friendly port given our current heading and the nature of the winds in this airband. I can hear her engines straining slightly. They are running under just enough load to give them a workout without redlining. Which is good, because the rest of this vessel is about to fall through the sky, carrying us all with it.

At least we beat those rat bastards off.

This time.

Laying down the last of my blades, I begin cleaning my right hand with my left. It is fastidious, demanding work. My Maker would have been proud of my diligence. His apprentices would have been appalled. "Don't make so much work for us, Jakesia," they used to whine.

I stare past the rail a moment, tempted by memory and old pain until my eyes lose their focus against distant, empurpled clouds.

Shadow is returning. No matter how many rat bastards we fight, there will always be more.

Meat breeds. That's what we Tocks always said, when we were just whispering intelligences, unsighted and benchbound

240

in the earliest days of our creation. Meat breeds. And it always breeds faster than Tocks build.

My hand is sticky and stiff. Carefully I pick flecks of cruft out, that were some rat bastard's heartsblood not so long ago, and try not to think too hard about the breeding of Meat. I try even harder not to think about the fact that I am now in command.

Cʒ�

The shipyards that birth our aerial vessels are as shrouded in secrecy as our very origins themselves. Ask anyone where the airships are built, and you will receive a vague wave and the answer "somewhere spinward." But have you ever met someone who travelled far enough to the spinward to find the answer first hand? I certainly have not.

The airships simply migrate antispinward, being handed from captain to captain through the vagaries of succession, trade or piracy. Perhaps they gather in secret conclaves to re-create themselves in a new generation of similars, much as Tocks are said to do. Or perhaps the airships have always been here, before either Meat or Tock came to these skies.

Who can say?

– Skyborne University Inquisitor C.S. Cole, *Lectures*, vol. 3

CʒʙꙄ

Palacio Sarita bat Mardia, Skymistress of the Lesser Port of Grand Reserve, watched the airship *Entwhistle* beat across the wind into the eastern slips. She stood on the observation deck of the Eastmost Tower, clad in the wool-padded leather of any common dockhand. The formal robes of office with their cerise banding and lacework fringes were too damned prissy for real work. Plus they picked up grease like nobody's business.

If there was anything Lesser Grand Reserve had, it was grease. In copious amounts. At least up to now. Without grease, they would have been nothing but a bunch of starving people on a too-small island in the sky.

The scent of the pits was as always omnipresent. So far as Sarita knew, there was nowhere on Lesser Grand Reserve where one could escape from that odor. Tall as she was—well over six feet, unusual for a woman of this or any era—in her time of service, even she had crammed and folded herself into all but the smallest passages and bilges all through the island's keel and decks and towers.

A Skymistress was expected to know her domain. While the endless kingdoms of the air were beyond any woman's knowledge, her home was as familiar to her as a hutch to a rabbit.

Her tools lay beside her, racked and fastened as proper in their filigreed brass and balsawood case. Sarita brushed her fingers over them in their familiar order. Telescope, range finder, electrical divinatory, telelocutor, flare pistol and shock prod. See, signal and shoot.

Of course they were old, as all the best equipment was. Of course they were worn, as all the most properly used equipment was. Of course they were slightly slick with the ambient grease of Lesser Grand Reserve.

She wondered what would become of them. Likely there would never be another Skymistress of the Lesser Port of Grand Reserve.

Panjit, her chief acolyte, snapped his own telescope shut with a crisp movement that telegraphed bored mirth. As always, he struck a pose. No leathers for him. No, Panjit favored the full regalia, identical to her own neglected cerise robes except for the azure dye and shorter fringework. He was not shy about remarking on how well cerise would favor his magnificent dark complexion and patrician nose.

Not in this lifetime, she thought. *Or at least, not in my lifetime.*

But what was a Skymistress without a port?

"You watch, they'll clip the number three east boom on the way in." He sounded remarkably satisfied for a man predicting a minor disaster. "That'll bring a good levy."

"The state of her gasbag and rigging says otherwise," observed Sarita mildly. "No matter how great the fine, we cannot wring payment out of someone who's already wallowing in penury."

"You underestimate the value of salvage, Skymistress." Panjit's tone was so smooth and self-assured that she wanted to slap the words from his face.

Sarita didn't bother anymore to ask herself why she was stuck with this dreadful little climber for a chief acolyte. Everyone of worth and potential had emigrated over the past two years. Once the state of the grease pits had become general knowledge, anyone with sense had been able to see which way the wind was blowing on Lesser Grand Reserve.

Due wrong, in two simple words. The wind was blowing due wrong.

The problem with basing your entire economy and raison d'être on a constrained resource was that eventually you ran out of the resource in question. Decisions which had seemed canny two centuries ago during the bright days of the port's founding and initial construction were now foolhardy in the blindingly obvious light of hindsight.

For the past thirty years, they'd actually been *burning* the grease to make electrical energy. On ascending to the post of Skymistress, she'd put a stop to that, and nearly lost control of Lesser Grand Reserve's governance in the ensuing spat. Now the few Master Mercers yet remaining in port quietly praised her foresight in doing so, and even more quietly grumbled that she hadn't seen through the problem sooner.

Logic was not an essential element in politics, Sarita had long ago learned to her displeasure.

"Panjit," she said, her voice filled with the regal snap of authority. Not to mention the cold edge of the air on the Eastmost Tower. "Take yourself down to the east slips and present my compliments to *Entwhistle's* captain. Dinner in my apartments, should they be so inclined."

"We would be better showing them the back of our hand than our open palm," grumbled the acolyte.

Sarita stroked her shock prod fondly, not trying very hard to keep her impulses from her face. "Are we so rich in visitors these days that we can afford to turn anyone away?"

"No, Skymistress." Without making the proper obeisances, he turned on his heel and strode away.

Little bastard never had believed in the grease crisis, she knew. Panjit still thought it overblown, still believed that if you bullied and bribed the surveyors enough, they'd come back with better estimates of the depth and grade of what remained embedded within the caverns hidden at the heart of Lesser Grand Reserve.

Sarita watched the airship a while longer, pleased to see that *Entwhistle* beat past the number three east boom without incident. She finally went below herself to review once more the remorseless reports that charted the death of her city in the sky.

Cখ∞

One for wood and one for oil
One for sheep and one for soil
Wheat and barley, water and rye
Everything grows here in the sky

— Children's rhyme

CЗ8Ɔ

Having arranged the good airship *Entwhistle* to be tied up to the waiting slip and boom-braced until her gasbag is no longer under load, I am now reduced to watching the local Meat whine and caper alongside our battered hull.

The Lesser Port of Grand Reserve is a friendly port, her slips and galleries open to us, but that does not make her welcoming. It simply means that in the war of Shadow, she does not shelter those who hunt us across the endless sea of skies.

Meat does not hate Tock here, except in the vague way that all Meat fears and despises Tock. It is something in their monkey flesh, buried deep beneath Meat's quick, erratic mind, that leads them to such animosity.

I no longer care. My hand rusts, my captain is lost, and my ship is wounded. Any of those things would distress me. All of them together overwhelm.

"You," says the most important Meat on the slipside. I know he is important Meat because he is dressed like a fool and doing no work.

I meet his eyes, my own glittering stare encompassing the liquid brown of the man's gaze. He needs no response from me, he knows he has my attention.

"Where is Captain Armature?" the Meat continues.

"Falling," I answer. I am laconic truth, and find the depths of my despair yawning below me like the bottomless sky.

This imperious Meat blinks a moment, thrown off whatever script he has prepared. "An air sailor's death, to be sure. Then who commands here?"

Fool, I think. *Tock do not die. We are stopped.* Meanwhile, three of my deckhands drift close. Two bear blades loosely sheathed, the third carries a long iron lever bar. The Meat grows impatient.

GRINDSTONE

"Jakesia," I finally say. Swift grins chase one another across the faces of my crew.

Anger flashes in the Meat's eyes. This one is important, unaccustomed to a lack of cooperation in others. "Summon him."

"*She* is here." I rise and bow, the bad servomechanism in my left hip whining briefly in counterpoint to my indifferent dignity.

Three of the port's dockhands bring over a water line, hup-huping in time as they coordinate with my own deckhands. Our credit is good enough here for a resupply without advance guarantees. I am certain we will not be treated this well again.

The important Meat turns and walks away. In showing me his unprotected back he is telling me how insignificant I am to him. This is fine with me. He is not a rat bastard intent on claiming my life, nor is he a minion of Shadow. Therefore he is insignificant to me as well.

CB&ECO

When fades the light, comes the night
And brings the realm of ghosts and Shadow
When fades the day, good men stray
Into the night of ghosts and Shadow
When fades our world, flags are furled
All are ghosts in the realm of Shadow

–Traditional dockhand ballad, attested on multiple islands

CB&ECO

Skymistress Palacio Sarita bat Mardia strode down a deserted hallway. Pale patches on the wall betrayed the long tenancy of portraits recently removed. Dust, flecks of paper, scraps of cloth and grit were scattered across the polished floor. She could remember when this had been a busy thoroughfare. Now it was as deserted as any dockside lane when the airships were away.

She took a deep breath and allowed the smells of this place to settle into her nose. Grease, of course. Everywhere the grease. If there was one benefit to the not-so-slow death of the Lesser Port of Grand Reserve, it was that she might someday soon escape the perpetual reek of grease.

Beyond grease, there was the faint, murky scent of mold. As if water had gotten into some nearby carpets. Sweat, too, of dockhands working hard to shift loads while there were still decks to shift them to. Someone's old cook fire, rancid oil and burnt beans. But mostly the dusty, silent reek of emptiness.

Already well over half of Lesser Grand Reserve's population had departed. Most of the early migrants were from the monied classes. People with the funds or education or skills to easily find passage aboard some airship or another with reasonable expectation of new employment at their next port. Or possibly the port after that one.

Those who remained were the poor, the stubborn and the terminally optimistic. Along with a few operators like Panjit who saw, or thought they saw, ways to profit from the collapse of a once-proud port.

The last major port failure had occurred when the springs on Flymonkey Island had dried up unexpectedly. Within a handful of months the city there had been reduced to empty ruins. Not even pirates could harbor there in later days.

Sarita had been a girl then, well into her own apprenticeship at Port Lamassu. The collapse of Flymonkey Free Port had been a subject of speculation and rumor for months.

The Lesser Port of Grand Reserve was a much more important place that Flymonkey Free Port had ever. But she both hoped and feared its fall would be less remarked upon.

Someone—or something—had been hunting airships out in the airbands, pulling the stricken vessels to their deaths among the clouds. The disruption to communication, trade and migration was impossible to ignore.

Shadow was coming, the laborers whispered in their dormitories and refectories, but Sarita placed little faith in such rumors. The fears of small people everywhere could speak louder than any voice, and with less reason. Legends were just that: legendary.

If not Shadow, though, it was something. New and aggressive pirates. An invasion from distant airbands. *Something*.

And in the midst of it all, her city was dying.

The Skymistress passed quickly through a cleaner hallway and into the elegant dining room where affairs of state were often conducted, and even occasionally settled. The table awaited. Oil cups and troughs were set on one side for Tock, plates under domes on the other side for Meat.

It was set for three, she noted sourly. She would not escape Panjit this evening.

☜❉

"Of course this is not our original home. How could it be? Were the bones of our first fathers and mothers made the air? Why do we have words for 'dog' and 'horse', and even paintings of them, when no one in recorded history has ever seen such fabulous creatures?

"The question isn't where we came from. Somewhere else, obviously. The question is, where are we going?"

– Binyan the Wanderer, Sermon at Port Ruin

☜❉

I sit in a gilded room with two Meat. We are surrounded by statues of heroes of yore, and a carpet thick enough to bury corpses in encloses our feet. History and art and money reek about me. Amid their glory, I ignore the Meat blood still crusted in the joints of my right hand. They dine in the fashion of their kind. Steaming food is clutched in their soft, clever fingers and shoveled into their pursed, damp maws. I try to imagine what it would be like to have teeth. Excrescences of bone within one's jaws. Brittle, fragile, hard and sharp.

Much like Meat themselves.

The important Meat who met me at the dock ignores me. He pretends attention and respect to the woman he sits with. Even I, a simple Tock, can see she has no use for him. She does not bother to hide her corresponding lack of respect.

She I must focus on. She is the Skymistress. It was her order that permitted *Entwhistle* to dock at the Lesser Port of Grand Reserve. It is her forbearance that permits us to take on supplies even now in advance of our letters of credit and our limited funds.

The Skymistress has a name, but Meat always has names. They never seem to last long enough to earn them. Still, I attend to her. She is at least polite to me. The Skymistress meets my eye, when she is not looking at her glistening, crumbling food. She listens to my mumbled words. She seems interested.

Too interested, perhaps.

Finally she places her little stabbing fork down at the left side of her plate and her dull knife down at the right. "Captain Jakesia," the Meat says in that clear, strong tone of voice Meat always uses to announce something unpleasant. "I must ask a difficult question. In the interests of my island."

"Ask." I am not long on courtesy, but then I am not long on much of anything these days.

"What became of Captain Armature? Who did such terrible damage to your ship?"

"*Entwhistle* is airworthy," I say almost automatically. A sky court might find differently, especially if I were ever heard to express fears contrary to that basic sentiment.

"I do not seek to … challenge … you." She leans forward, her hypertrophied chest glands straining against the curdled red of her robes. "We live in a time of adversity. Especially here on Lesser Grand Reserve." That earns the Skymistress a hard look from her Meat companion, the important one that I have already come to dislike in a most collegial manner. I grudgingly admire the way she simply ignores his hostility.

"We were attacked," I say. Truthful but unhelpful. That is usually best with important Meat.

"Stupid Tock." The other Meat's impatience practically spills across the table. "Her language facilitator is on the blink."

I meet his eye and hold him with my gaze. I am Tock, I do not need to blink. In time, he does. "There is nothing wrong with my language facilitator, you ignorant dolt. I am merely parsimonious with my words."

"Attacked by who, then?"

"Whom," I correct him. "Attacked by *whom*."

The Skymistress bursts into noise that after a moment I recall is Meat laughter. It has been a long time, and very little is amusing to me anymore. "Panjit," she says with a bright smile, laying one hand upon his arm, "you will not best this one."

I trace my fingertips in the remaining pool of my machine oil, a lovely 000 light vegetable base. "No, leave that to the rat bastards. They bested us all too well."

She leans close again, pressing her glands against the table edge so that the other Meat's eyes slide sideways despite his hostile focus to me. "Who are the rat bastards?"

Now there is a question. I take another long hard look at her assistant Meat. He is a dangerous fool, but the Skymistress holds the lines of power here. Also, I have little left to lose. Armature is dead, *Entwhistle* is stricken.

"The rat bastards are servants of Shadow," I say. "They sail in small ships, some of them just wings without gasbags. They live hard and close to the wind. They come from the east and antispinward. They attack ships far out in the airbands, or traveling within the clouds. I have never heard of one attacking an island or a port or a city."

That is the longest string of words I have spoken since before Armature went over the rail with three rat bastard lances in his chestplate.

"They prey on trade," the Skymistress says in a thoughtful voice.

"Your trade is gone anyway," I observe. "Your slips are idle, and most lie long unused."

Unexpectedly, the other Meat speaks. "Too many believe our grease mine has failed."

I know a state secret when I hear one. "Your port is dying," I tell them. "My airship is dying. Will you repair me?"

"Will you bring back our trade," snarls the other Meat. The Skymistress stares him to silence before returning her attention to me.

"I thank you for the information." Her voice is grave. "Our crews are diminished, but we can still provide repair parties and supplies."

Grudging honesty forces answering words from me. "Payment may be slow."

She spreads her hands. "Where would we cash your credit draft?"

That provokes a chuff of steam and a wheeze from me. Laughter, indeed.

Disgusted, the other Meat rises from the table and leaves

with great ceremony. His exit is clearly intended to provoke us, or possibly make a point.

"Your life would be improved by killing him," I tell her.

"Unfortunately, he is the best of those remaining to me." She sighs and sags a bit in her chair. Becomes more human, more like me, in that moment. "Will they come in time, these rat bastards?"

I opt for the truth. "Come the Shadow, comes the rat bastards. In the darkness, they will shit in your halls and shatter your windows and howl from the tops of your towers."

"Shadow is just a rumor." Her voice is uncertain.

"Shadow is the end of all things. They are just its servants and heralds."

She watches me a little while. Then: "You are very angry."

I shrug. Human is as human does. "No one craves their ending. Meat ages and dies. Tock can fail without proper maintenance or too far from fuel and grease. But Shadow? Shadow is the failing of the entire world, the dying of the light."

The Skymistress is aghast. "How do you know?"

"Because of the coming of the rat bastards. This has all happened before. It will all happen again."

"How do you know *that*?"

I tell her my deepest secret, one that runs back to my Maker and my very making. "Because I remember the last time."

Her voice drops to almost nothing. "How old are you?"

"Older than the light itself."

With that I rise and begin my walk back to *Entwhistle*. It won't matter soon. The Lesser Port of Grand Reserve is dying, as surely as the light is dying. As surely as I am going to fail.

If Tock could cry, I would weep.

☙❧

Meat and Tock
Hand and clock
Rise and walk
Meat and Tock

Tock and Meat
See and greet
Have a treat
Tock and Meat

– Children's rhyme

ᮞᮞ

Skymistress Sarita returned to the observation deck of the Eastmost Tower, trailed by two silent servitors. The best of her household were gone. A few more departed with every one of the increasingly infrequent sailings.

Soon, the Lesser Port of Grand Reserve would have too few people to maintain the docks and keep the island's businesses running and supplies moving. The grease mines wouldn't matter then. They people would continue to shelter a while – there were still springs, and granaries, and orchards – but without grease, and money, there was no trade. Without trade, there were no new supplies.

As she'd promised, repair crews were about *Entwhistle*. In truth, the dock masters were glad enough of the work. It was something to do. The airship was listing slightly in her slip even as men and women swarmed over the rigging and along the decks. Hoses snaked from the gasbag to pumps brought out on trolleys.

A cold wind picked at her hair and made her eyes water. It blew from antispinward. She thought hard on Jakesia's words about the rat bastards and the coming of Shadow.

The actual darkness might be a nursery tale to frighten children, but surely Lesser Grand Reserve was falling into its own Shadow.

Metaphor or not, the Shadow was real.

"What if I just boarded the ship and sailed away with them?" she asked the wind.

Meat and Tock usually did not mix in crews. The demands of everything from watchstanding to what was required of each sailor were too different. Tock did not sleep, and were hideously strong by the standards of ordinary men. They could sail with half the complement of a Meat ship.

But any ship would take passengers for the right fee, under the right circumstances. Any ship would take *them* on.

"Alfons," Sarita said aloud.

Her servitor stepped forward. "Skymistress?"

"How many persons remain on this island?"

"A moment, please." He retreated indoors, searching for records.

Her old steward would have simply known.

She watched *Entwhistle* and listened to the wind a while. Eventually Alfons came back. Bald, stooped, one eye drooping, he was at least sharp of mind. "One thousand and one hundred natural persons, Skymistress, and six hundred and forty made persons. That is the current estimate."

"Of which we could put perhaps forty aboard *Entwhistle*," she said. "It will take fifty more like her to carry everyone away." And long before that the great steam engines and electrical generators and water pumps that maintained life on the island would fail for reduced maintenance and lack of tenders. Were fifty more airships ever going to call at the Lesser Port of Grand Reserve?

"They are unlikely to pay for the services we provide," Alfons said lugubriously. "You may as well demand forty passages as compensation."

Something in his voice caught her attention. "Would you go?"

"No, Skymistress." He protested loyalty, but she knew he did not mean it.

Nobody did. What was there to be loyal to? The city was dying. And Shadow was coming.

Sarita wondered what had become of her loyalty. Evaporated under Panjit's ambitious glare and the burgeoning decay of the port city in her charge. Nothing remained but old habit, it seemed.

She watched the horizons of air eastward and antispinward a while, looking for the swirling dots of a flight of rat bastards, or some other harbinger of Shadow. All Sarita saw were storm clouds trading lightning in the distance. All she heard was the lonely voice of the wind.

"We shall be ground as dust." Her words slipped out aloud once more.

Alfons spoke, so close to her elbow that she startled slightly. "Every grain breaks upon the grindstone, Skymistress. That is the fate of grain."

"We are more than wheat and chaff," she replied, but did not believe herself.

CB&O

"There must be people in the world beyond simply Meat and Tock. They are rarely seen. Legends, to most of us. But the sky is infinite. There are always more islands floating in the airbands. How can there not be both angels and orangutans somewhere? It would be stranger if there weren't."

– Binyan the Wanderer, Sermon at Port Ruin

CB&O

I stare across my deck. My hand is clean, finally. It took a wire brush and foolish degree of patience, but I am clean. Even rat bastards have mothers. How different is that from me cherishing memories of my Maker?

Those other memories, from the beginning, when the light first came back–those I do not cherish.

The deckhands assemble. Bosun Shimwater nods to me. All are accounted for.

"We are ready to sail soon," I call out. "We have taken on no cargo. There may be passengers, though perhaps not once I have seen the Skymistress again."

They all stare at me, eyes bright and marbled with expectancy, servomechanisms whining slightly as weights shift, eddies of steam from odd vents. Tock is never so still as Meat can be, because Tock never sleeps. We move or we die.

I pause, considering my next announcement. "Captain Armature had plans, but he is lost to us. *Entwhistle* is a ship without home port or purpose. Too many of us were lost as well. Her boilers are sound, her gasbags tight, her engines strong, but her heart is broken.

"As is mine."

Still they stare at me, glittering and feral. No one turns away. No one seeks to shout me down.

"I have a plan as well. *Entwhistle* will sail antispinward. I want to face the Shadow as it comes, and press my blades into the faces of the rat bastards. We will not drive them back. We will not stay the coming of darkness. But we will meet it with eyes open and arms raised.

"Will you come with me?"

There is no great shout, as a crowd of Meat might have done. Neither is there a rippling tide of those slipping away. Everyone just stands and stares. Bosun Shimwater. Leftscrew the junior pilot. The Leyden Twins, connected by spark and cable as they were. All twenty-three of my surviving crew.

No one answers, no one steps back.

They just await orders.

In that moment, I love Tock all over again as if I never have before in all the centuries since my Maker first unbound me from my birthing bench.

"Captain Jakesia."

I turn to see the Skymistress on the gangplank. She has presented herself without the foolish, important Meat who follows her around. Only with a servant bent and palsied with the age that afflicts all Meat after a few years.

To my surprise, her name comes to me. "Sarita," I say, forgetting the honorific.

I realize she has left behind her blood-colored robes. This Meat woman is clad in stout leather with wisps of wool peeking from her collar and cuffs.

"May I have your permission to come aboard?"

With a bow, I welcome her to *Entwhistle*. In setting foot on my deck, she comes under my rules. "Welcome."

She glances up as the old man crowds behind her. The important Meat stands on the tower, glaring down at us. Though even I cannot see his eyes from this distance, I can read the set of his body in his blood-colored robes.

"Your rank is no more?" I ask politely.

"I am just Palacio Sarita bat Mardia." She bows slightly in return to me. "I would work my passage wherever you are bound."

"Toward Shadow," I tell her, "And the dying of the light, amid the swords and spears of the rat bastards."

"We all sail into Shadow," she says. "And every woman's light dies someday. I would face it in good company."

The servant cackles. "Not with Panjit back there. Peacocked fool."

"The winds of time are turning foul," I warn her. "They will not turn fair again in our lives."

"We are all grain," she says. "The world is our grindstone."

"Can you haul a line on command?" I ask.

Sarita, once Skymistress of the Lesser Port of Grand Reserve, smiles.

Very much despite myself, I smile back.

I check the springs of my hand one last time, then I give the orders to cast off.

Raising The Dead

by James Dorr

Love, like hope sometimes soars farther than one can reach.

ೞೞ

SHE HAD THE SMELL OF DEATH ABOUT HER. This we could tell as soon as we saw her, a scent unnatural even here in the Tombs where death surrounds us. We care for the dead here, the dead of New City across the great river; we guard them from those of the ghoul-haunted Old City to west and south of us, blue corpse-lights flickering under a steaming moon, who would despoil them.

But *she* was still living.

And other things, too, seemed odd about this woman who walked the causeway, from east, to approach us, and pulled the bell-pull *once*. She wore her black, all-encompassing day-*chador* although it was still night, her sun hat and day-mask—the mask, we could see, of a *beautiful* woman. At least we assumed its shaped features were her own, protecting those underneath from the sun's searing rays should she not find shelter by the dawn's rising.

Of course we *would* shelter her, even as we ourselves descend to tomb-tunnels, crypts, and mausolea, to rest with our charges from daylight's actinic glare. *Knowing* the dead, you see—we who live with them.

It is our vocation.

And so it was I, Philac, one of the gate guards, who asked, as we let her in: "What brings you here, lady? And why alone like this, and not with the corpse-trains that ply our bridge nightly, the last just departed to seek, perhaps, one more load.

"Do you come here to mourn?"

She nodded—then shook her head. "I do not know," she said. "I come to seek a tomb. That is, a *new* grave."

"For one just deceased, then? I understand, yes." I motioned for one of the other guards to run, to fetch a curator—one who had knowledge of Tomb-lore both past and now—because the fact was I did *not* understand her. Why had she not dealt with a corpse-train master, whose duty it was to make such arrangements, for digging, for grave gifts, locations, and carvings? The myriad details that accompany a burying.

I then had her come with me into our guards' quarters, seeing to east the first signs of the sun's ascent, bloated and poisoned—each new summer hotter than that which preceded it—and saw, as she walked, although limping and tired, that she carried herself as a person of quality. One who had riches.

She spoke with the accent of one who was used to wealth.

And, yet, she walked alone—a practice dangerous for one such as her, especially a lady. Ghouls had been active within the Old City. We saw them from our walls. More active lately than for many weeks now, as if they planned something—a major attack on us? Or otherwise engaged in some great project. Not *this* night, mind you, but nights just before.

Just two nights past we had seen, as if a star, a light rise from the south—from within the ghoul-lands, reflected as well in the river's black water. A trick to distract us?

But that was the past, and this night all had seemed calm. I bade her, thus, to take off her travel garb, but she declined to.

I offered her berry wine, fermented from bushes that grow in shadow, to north of tomb-structures. In hollows where mist collect.

"How may I address you, my lady?" I asked her.

Her day-mask still on, she said: "I am Delphinion. As I say, I have come to seek a grave plot. I have come some distance ... "

A clatter, then. The curator had arrived!

"Go on," he said for me, he, too, in day-gear, as he found himself a chair facing across from her.

"As I say, my name is Delphinion. I have been married—my husband was Rhodrar, a man of standing within the New City. A friend of its mayor."

The curator nodded.

"And I, too, have standing, not just from my marriage. My father was rich as well, and I his only child. He is among those here—I have been to his grave. I have made offerings, as has been proper."

The curator nodded again. "And now?" he said.

"Ah," Delphinion said. She loosed her *chador* below her mask's neck-piece, to show, within the cleft between her breasts, a flash of diamonds. Of rubies and gold fittings.

"There is more," she added, "about my person, as you shall see soon enough. All that I wear may be considered a funeral donation."

"And grave goods as well ...?"

She shrugged, fastening her front again.

"I see," the curator said. "Then, for your husband ... "

Delphinion nodded. "We were not long married, Rhodrar and I, but for all that, we loved each other deeply. Perhaps all the more so. It was, as you scholars say, our *z'étoile*—our fate-star to do such. It has been explained to me by another, if not a curator of the Tombs like yourself, a scholar nonetheless.

"One from the *Old* City."

I and my fellow guards shrank back somewhat at that. Several, instinctively, grasped for their ratpicks, some for their iron-shod staffs—*from the ruins to the south?*

"Ah," the curator sighed.

"Yes," she said. "I have been among the ghouls. I have consulted a Necromancer, one of those who rule them.

"I needed a favor—and, as you've seen, I could pay."

"Go on," the curator said.

"Rhodrar died just last week. Suddenly. In the day, when we were sleeping. A weak heart, perhaps, or some sickness inherited—there is a legend his family had some river blood in its ancestry, that of the boat-gypsies who die young also. I do not know what caused it.

"But I knew this—that I loved him deeply.

"It was not *fair*, you understand, that he should die so soon, with us scarcely married. Not even a month by then. I told his parents this when they would have me arrange for his funeral—that I would not give Rhodrar up quite so quickly.

"Instead, I would save him.

"You see, I knew some things taught me by my father, things not every girl learns. About the Old City. Of science and theosophy. Of the parts of the soul—"

"Of the *z'toile*, yes," the curator broke in. "You already mentioned it—that which determines the destinies of us all, but only broadly. You must understand that. It does not force us to paths, but, at most, shows us ways—"

Delphinion answered: "And other soul-parts too, though. *Psyche* and *animus*. The first of these which gives form to one's will—making one who one *is*. And the second which gives motion. The former which hovers about one's body, sometimes for weeks and more, until it can be sure that it is truly dead. For one may *not* be, you know.

"Thus there are *Walkings*—'ghosts' as they have sometimes been called by the Ancients. And, sometimes, more than that.

"Corpses re-vitalized."

"Yes," the curator said. "But now you speak of myths. Of ancient stories. Of Gombar and his corpse-bride, the Emperor's daughter, dead three thousand years or more—"

"Brought back by love's power," Delphinion said.

"And that of science also," the curator answered. "And other tales as well. But the point is, these *are* legends. Stories of olden days, when people braved the sun without their flesh blistering. When mutations were still rare. Not like our modern times, when neon searchlights course from the New City. When waste lands surround all. When—"

"Be that as it may be," Delphinion continued. "Old times or modern times—*love* has not changed so much. And my love, especially, had yet to be satisfied.

"So I sought one who would—who could save my husband. Yes, a Necromancer. I knew the limits of New City's scientists. So, Rhodrar's corpse on my back, already stiffening, I sought relief to the south, passing the plaza where the New City's poor leave their own dead, sometimes, in that way to appease the ghouls. Clothed as I am clothed now. Crossing the dry stream that marks the border between us and ghoul-lands.

"I passed the ruin-portals, into the Old City, ghoul-lights now surrounding me. Flickering blue corpse-flames.

"I heard the whispers: 'Why comes she, thus, here?' 'Does she bring an offering?' 'It cannot be for *us*—see how well she is dressed. She and the corpse also.' 'But, if not for us, *who*?'

"'Who,' indeed!

"Thus, at last, they—just as you here have done—fetched one who might know, or who at least might understand the right questions to be asked: Not so much 'who?' as 'why?'

"Or, perhaps, this time '*how?*'

"I was on strange ground: I knew not the answers. Trembling, I waited as one cloaked in *shadow* approached me, mincingly. Black, indefined—as if clouds of an acid-storm, such as we have in fall. Drifting, you see, that way.

"Not walking, as a man.

"Hooded. *Chador*ed. No face within that hood—only more blackness when, then, the ground *shook* with voice.

"*'Am I what you seek, child? A Necromancer?'*

"I nodded, dumbly.

"*'Then come,'* he motioned. I say it was *he*, although I do not really know that. A 'he' or a 'she'—or 'it.' Nor do I know his name. I do not think they have *names*, such as you and me.

"Frightened, I followed, Rhodrar's corpse on my back. Stammering, I explained ..."

Here she fell silent a moment. Sobbing. The curator motioned for us to bring more wine. A stronger wine this time.

He offered her some to drink.

"Thank you," she finally said. "You understand me. It pains me to recollect.

"Nevertheless, I *must* tell you my story. I told him why I had come—about my husband. How I could pay richly to have Rhodrar back again.

"Back with me, living.

"This time his voice gentled. 'It is not so easy,' he said, 'to bring lovers back. That is, the soul entire—not just the moving force. That latter we can restore practically with just the snap of a finger, to form what you New Cityers call, sometimes, *le zombi.*'

"He spoke in the formal French.

"But he continued: 'That is not what you wish, I think, but I will do one thing now to halt the corpse's rot. That will be easy too. But, for the other ... '

"*'Oui, seigneur?'* I prompted. I spoke in the French as well.

"For the other, the true soul, that will be much harder. But you must realize that even we Necromancers know what love is. How it must be fulfilled.

"'And so there may be a way—'"

Here she fell sobbing again, while we tried to help the curator to comfort her. Finally, she nodded.

"This 'way,'" the curator said, "might it have something to do with two nights ago. That is, before this one. In the south, we saw a light, one high up in the sky. We saw it rising."

She nodded once more. "Yes. Illuminated with corpse-gas searchlights, so those on the ground could see. We in the New City are not the only ones who can project light beams. But also in hopes that a soul might be beckoned.

"Instead of what *did* come ... "

"We saw it rise higher," the curator said, "beyond the ground's light beams. Still glowing, however, as if with its own lights.

"But then a blackness."

"Yes," she answered. "What you saw were its running lights, that which the Necromancer and I had built. And something else as well. It was a flying thing—souls, you see, mostly inhabit the air. They are not ground-bound, as *we* are. Therefore, to seek one, or so the Necromancer explained to me, we must fly too. Or, at least, rise up to it.

"So he had ghouls under his command build a keel, as if to make a boat. But on this keel he had built a great framework, of hoops and circles, from the wing-bones of huge birds, both lightweight and strong and stiff. These he had bound with wires, twisted, thin metal to form a netting, within which he placed skin bags—huge, too, and air-tight.

"*Ballonnets*, he called them, speaking the formal French. Trapped thus within the wires.

"With river-reeds, dried and tough, he had his ghouls weave baskets, two of them, each large enough to hold a man. Or, rather, one for a man *and* a woman—this to be in the front, containing Rhodrar and me. While in back, one with him, from which hung ropes to a device above the keel which he would steer with.

"Below this one, also, he had constructed a clockwork machine, but with screw-blades instead of hands. This to give power, to move through the air with. Or so he explained to me. And, *between* the baskets—connecting them, as it were—a kind of catwalk with a weight attached to it, that could be slid back and forth. For 'trim control,' he said.

"I did not know these words. Even in French: *Direger? Équilibrage?* Not the way *he* used them—although I would, later.

"As, on that night *you* cite—two nights ago, you say? I have lost track of time. Anyway, on *that* night, one of oppressive heat, of still, heavy air but with rumblings to north and east, he ordered his ghoul-helpers to bring up great pipes to these frame-enclosed air-tight sacks. He had me place Rhodrar's corpse in the fore-basket, and climb in myself with it.

"He had *corpse-gas* pumped into these *ballonnets,* or so he called out to me, himself in the back-basket.

"The frame strained above us, bone-hooped and coppery. While ghouls, below us now, clutched ropes to keep us down. Unhooking, now, the pipes—

"I nearly lost *my* soul!

"The ghouls had released us. We shot into the air, the pin-pricks of lights below—these were the *searchlights!* The great river which divides the Tombs from New City, it seemed just a stream now. New City itself, drifting from us to the north, even though our clockwork *moteur* kept us pointed toward it—even with *its* lights blazing red, purple, gold, topaz, and emerald—seemed but a village.

"Then: 'Look up, above us!' the Necromancer called, from his nest behind mine. Mine that I shared with the corpse of my Rhodrar.

"I looked above. *Blue sparks crept over our framework! Crackling and flashing!*"

"The *second* light, then," the curator broke in. "The one we saw after. When you were too high to be seen in the search-lights, yet brighter and larger than your running lanterns. The ones that you carried."

"But was that not dangerous? That is, does not corpse-gas burn?"

She nodded. "Yes, I think. That is, the Necromancer explained it—but I was too frightened of *everything* then, you see. What were the words he used?"

"Yes. *Le feu Saint-Elme.* He said it was soul-charged, akin to lightning, because we attracted it. Crackling with storm-fire. You know the feeling, before there's to be a rain, your skin's sometimes all prickly. Because *souls* like lightning, too, slipping in cloud-layers, riding wind currents there. Because that's what souls *do*—so he explained it to me.

"And as for our *ballonnets*, they would be safe enough, because our metal-wired framework carried the sparks *from* them. Down to our baskets.

"Or, more properly, *my* basket—where Rhodrar lay with me, his head cradled in my lap.

"Blue sparks surrounded us—I thought I saw him *move*. An eyelid flutter! I kissed him on the lips.

"But, once more, the Necromancer shouted. '*Something is wrong!*' he screamed. 'That cloud approaching—'

"I saw it. All black. But amorphous and moving, splitting and shifting—not like a *cloud* at all.

"Then it was on us. A storm not of rain, but birds! Carrion birds! Night birds! Owls and juggers! King-vultures, ravens! Of hooked beaks and feathers.

"They tore our *ballonnets*. They stole—they *ate*—Rhodrar, right there where I sat with him.

"I could not stop them.

"I called behind me, to the Necromancer, but he, too, was helpless. Surrounded, too, by the birds, fighting to keep our *machine* from falling.

"And yet we did go down.

"I landed, hard, but the basket was flexible. Strong and yet yielding — the fall scarcely harmed me.

"I could not find Rhodrar, not even a bone left. Nor the Necromancer, although I searched for him. I do not know if he came down in his basket, but fled before I did. Or if the birds ate *him* too.

"And so I wandered. I saw, in the great distance, the lights of New City, so I took that as my guide. Threading my way through the alleys of Old City, its ruins and tunnels.

"At dawn, the ghouls took me in. They did no hurt to me — it is their law, you know, that they are not to murder the living, unless in a fight or for some provocation — though I did not eat their food. Then, the next night, my journey continued.

"I think it was that night — or was it the one after? *This* night, just passed, that I came to the causeway. I knew it was almost dawn. I saw the last of the corpse-trains departing, its high-wheeled carts passing me. Emptied of cargo.

"I walked the causeway, alone, as you saw me. And pulled on the bell-cord once.

"And so I am here now."

"Yes," the curator said, helping her when she gestured her wish to stand. I had not realized myself, until then, how weak she had become, both from her journey and what she had been through before. She who was wealthy, of stature in the New City, and yet as fragile herself as a flower — such as we heaped on graves.

I watched as she trembled at the curator's next question: "Why, then, the bell-pull? The train masters, as you know, pull it once for each corpse, so we will prepare for the number they carry. But you come to us alone, your husband's corpse taken, already, from you."

She nodded. She reached up. She took off her day-mask

and loosed her *chador*, letting it fall to the ground at her feet. Her body beneath it, bare, save for her jewelry. Encrusting it, breasts and hips, covering her over. More fully than clothing.

But it was her *face* we saw, *half eaten by the birds!* The flesh pecked away from it, half-destroyed in their greed.

The half she had pressed to her husband's own head, in vain to protect it.

The other side beautiful, still — and, in that way, perhaps all the more grotesque. Especially when she smiled: "They did not hurt my *soul*. Nor did they Rhodrar's. I know now he waits for me.

"What he will see of me is what I was before. What we *both* remember."

Her body, too, half-torn.

"Yes," the curator said, after a pause. "And I understand, now, what you meant of *z'étoile*."

She nodded again. "I would have my tomb look south, toward where we met briefly, once more, in that basket. To where I last left him. And the roof above it to be windowed, of course, to be open to the sky."

The curator motioned to me. To the others. To fetch diggers. Builders. Whatever might be needed.

"Of course," he answered.

ABOUT THE AUTHORS

GARY CUBA lives with his wife and an unruly horde of domestic critters in South Carolina, USA. Now retired, he spent most of his career working in the commercial nuclear power industry, and holds several US patents in that field. His short fiction has appeared in more than eighty magazines and anthologies, including *Baen's Universe*, *Flash Fiction Online*, *Universe Annex* (Grantville Gazette), *Penumbra* and *Nature Physics Futures*. Visit http://www.thefoggiestnotion. com to learn more about him and to find links to some of his other stories.

CHRISTINE PURCELL is a neuropsychologist, coffee aficionado, and Scrabble demon living in the Great White North (in southern Ontario, where it's actually quite sunny). Her first novel, *The Emerald Key*, co-written with Stewart Sternberg, will be released in February 2015 from Ticonderoga Publications. Her short works have most recently appeared in *Apex Magazine* and *Grievous Angel*. She was previously the Acquisitions Editor for Elder Signs Press. She is an active HWA member.

MEGAN ARKENBERG is a student in Wisconsin who will hopefully be able to call herself a teacher before too long. Her work has appeared in *Asimov's*, *Strange Horizons*, *Shimmer*, and dozens of other places. In 2012, her poem "The Curator Speaks in the Department of Dead Languages" won the Rhysling Award in the long form category. She procrastinates by editing the fantasy e-zine *Mirror Dance* and the historical fiction e-zine *Lacuna*.

CORA POP has a life-long love for spinning stories, mostly from the yarn of the science-fiction and the fantastic. She's acquired it by reading such masters as Edgar Allan Poe, Jules Verne, Jean Ray, Joseph Sheridan Le Fanu, Edgar Rice Burroughs – to name only a few. Her stories have appeared in *White Cat Magazine* and *The Lovecraft eZine*. Her collection of strange tales and poems, *Wanderings on Darker Shores*, is available in paperback from all online stores. In "real" life she has a Master's degree in Aerospace Engineering, though she much prefers her imaginary life. She lives in Montreal, Canada, with her husband, their two young daughters, and a shy cat named Blues. Visit her online at http://www.chickwithaquill.blogspot.com

CAT RAMBO lives and writes in the Pacific Northwest by the shores of an eagle-haunted lake. Her work has appeared in such places as *Asimov's*, *Clarkesworld*, and *Tor.com*, and has been nominated for the Endeavour, Nebula, and World Fantasy Award. In 2015, her first novel, *Beasts of Tabat*, and third collection, *Neither Here Nor There*, are both forthcoming. For more information and links to other stories, see http://www.kittywumpus.net

FERREL D MOORE is a Michigan writer specializing in dark fiction. His stories have appeared over the years in anthologies from Elder Signs Press and Sams Dot Publishing. A lifelong passion for the martial arts and esoteric pursuits frequently find their way into his writing. He is the author of *Tainted Blood* and *The Ghost Box* published by White Cat Publications, LLC. Currently he is working on the sequel to *Tainted Blood*, which is tentatively titled *The*

White Death. You can contact him via his website at http://www.ferreldmoore.com

NGHI VO currently lives on the shores of Lake Michigan, and her fiction has appeared in *Strange Horizons*, *Expanded Horizons*, and *Alien Skin*. Her current interests include Vietnamese ghosts, Turkish food, intricate hairstyles, and medieval medicine. Her first official job was at a university library, where she decided that she could easily spend the rest of her life. That proved to be impossible, so she became a writer instead. Her love affair with the Oxford comma will go down in history as one of the great romances of the twenty-first century. She can be contacted at bridgeofbirds@gmail.com.

ALMA ALEXANDER's life so far has prepared her very well for her chosen career. She was born in a country which no longer exists on the maps, has lived and worked in seven countries on four continents (and in cyberspace!), has climbed mountains, dived in coral reefs, flown small planes, swum with dolphins, touched two-thousand-year-old tiles in a gate out of Babylon. She is a novelist, anthologist, and short story writer who currently shares her life between the Pacific Northwest of the USA (where she lives with her husband and two cats) and the wonderful fantasy worlds of her own imagination. You can find out more about Alma on her website (http://www.AlmaAlexander.com), her Facebook page (https://www.facebook.com/pages/Alma-Alexander/67938071280) or her blog (http://anghara.livejournal.com).

JAY CASELBERG is an Australian author based in Europe. His work has appeared in many venues worldwide and in several languages, both at short story and novel length. Not restricted to any particular genre, his work ranges across sci-fi, fantasy, horror, literary, and many things in between He also writes poetry. His latest book, *Empties*, a novel of brutal psychological horror is available now from White Cat Publications, LLC. More details can be found at his website, http://www.jaycaselberg.com

MICHAEL J. DELUCA is a fernlike, woody perennial native to the Eastern US, found on hilltops and in woodland clearings from Massachusetts to Michigan. Leaves astringent; strongly tannic; used in teas, to flavor ales and as an aromatic smudge. Flowers late summer in cylindrical catkins. Recent fiction in *Ideomancer, Phobos, Betwixt*. Tweets @michaeljdeluca.

E. G. GADDESS lives in Norfolk, Virginia with her husband, daughter, dog, and the cat that rules them all. She has always put pen to paper and let the story leak out. Her first independently published book, *Dhampyr Heritage*, was done at the instigation (nagging) of her daughter; there are no regrets. The pen name is an amalgamation of the names of her deceased grandparents; she wishes they could have seen the book in print. She has published the sequel, *Dhampyr Journey*, and is furiously battling the brick wall that has become the third book in the series. Who knows? There may yet be a fourth. A longer work of steampunk fiction is also in the works—one that continues in the future of the world of Huddy and Dumaka. You can find her on Facebook at http://www.facebook.com/eggaddess.

ERIC DEL CARLO's short fiction has appeared in *Asimov's, Strange Horizons, Shimmer, Perihelion*, and many other publications. His novels, solo and collaborative, have been published by Ace Books, DarkStar Books, Loose Id, and other houses. His latest novel is *The Golden Gate Is Empty*, written with his father Victor Del Carlo, and available through White Cat Publications. Find him on Facebook for comments and questions.

DARIN KENNEDY, born and raised in Winston-Salem, North Carolina, still remembers watching *Star Wars* at the local drive-in when it came around the first time and it's all been downhill from there. He served eight years as a United States Army physician and wrote the majority of his first novel during his yearlong deployment to Iraq. He has published eighteen short stories in various anthologies and magazines and is currently working on his third novel. Doctor by day and novelist by night, he lives and writes in Charlotte, North Carolina. He is represented by Stacey Donaghy at Corvisiero Literary Agency. Find him online at http://www.darinkennedy.com.

JAY LAKE (1964-2014) lived in Portland, Oregon, where he works on numerous writing and editing projects. His books for 2012 and 2013 include *Kalimpura* from *Tor* and *Love in the Time of Metal and Flesh* from Prime. His short fiction appears regularly in literary and genre markets worldwide. Jay is a winner of the John W. Campbell Award for Best New Writer, and a multiple nominee for the Hugo and World Fantasy Awards. He is deeply missed.

JAMES DORR, Indiana writer of *The Tears of Isis* was a 2014 Bram Stoker Award® nominee for Superior Achievement in a Fiction Collection. Other books include *Strange Mistresses: Tales of Wonder and Romance, Darker Loves: Tales of Mystery and Regret*, and his all-poetry *Vamps (A Retrospective)*. With nearly 400 individual appearances from *Alfread Hitchcock's Mystery Magazine* to *Yellow Bat Review*, Dorr invites readers to visit his blog at http://jamesdorrwriter.wordpress.com.